CUT
OUT

ALSO BY

CUT OUT

MICHÈLE ROBERTS

SANDSTONE PRESS

First published in Great Britain in 2021 by
Sandstone Press Ltd
PO Box 41
One High Street
Muir of Ord
Highland
IV6 7YX
Scotland

www.sandstonepress.com

ISBN: 978-1-913207-47-2
ISBNe: 978-1-913207-48-9

Sandstone Press is committed to a sustainable future.
This book is made from Forest Stewardship Council ® certified paper.

Cover design by Nathan Burton
Typeset by Iolaire, Newtonmore
Printed in the UK by CPI Group (UK) Ltd, Croydon, CR0 4YY

For Charlotte, Danny, Helen, Jo and Sam

1. Young women in church, Nice

CLÉMENCE

Sunlight glittered on the gravel underfoot, glossed the lip of the well. Berthe and I crunched across the courtyard and perched on the low stone parapet flanking the entrance to the chapel. Ten minutes to go. Berthe unfolded a black lace mantilla, draped it over her hairdo. Ridged curls held by lacquer smelling of burnt sugar. I'd snitched a headscarf from my mother, a yellow cotton square patterned with blue paisley. I knotted it loosely under my chin. Berthe said: I'm dying for a quick cigarette. Got any on you, Clem? Sorry, I said, I thought you'd given up. When did you start again?

Oh, she said, I don't smoke really. Just now and then.

She wore green rayon, carried a bag to match. I was wearing a white dress with polka dots that my mother had run up for me, and peep-toe cork-soled slingbacks that I'd re-painted the night before, to make them look less shabby. After a stroll together along the boulevards, Berthe and I had got to work back in our rented room in the old town, using nail varnish. Berthe painted one and I did the other. Choking smell of pear drops and carnations. Next we fixed up Berthe's wedges, coating them with tennis-shoe whitener. We propped the sandals on the windowsill to dry. I had no other shoes with me, and no money for drinks, so I stayed in, and Berthe kept me company. We spent the evening barefoot, sitting by the open window, looking down into the little square. At dusk, we turned the light off, to discourage mosquitoes. Once it grew properly dark outside, yellow lanterns strung from criss-cross chains lit up the wooden platform outside the café opposite. The band struck up, and people began dancing. We ate our picnic. Saucisson, tomatoes, olives, bread, that we'd wrapped as a parcel to smuggle past the landlady, plus a bottle of beer. Toothmug toasts. Well then, I asked Berthe, so how's the little one? Berthe said: he's doing fine. My mother-in-law's gone over to look after him. Roger didn't think he'd cope on his own.

The courtyard began filling up with people. Berthe fiddled with her mantilla and yawned. We'd shared a room to save money, slept badly on a sagging mattress. Berthe stuck the bolster down the middle of the bed, to fill the dip, and so that she wouldn't kick me in the night. She kissed me across it: good-night, Clem dear. The bolster wore a long white nightshirt, its frilled collar tied with a pink bow. Goodnight, sir, Berthe said to it: sleep well. Sweet dreams in between us!

Heat struck down. We moved further inside the chapel porch, to shelter from the glare. Berthe pulled on a pair of black lace gloves. We both draped cardigans over our bare shoulders.

Monique's mother, sister and brother turned up just as the bells began to ring and the frock-coated verger stepped forward and banged his staff. We left the brightness behind, filed in to the dark interior smelling of dust. Like an old coat folding round you, smothering you. Berthe dipped her fingers in the holy water stoup, crossed herself. She genuflected in front of the altar. I just bobbed.

We rested our feet on the wooden kneeler, held our missals on our laps. Berthe was lending me her spare: I'd sold mine to help pay for my shoes. The organ idled and hummed. Monique's mother in the pew in front put up her hands to twiddle her hat of woven black straw. Under it her hair coiled in a bun at the nape of her neck. Monique's little sister wore a beret crammed over her dark curls. Her brother sat stiff and upright beside her. His close-cropped hair shone blackly with hair-cream. He looked like a soldier already, poor little sod.

Berthe fiddled with her rosary. I crossed my arms and stared around. To our left, Our Lady drooped on a cracked plaster plinth. Near her, St Joan of Arc, in helmet and armour, posed chin up, her hands clasped on the hilt of her sword. Lace-edged cloths, spotted with rust, hung down. Black oak confessionals clumped in a corner. Holy old junk shop, this place. Looked as though it hadn't changed for a hundred years.

Clink, clink of a swinging censer sending threads of sweet-smelling smoke through the clammy air. The dimness shifted. Something rustled behind us. We turned round.

The side door at the back of the chapel had opened and sunshine streamed in. The bride appeared inside the stone archway, surrounded by light. She paused inside this radiance, looking down at the ground, while we stared. The light removed her from us, held her in a gold cocoon. Inside it she was wrapped in white.

Such changes of clothes! Volunteering at my school to run the Girl Guides, Monique had worn the uniform of dark serge skirt, blue shirt and blue beret. By day, a probationer nurse's outfit, her starched white head-dress spreading out in a triangle. Just one year of nurse's training and she had to put on mourning for her father. After that, working as a nursing aide, she wore a version of a nurse's uniform again. Once, just once, in the Hotel Regina, I saw her got up in an evening frock, a low-cut affair in coral chiffon pulled from the Master's dressing-up trunk. Black velvet high heels, a string of pearls around her neck, salmon-pink fake orchids pinned in her hair. She lay on the divan set by the tall window with its long blue shutters half drawn. She lifted her chin. The Master admires my neck, he says it's a white column, what do you think, Clem?

Today Monique wore a long-sleeved cream dress, buttoned at the throat, with a bunchy gathered skirt dropping to her ankles. A wreath of cloth daisies balanced on top of her net veil. The kind of costume I'd worn for my First Communion. What would the Master have made of that? The outfit in which he'd wanted her to pose had been much more glamorous, as she described it, the Greek goddess look, in grey-mauve pleated tulle, with gold shoulder clasps, a gold belt. A plunging neckline. Sleeveless, to show off Monique's arms. Had he ever made that painting? Had he had time? I didn't know.

The organ halted, paused, began piping a new tune. The choir's voices sprang up. The bride paced forwards between the packed pews, the tunnel of bodies in dark formal suits and dresses. Women wearing puckered hats like candle snuffers. Men clutching their caps on their knees.

Berthe and I sat at the aisle end of our pew. As Monique approached I willed her to raise her eyes, glance aside. Her two old friends. All I wanted: the tiniest twitch of her lips.

A swish of skirts. She passed us.

That gauzy whiteness falling down her back: a curtain that separated us. It was my own choice, Clem, she'd insisted, my own free choice. He asked me, and I said yes.

My parents had both been in the shop when I brought in Monique's letter enclosing the invitation and read it to them. My father slid a card of pearl buttons into place, clapped the drawer shut, muttered. My mother, counting receipts at

4

the till, swung round on her high mushroom stool. She said: I'll make her dress for the ceremony. That's something I can do. Dad said: there's no rush, is there? She may change her mind. Nonetheless he reached behind him, took down a roll of white poplin and flung it on the counter, pulling out one rippling length after another. They billowed up from his hand, flopped into a soft white heap. That enough? It's the last of the bale, in any case. Later, Mum pinned the paper pattern onto the spread-out material. Give me a hand, Clem. You know how to do this well enough. We marked outlines with tailor's chalk, set to with dressmaking shears, cut out white shapes. Three-quarter-length sleeves, d'you think, Clem? Yes. Once the panels of the flared skirt were trimmed, exact, she tacked them to the bodice. I stood on a chair and modelled the dress so that she could level the hem. She stayed up late several evenings running, hunched over the black and gold sewing machine. The finished creation dangled in my bedroom, swathed in a sheet. It whispered to me in the middle of the night, rustling sentences. Don't cry, Clem. What's done is done.

The white figure neared the pots of white lilies set at the low step in front of the railings guarding the sanctuary. The bishop in his gold cope stood with his back to the sanctuary gates, waiting for her to swim closer. The fisherman. His crozier with its curled-over end: a hook in her mouth. Reeling her in.

The organ music and the singing stopped. The bishop came forward to greet the bride, his arms outstretched. She knelt in front of him.

His stiff golden clothes held him up. His voice came from somewhere inside all that gold thread, gold embroidery. Our brave little sister, a soldier of Christ. Shield of humility, sword of obedience. Her heroic assault on heaven. The golden citadel.

The trumpets shall sound. By God's grace she will not be defeated.

Had the glory of all that helped to lure her? She was a soldier's daughter, after all, brought up to military life, schooled to obedience by harsh discipline. Over the years she'd flung out bits of her story to Berthe and me. The family shuttled from one bleak barracks to another. Often ill as a child: a weakened lung. Forced to flee the north-east at the start of the war, piled into a cattle truck with other evacuees. Their home and all their possessions lost. Down south, the father died, broken by the war, by tuberculosis. Once Monique signed on at the agency as a *garde-malade* she was able to support her mother and siblings, help them survive their bad patch. Did they mind that now she was leaving them? I minded that she was leaving me.

Holy poverty, said the gold-brocaded bishop: the renunciation of the modern obsession with material things. Berthe folded her arms. I turned my head. Her lips shaped a soundless blah blah blah. Last night, sitting on the bed painting her fingernails with the last of the varnish, she'd listed the goods provided by Roger on Hire Purchase: the washing machine, refrigerator, floor polisher, vacuum cleaner. She blew on her nails delicately, to dry them.

An altar boy in red cassock and white cotta approached, carrying a red silk cushion. On it lay a pair of golden scissors. The bishop took them up, stretched out his hand. His jewelled ring flashed. He cut off a single lock of Monique's hair.

The bishop spread out his arms. One of the company of glorious virgins! Pure, intact, untouched. Following Our Lady's perfect example.

No more kissing for Monique in shuttered hotel rooms.

Would she mind? No: her vow of chastity would give her a high rank, far above that of ordinary women. My mother had grumbled: nuns have no responsibilities, nothing to worry them. They know nothing about real life. My father had said: women are made to have babies. What a waste of such a beautiful girl. I'd snapped at him. Women can do other things too! He put his arms around me. Hush, dearest, you're back home with us now, you had your adventure, now you're safe. In our rented room Berthe flourished her shining fingernails and spun round in her crackly petticoats. Come on, Clem. We danced to the band music coming up from the square below. When the people next door thumped on the wall we stopped and got ready for bed. Berthe wore a lacy coffee-coloured nylon nightgown, bought for her honeymoon. I wore the blue cotton one Mme Matisse had given me.

The bishop with hands upraised began intoning a Latin prayer. Beside me, Berthe shifted to and fro in the cramped space of the pew boxing us in. Family houses or convents. You had to choose. As a child I'd lived my real life outdoors: building dens in the scrub by the river, climbing trees, roaming the hills, going swimming on Sunday trips to the coast. In my days at secondary school, recruited by Berthe into Monique's troop of Guides, I'd gone hiking and camping. We laid trails, lit fires, lashed up tripods. At night Berthe and I crept into the woods, hoping to spot badgers, pine martens. Sooner or later Monique would turn up and chase us back to our tent.

I nudged Berthe. D'you remember?

Berthe peeled off her black lace gloves and spread out her fingers, flexing them. She tilted her left hand so that candlelight from the tin wreath dangling above caught her wedding ring. Thin gold, and next to it a strip of silver set with a chip of

7

diamond. Why did she have to show off? She leaned against me, patted my hand. Once, twice.

Soon they'd be fitting the white coif and veil of the novice over Monique's shorn scalp. They'd cut off her old name and give her a new one. She'd be cut off from the love of worldly creatures. In the convent they called it becoming dead to the world. So the white outfit was a shroud.

Monique was not in fact wearing the elegant wedding dress Mum and I had stitched then posted off in a long cardboard box. Monique had explained why in her letter we received just before I left for the ceremony. The nuns gave the dress away to a parishioner in the town who was getting married and couldn't afford a frock. To teach Monique not to be proud, they chose her a plainer, second-hand dress from the collective store.

Just visible behind their grille to the right of the altar, the rows of kneeling nuns gazed calmly ahead. These new sisters would take Monique by the hand, not let go. Ranged alongside one another in their stalls they looked like those paper dolls you cut from folded newspaper then pull out to stretch fingertip to fingertip in a joined row. A string of nuns, all identical.

Monique lay down, arms outstretched, the shape of a cross, at the bishop's feet. He flung a black cloth over her, covering her completely.

Later on in the afternoon, at the *vin d'honneur* outside in the courtyard under an awning, Monique posed in her white habit and black scapular. White coif, white veil. She stood up ramrod straight between her mother and siblings. All four at attention. I took photographs with my father's Kodak he'd lent me. I promised Berthe to send her a print once she was back in England, for her album.

I got the exposure wrong: you couldn't see Monique's face

at all. She looked like a white crayon. That might have pleased her: she wanted to become an instrument in God's hands; he'd use her in his grand design. He'd scribble with her until she wore out.

Oh, my dear Monique. I thought I knew why she decided to become a nun, but not why she chose the Dominicans. She could have joined the Order that ran my school, Notre Dame de Bon Secour. She knew those nuns well enough. Perhaps she'd wanted to get away from them; too much like family. Perhaps those Dominican nuns were simply there, and so in she went.

People were standing awkwardly about, making small talk. Monique broke away from her family, came towards Berthe and me. She stood at the correct nunlike distance. The white coif, jutting out, half-hid her cheeks, the wimple swathed her neck. This person in disguise beamed at us. We raised our glasses, toasting her.

She said: I'm going to be transferred shortly, up to our new foundation in Vence. There's no chapel there yet, just an old warehouse, fallen into ruin. We need to turn it into a proper chapel. Something modern and beautiful. And I know exactly who could design it.

2. The Wardrobe

DENIS

Hot water steamed in the steep-sided enamel bath. I stood shivering on the cotton mat on the green-marbled lino. My mother, flushed from cooking, in a tightly tied apron, her dark hair swept up with combs, evaded my hands, laughing. She opened the airing cupboard, pulled out a clean pair of pyjamas, a clean towel. She dropped them onto the cork-topped dirty-linen box. There you are. I've got to keep an eye on your father's supper. I'll come back upstairs to hear your prayers in ten minutes or so, once you're in bed. Get a move on.

The door shut behind her. The bathroom heater had broken and my father had not yet repaired it. I felt too cold to undress. Instead I wandered out, into my parents' bedroom. I switched on the electric fire, watched its bars glow red, turned, to let them scorch the back of my legs. Warmer now, I shed my shorts, my Aertex shirt.

I opened the door of the fitted wardrobe. Darkness, smelling of camphor and lavender. The press and jostle of Mum's clothes: ladies in waiting. Waiting to be chosen by children in need of disguises. I poked my hands in and out of skirt and jacket pockets, fiddled with buttons. I undid hooks and eyes, tugged zips up and down. I edged along the row as far as my mother's fur coat, half-covered by her old pregnancy smock. I slid my hands in under the cotton, found that tense animal hiding there. I lowered it from the hanger and put it on. I donned her fur scarf too, a flattened dead fox: dry pointed muzzle at one end and thick soft tail at the other; lined with a strip of brown silk; fastened by a big hook and eye wound with twill. Coat and scarf fused, came alive. Beast that shielded my back, stroked my cheek, dangled its paws over my shoulders. Chilly silk lining slithered over my hands, against my legs. I'd been born deep in the forest, I didn't belong here, I was wild, a predator slinking out to plunder and kill, I tore a rabbit apart, its guts and flesh, I had a bloodied mouth, the red ripped body dangled from it, then at the call of the mother-hunter downstairs I returned to myself, barefoot on the rug in front of the glowing red fire.

3. Colour photograph (precise date unknown) by Yvette Martin of Matisse working at the Hotel Regina, Nice

The photograph shows a wide view of the angle made by the meeting of two walls. Presumably a corner of the large hotel room Matisse uses as a studio.

Vividly coloured pinned-up paper cut-outs, crammed together, take up most of the space. Almost abstract images, suggesting acanthus leaves, fronds of seaweed, apples, a parrot. Fuchsia pink, dark blue, purple, fir green.

The white-haired artist appears at the lower left-hand edge of the photograph, just inside its frame. Clad in loose white jacket and trousers, white slippers, sitting in a wheelchair, he cuts with a large pair of scissors into a sheet of orange paper.

On the lower right-hand side of the photograph, a youngish man bends his head and peers down into a camera, pointing it at bright fragments of cut paper lying on the floor in front of him, painted in coral pink, sky blue. A tall brown wooden ladder stands splayed in the corner.

A third person has almost completely vanished into the flat, cutout forms fastened to the wall behind her. She has become part of the design. Her skirt seems merely a lavender blue shadow. Her white blouse melts her into the white background. She holds out some drooping pieces of paper Matisse has already cut. A butterfly, a pale, flopping octopus.

She stands between the man concentrating on his camera and the man concentrating on his cut-out. She appears. She vanishes. She reappears.

4. Figures in the Vineyard

CLÉMENCE

The plates clinked as I lowered them into the enamel bowl in the sink. Dad stroked my shoulder as he passed behind me. And what's my girl going to be doing today? Helping your mother, I hope.

I said: I already am.

I might have left the nuns' school three months back, but timetables still organised my life. Monday: wash-day. Tuesday: ironing. Wednesday: baking. I followed my mother's orders. Monique in Nice, training as a nurse, obeyed the orders of her superiors in the hospital. Berthe, however, an au pair for an English family based at the British Embassy in Paris, only appeared obedient. At night, she skipped her English language classes and slid off to nightclubs. She'd met an Englishman, Roger, who worked for the trade department of the Embassy, and was practising her English on the dancefloor. She wrote: get some paid work, Clem, save up enough for the train fare, come and visit, we'll find somewhere to put you up.

Thursday: the kitchen turn-out. Walls, shelves and floor to be scoured, windows washed. Mother and I upended the chairs on the table, knotted up the curtains. At midday, she went next door into her workroom to finish a job for a customer, and I carried on cleaning alone. The trundle and clatter of her machine made a regular music. I turned on the radio to drown it. Jazz sang out. Mop hopped into my arms, swung me round. Broom beat a tattoo.

By mid-afternoon my hands and forearms itched from contact with cooling soapy water. The kitchen smelled of wetted ash and dust mixed with carbolic and linseed oil. Mother stopped her machine and sat down to rest for ten minutes in the back yard. I shouted I'd go for kindling, and bolted into the street.

My damp work apron, heavy around my knees, slowed my pace. After ten minutes of sun and wind it dried and loosened, let me walk freely. Housework broke off me like a crust of soot. I ran my hands through my sweat-clotted hair, to let the air get at it.

I left the village by the road leading north between olive groves. The landscape stirred, came alive, flushed with colour. Each day it changed, as the weather changed. This afternoon, grey cloud lay along the horizon. Glimmer of milky sun. To my left, rocky outcrops separated groups of wind-stunted pines. To my right, a low stone parapet braced the side of the road. Just beyond it, the terraced vineyards began, ripples of scarlet and crimson stretching away to the far mountain.

I climbed over the wall, jumped down over a sprawl of wild thyme, landed on the path of gritty earth flanking the vines. I was trespassing. If I got caught I'd just talk my way out of trouble, just spin a line.

Between the long rows of low, gnarled trunks stretched along wires grew parallel lines of wild rocket, big clumps in ragged white flower. The leaves were supposed to be picked young, when they tasted not too peppery, but I gathered some anyway.

In my skirt pocket I carried a stub of pencil, a couple of empty blue sugar bags filched from the kitchen drawer. Good rough surfaces; they took the soft lead well. I perched on a handy boulder and started drawing.

The smell of woodsmoke rose from below. Colder now, the whole sky turning blue-grey. Down in the village women were stirring up their fires, starting to cook. The church bells began ringing the Angelus. Time to go home, make excuses, make supper.

What to collect for kindling? Heaps of vine clippings from the summer pruning, nice and dry-looking, lay tossed down by the wall. I pinched up the corners of my apron for a makeshift bag, collected as many knotty twigs as I could carry, tucked my drawings on top. I filled my big handkerchief with pinecones fallen under the stand of pine trees at the vineyard's edge.

Clambering back over the scratchy, pungent thyme, the piled stones, I heard voices just below. The voices lilted closer. A twist of tones: deep and light.

Two strangers rounded the curve and walked up towards me. He in a felt hat, the brim pulled low, a grey overcoat, a stick in one hand. She in a calf-length blue skirt, a long blue woollen jacket open over a loose white blouse. Tourists, presumably, out for a stroll. Mostly they arrived in summer, departed again like swallows at the end of August. Parisian swallows, flying north.

I rather doubt, Camille, the man was saying to the young woman: that we'll find entire houses to rent in such a primitive place. We'll be fine where we are.

Her glance swept over me. She crooked her arm through the man's, twisted her rouged lips in a half-smile. Just look at that. What a picturesque little thing!

I played dumb peasant, staring back at her. Smooth, powdered face, plucked, high-arching eyebrows pencilled in black. That reddened mouth. Blue shoes with pointed toes and high heels. The blue ribbon twist of her little turban bore a brooch set with stones hard and sparkling as her blue eyes. On her left hand she wore a pale grey kid glove cut into lace at the wrist and fastened with pearl buttons. She carried the other glove, leaving her right hand bare.

The gentleman doffed his hat. Good evening, mademoiselle. His brown hair stood up stiff, like bristles on a brush. Lively brown eyes. Clean-shaven. Quite young. A carved-looking face. Sunburned skin.

He glanced at my apron-bag I clutched shut in one hand, the bulky knotted handkerchief balanced on top. Don't let us keep you. But you live down below in the village? Then perhaps you can give us some information.

My mother had been out to the allotment, where she had felt obliged to put in an hour's digging. Oh, now I'll pay for it. Oh, my poor back.

I dumped my bundle by the fireplace. She carried on grumbling. You're late, Clem. What have you been up to? You should have been home an hour ago, to give me a hand. Oh, my poor bones. I'm aching all over. I patted her arm. Poor Mummy. Sorry. I forgot the time.

She began rubbing her waist. Your father wouldn't like it, but I shan't tell him, or we'll both catch it.

I crouched in front of the chimneybreast, laid the grate with crumpled newspaper, pine cones, vine twigs. My fire took easily, flames darting at the broken pine branches I piled on top. The resin hissed and sang. See? I said to the blue-turbaned woman: there are some things I bet I can do far better than you. Her white blouse, fastened at the neck with flat white buttons shaped like birds, had tiny pleats fanning out from the yoke. Her bare right hand was plump and smooth, her oval fingernails painted pale pink. At the sink I took up the cracked sliver of soap, the nailbrush, and scrubbed at my dirt.

Mum had picked a couple of squash. She shook her head at my posy of rocket: too coarse for salad. I put the limp flowers in a jamjar of water, placed it on the mantelpiece. All through the war the photograph of Marshal Pétain had stood there, next to the picture of St Joan. Marshal Pétain had gone, but St Joan remained, guarding the photo of my white-frocked baby brother on his white-covered bier.

Mum carried on complaining about the pain in her back, her shoulders. So sit down for a few minutes, I exclaimed, have a rest. She shook her head. Too much to do. I dug my fingernails into my palms, yelled in silence. Stop being such a martyr!

The woman in the blue turban had asked whether I could cook. Stupid question. Mother had started teaching me as a child. Aged six, I could prepare vegetables, make white sauce. During the war, a boarder at school, I'd hung around in the convent kitchen, watched the lay sisters boil up bean pods, turnip tops and parsley stalks for soup. Now I cooked most of our meals.

Make a gratin, mother said, your father likes that.

While she fed the hens out the back the bowl of peelings, shut the squawkers up for the night, I got out the last of yesterday's loaf, laid the cloth. She returned as I finished washing up the mixing bowl and knives. She lowered herself into her chair next to the hearth. You're a good girl, Clem.

Sometimes, I said. I put my arm round her, kissed her cheek. She had black hair going grey, lines carved on her forehead and about her mouth. Only forty, but she looked fifty.

You're my treasure, she said: my only treasure.

Impossible to live up to my brother. The son, the adored firstborn, the little angel, sleeping the night through right from the start, no colic, teething just when he should. Dead before he could tarnish his halo. He'd needed me before he died, to play with him, carry him about, change his nappy, bath him. He needed me still. To console my mother.

Dad arrived from the bar, where he'd dropped in to read the newspaper and sink an under-the-counter pastis. He sat down, smoothing his moustache. He tapped his fork on the side of his plate. Well, let's see. He explained: from his chums he'd heard the news of the strangers' arrival. So had my mother, from the next-door neighbour met at the allotments. Over supper they pooled accounts. An artist and his wife, Parisians, staying at the baker's. The baker's daughter had left to be postmistress forty kilometres away, and the boy was doing his military service, and so the baker was letting out their rooms. Odd time of year for a holiday, surely? No, not a holiday. A work trip. So that he could paint the autumn colours. The baker's wife had no time to look after them, and so the visitors were in need of domestic help. Primarily someone to cook for them.

I didn't mention that I'd met the Parisians. Nor how, as I turned to leave them, the wind caught the pieces of sugar paper tucked on top of my apronful of vine prunings and lifted them. They scudded along the road. The man ran after them for me, picked them up, glanced at them. You did these? Not bad at all. Really promising. He handed them back to me, gave me a little bow. Was he mocking me? I went on down to the village.

To my parents I put forward a solution, hesitantly, hiding my interest. Yours truly, only too glad to take a temporary job and thus contribute a bit more to the household.

Dad rested his fists on the tablecloth. He took some convincing. He wanted me to continue helping my mother but also to work with him in the shop, counting out hooks and eyes, measuring lengths of ribbon. What did we know of these strangers? Nothing. Mum pointed out I'd be home every night and that working for the tourists I'd be under the eye of the baker's wife and could come to no harm. The extra money will be handy, she said, dishing out squash gratin: we can manage without Clem for a bit. They won't stay long. Once it turns colder they'll be off, you'll see.

After supper, Dad put his jacket back on and went along to the baker's, to interview the Parisians and check their respectability. Also to get in quick before anybody else's daughter had the same bright idea. Mum and I cleared the table and washed up. Then we took up our posts by the stove. While she knitted, I darned a sheet. Dad was late home, so we said the evening rosary without him. I convinced Mum to stay in her chair, not to kneel on the concrete tiles and hurt her knees worse. I knelt for both of us.

The Hail Marys smelled of burning pine, resinous and incense-sweet. I made up my own Joyful Mysteries. The Annunciation: an angel haloed in grapes raised his forefinger and promised that my life could change. The Visitation: the woman in blue winked, taught me to play poker. The Nativity: my brother was born with no trouble, and survived measles, whooping cough, scarlet fever.

Dad banged in. He had gone back to the bar with the stranger, who'd bought him a drink or two. Bit of a show-off: he certainly seemed to have money to chuck around. Collecting local colour? Dad could give him local colour, no problem. The wife had come too. She'd sat there, quite at ease, the only woman in that crowd of men. It was all sorted out, and I was to start tomorrow.

He pulled me onto his lap. His arm curved round me. I leaned against his shoulder. He said: I'll miss you, little Clem, when you go out to work.

I patted his chin. My dear papa. I stroked his moustache, smoothing it, as I did as a small girl. Tidying him. You'll get used to it, I said.

His arms tied me up, knotted me to him. Give your papa a kiss.

I dabbed my lips to his forehead. He smelled of aniseed and tobacco. Outdoors had smelled of sun and wind. When the artist bent towards me, handing me back my drawings, I'd caught the fresh smell of his soap. I said to Dad: now that I'm going out to work I'm not your little girl. He snapped his fingers round my wrist. You'll always be that.

I'd left my drawings on top of the dresser by the door. Mum lifted one up, turned it round. How nice. Girls always love drawing. I was just the same. But you've left school now, dear. You'll have to be thinking of other things.

She held it out to Dad. He said: but what is it? What does it represent? It's all wonky. That tree's going to fall down soon, that's for sure! And this one, it's just lines of scribble.

I went upstairs. Outside, the owls hooted. Flying out into the dark blue night sky to hunt, plummet down, grip mice and voles in their sharp talons, tear their heads off, devour them. I was an owl, hunting for what? I didn't know. I slid into my bed under the eaves.

5. Still Life with Artichokes, Carrots and Fennel

DENIS

Women in red sleeveless dresses danced in a snaking circle, silk skirts shuddering around their calves. Wail of violin and accordion. Bare feet thudded on wooden boards. One dancer broke free, opened her arms to draw me in. Crushed against her. She cradled me, a second of heat, then tossed me over her head. Her companion balanced me on her palm, flipped me up like a coin. Heads or tails? I spun between their flicking fingers and thumbs. Which one would catch me? If I fell they'd trample me.

A change in the air stroked me awake, Freddy fidgeting himself to the edge of the bed, taking the duvet with him. I grabbed a fistful of down, held on. A soft wrestling match, which I lost. Freddy unwrapped himself, pushed the duvet further off, began to slip out from under it. I reached for him, halted him. His back a wall. You're going already? But it's Saturday. It's only seven o'clock. I sat up and kissed his shoulder: don't go just yet. He stretched his big, milk-white arms. Got to. Lots to do.

We could have breakfast out, if you like, I said. Try that new Portuguese café down the road. Gathering his clothes from the floor, he flicked me a calm glance. No time. I'll have breakfast at home.

My bed was a bucket of warmth. We'd heated it last night, heated each other. Third time we'd been out together. Two weeks in between dates, at Freddy's insistence: no rush, let's take it gently. First time he'd stayed. This should be enough, I'd told myself, watching him undress. Don't ask for more. Ideal pattern for lovers: a dance two people improvised together, as equals. Something red? The dream tore to rags, vanished. No. Freddy had already taken over as choreographer. Exit Freddy stage right. Before leaving he said: don't take this the wrong way, but this won't work out. You're not right for me. Sorry.

He meant: too old. Wrinkled and sagging. Old people shouldn't want sex. They were disgusting if they did. In the dark, though, I'd been thirty years old again, I'd known that joy of giving pleasure to someone I desired. The front door slammed. I fell back on the pillow dented by his head. The sheet smelled of him. I reached for sleep, to muffle his absence, but could only doze. Two hours later I heaved myself up. I slung on my jogging things, zipped my bank card into a pocket, let myself out into the rain-freshened street.

Ambulance sirens screamed in the distance. A police car tore past. Boys scuffled with a ball. Gaining the park, I ran past the little playground empty of children, a few crisp packets scudding in the wind. After a couple of circuits of the ornamental lake my weariness flaked off.

At the far side of the park I emerged onto the main road, opposite the supermarket. The chilly aisles smelled of baking bread, fresh coffee. No sign of either. I pulled out my list from my back pocket. *Milk, eggs, butter, cheese, sugar, vanilla, almonds.*

A howl cut the air. A toddler sprawled face down on the floor, near the vegetable rack. I longed to dump my metal basket, pick her up, jiggle her, croon to her. She'd hiccup, wind down her sobs. I didn't dare touch her. A woman rounded the corner, glared at me. She snatched the child's hand, towed her away. I selected flowers. Small, delicate lilies, in mixed shades between salmon pink and orange. I made for home.

Unlocking the front door, pushing it open, I halted. An envelope lay on the mat amid a drift of publicity flyers. A large white rectangle folded in two to be forced through the letterbox; now creased down the middle.

A pasted-on label: the envelope had been forwarded from the firm of undertakers who'd organised Mum's funeral. Above it, my name inscribed in black, wavering script. A handwritten letter? Only old friends sent me notes or cards in the post, when I'd cooked for them, or had them to parties. Some weird thank-you letter from someone Mum had known years back? Gorgeous wake, darling, and the French fancies provided the perfect touch.

So let it wait. Flat and smooth as an emptied hospital bed. Why such a gloomy supposition? Because Freddy had left my own bed so early this morning, glanced at me so coolly, dismissed me.

Several beloveds still remained to me, for example my dear Phyllis, due for lunch tomorrow. Certain dishes needed preparing in advance. So get a move on. I stepped over the clutter of junk mail, kicked the front door shut behind me, took my shopping through into the kitchen. I lowered the flowers into a tall glass jar of water, set this on the table, the salmon-rust colour of the blooms complementing the rich blue of the checked Madras cloth.

I showered, changed into jeans and T-shirt. The envelope summoned me, alive as that bawling baby in the supermarket, demanding to be picked up. I slid it between two cookery books on the shelf. I got on with whisking egg white, folding in ground almonds and vanilla sugar, then spooning the glossy mixture into two discs on two non-stick trays.

My mother used to make meringues for my birthday. Small individual ones, baked for hours in a cool oven; levered off the parchment brittle and crisp. Sometimes, busy marking schoolbooks, she forgot them, and they turned out overdone, the colour of milky coffee. They shattered when you crunched into them, shards of sweetness scattering. Domes sandwiched in pairs by thick whipped cream. With the yolks my mother made mayonnaise, a risqué novelty in our salad cream suburb, to serve with cold poached mackerel for supper. She skimped out the pale sauce, a teaspoonful per person. Berthe, my darling girl, my father would implore, don't be so mean. Roger, she'd retort, don't be so greedy. To my own mayonnaise I added minced green herbs, a few rinsed and chopped capers. As usual I made too much. Phyllis wouldn't thank me; she stayed thin by eating meagre helpings. In this she was far more French than I was. Far more like my dear French mother, who'd learned rigid self-control as a Catholic child and rarely let go of it. Her survival skill, which saw her through the war, stuck in that boarding school, helped her survive in Vichy France, cope with foreign armies sweeping in: the Italians, the Germans, the Brits. No collapsing; carry on.

Freddy's appetite, on the other hand, matched mine. I'd watched him savour canapés at that book launch, tip back his glass of golden fizz. The party was to celebrate a collection of recipes for which I'd done the index. The author was someone Phyllis knew, a TV cookery-show contestant turned author: *arte povera* meets thrift chic. Glam tricks for dealing with *asparagus stalks, beetroot leaves, carrot peelings and tops, cauliflower stalks*, and so on. Freddy returned my look with a humorous, self-deprecating one. I wandered across towards him. He held out his glass for a waiter to re-fill with champagne. We made conversation; like offering titbits to lions behind bars. Each of us a lion and each a titbit. After a while, Phyllis slid up. Such nonsense, this book, I'm ashamed of her. Poverty porn! Our mothers lived through rationing, they knew how to cook with vegetable scraps, it was common sense. Mothers don't make fashion statements, I suppose. She glanced at Freddy, nodded. She hugged me. I'm off, darling, you staying, good for you. At the end of the party Freddy and I left together, went out to supper in Old Compton Street.

In mid-afternoon, having set the cooked meringues onto the rack to cool, I took up the envelope. French stamp: a turreted chateau, printed in brown. French postmark blurred by wet; indecipherable. No sender's address on the back.

I sat down in the basket chair by the window, slid my thumb under the loosely gummed flap, and extracted an oblong piece of cartridge paper, painted mid-blue in what looked like gouache, with a large bulbous shape cut out of it, the resulting hole reaching almost to the blue edges, so that this remaining paper was no more than an irregular frame, slashed into at one side, around something missing. A huge lost teardrop.

I'd handled similar pieces of paper before, as a child, in my godmother Clem's house in southern France. She kept a loose pile of them in the drawer of the dining table, her secret store place concealed by the overhanging tablecloth. She took out a green scrap, an orange scrap, to show me one day, when it was raining and we were both bored, in need of amusement. I asked: what are they for? To play with, she replied. We cut them up, made collages. She pinned up our finished artwork in her bedroom, next to the framed drawing in black ink of the naked girl curled up like a caterpillar. The right-hand lower corner was signed: for Clem, with love. H.M.

The piece of blue paper talked. French words struck up inside me, salt-sweet, smelling of eau de cologne, thyme, sun-warmed melons, eau de Javel. They breathed and wavered, formed themselves into something solid yet soft, Clem's face close to mine.

She must have sent the coloured fragment. Why? We hadn't been in touch for many years. Perhaps she read *The Times*, perhaps she'd spotted my mother's death notice, with the undertaker's address given for flowers. But why be so mysterious? Another of her games? I wasn't in the mood for them. Mum had died too recently. Grief made me irritable. People offered sympathy and sometimes it scratched. They meant well but sometimes their brisk survival tips made me feel lonelier, sadder, than ever.

That night, again I dozed rather than slept. Dreams kept pricking me awake. I fell asleep sometime around four. A hoarse gasping roused me: a jay, perched close to my window, misled by the all-night yellow glimmer of the city, offering its rasped version of the dawn chorus. Lay off, chum. Give us a break. At seven, I got up, made coffee.

Sleepy, disinclined to run, I forced myself out, going the other way round the park for the sake of variety, bought the Sunday paper from the newsagent at the corner. The disused shop next door, now a pop-up church, resounded with the boom of baritones, soprano cries of ecstasy, the banging of drums, the ringing of clashed cymbals. My mother had taken me to decorous Mass every Sunday. Clem, never. She'd hauled me instead on walks up into the hills behind the village. When I lagged back on the steep path, she chided me. Come on, you can do it. Keep going.

What if now I kept going? Down the street, along the main road, jump on a train to the coast. Over the sea to France. Bolt: escape the bruise of Freddy. A long weekend in Paris. Even longer, perhaps. Travel even further away. I was in between freelance projects. Nobody needed me to do anything.

The praising voices soared. They rattled the makeshift chapel then died amid the roar of passing buses and lorries. Clem used to sing to me. Not hymns but classic chansons. Deep, slightly cracked voice, but she could hold a tune. Why had she sent me that scrap of blue paper? Why couldn't she have added a few words?

Back home, daydreaming over the food supplement, I ignored the time. I shouldn't have. I wanted everything to be tip-top for Phyllis, we hadn't seen each other for several weeks, unusual for us, but I was late getting started. I pulled out plates, a fistful of cutlery, put them ready on a tray. My two good wine glasses, inherited from my mother and kept for guests, looked dusty. I rinsed them, left them to drain.

Phyllis arrived early. She blew in through the hallway like a banner, grey, green and white. I've left my bike outside. Where are we sitting? In the kitchen? Of course. Lovely.

She thrust out a bunch of pink and blue hyacinths wrapped in white tissue paper. Where's your vase? Oh, it's got flowers in already. Never mind, you've got another, haven't you? Where is it? Don't tell me. I'll find it.

I kissed her on both cheeks, to pause her as well as greet her, and suggested a glass of prosecco, which she could drink while I finished my prepping. Shrugging off her green silk parka that matched her eyes, she clicked her tongue. D'you know, D., after all these years of drinking pop with you, I've decided I don't really like prosecco at all.

She fished in her green leather shoulder bag. Why don't you open this red I've brought? A nice Chilean Merlot, look. Where shall I put it?

She glanced at my table, the blue cloth pushed back into rumpled folds. On the wooden surface carrots lolled next to Jerusalem artichokes, a couple of fennel bulbs, a head of garlic, a bunch of parsley. A knife and chopping board lay next to them, a pink-striped tea towel flung down nearby. The glass jar of lilies jostled a tin of olive oil, a peppermill, a yellow eggcup full of coarse salt.

Screwtop, too, Phyllis said. You won't even have to find your corkscrew in all this mess.

I can always find my corkscrew, I said, and one person's mess is another's artfully arranged still life.

Don't play with your food, my mother had admonished me. Hard to do anything else with the fat-frilled, gristly lamb chops and watery Brussels sprouts she served up, that she supposed catered for my English father's tastes. In France we'd never eat overcooked meat, overcooked vegetables, my dear Roger, but that's how you like it and so that's that.

Clem piped up inside me: of course you can play with food. When cooking a pie she rolled out leftover pastry and cut ornaments for the lid in the shapes of leaping hares. She scattered orange nasturtium flowers from the garden onto the green salad. She arranged purple plums on a particular flat yellow pottery dish, cherished despite the cracks at its base, whereas strawberries always went into the speckled blue bowl with fluted edges, only slightly chipped, certainly not to be thrown away. Once the food looked right we could sit down to it.

Phyllis said: d'you like my hair?

It flicked up around her head, soft-looking silvery feathers.

29

Last time I'd seen her she had a sedate shoulder-length bob.

Nice, I said, really suits you, short like that.

Clem wore her straight chin-length hair parted on one side and swept across, fastened in place with a slide. For house-work she buttoned on a blue-flowered overall. To go out she donned a large navy overcoat, a man's beret if it rained. The heavy double-breasted coat swamped her, made her resemble a schoolgirl. In the back yard and vegetable garden she favoured rubber clogs, in winter zip-up flat brown ankle boots, and in summer a pair of espadrilles. She didn't seem to age. Her slenderness, her fine-boned face, open and eager: she remained like a girl.

Phyllis wandered over to the basket chair at the window, picked up the food supplement I'd dropped there, stared at the open page. Have you seen this ridiculous photo?

Mmm, I said.

Rustic chic for the bourgeoisie, Phyllis said.

I suppose so, I said, but for me, it brings back memories.

The supplement photograph displayed the ingredients for cassoulet. A heap of pink-streaked bean pods, an open Kilner jar of duck confit, a coil of raw sausages glistening with chunks of fat, a bouquet garni. Nearby stood an earthenware cooking pot with stubby handles, its dark blue glaze worn at the rim, exposing the reddish terracotta underneath. The upturned lid, blackened and crusted, lay nearby. The food stylist had posed the ensemble on a decorator's rough wooden work bench, with a haybale underneath. The bench stood on some yellow and blue cement floor tiles almost exactly like those in Clem's village house. Pattern of sharply angled blue and yellow stars. A la mode again; after so long. Modern versions: the colours crisp, the patterned surface undamaged.

That pot's unhygienic, Phyllis said. I'd throw it out.

She took a breath. Duck confit! It's terribly rich. In that picture it looks almost disgusting. The whole thing's just pseudo-peasant nonsense.

No wonder that earlier I'd let myself get behind with preparing lunch. The photograph compressed past years to star shapes. Summer after summer, day after day, I'd stood on that tiled floor, next to Clem, both of us leaning against the edge of the kitchen table as we sliced tomatoes and courgettes, peeled onions, topped and tailed beans. Above the table hung one of her paintings on brown cardboard; a black background and against it a pinkish-brown shape, curved like a violin, streaked with red. While we worked she tossed out scraps of stories. When I worked in the ateliers of the Folies Bergères. When I worked as a chambermaid in Nice. When I started my domestic science training.

Nostalgia is reactionary, Phyllis said, a repulsive kind of faking.

Mmm, I said.

D., you're in a dream, Phyllis reproached me.

I'm concentrating on lunch, I told her. Just give me a minute.

I chopped the fennel, artichokes and carrots. Rapidly, rhythmically, as I'd been taught by my godmother. Newly appearing, a kitchen ghost with a paintbrush in one hand, a knife in the other. She dipped her brush in olive oil and smeared a cake tin, she knifed on oil paint in thick layers. Scattered with thyme, interspersed with heads of garlic, into a wide roasting dish the vegetables went. I turned on the heat and shut the oven door.

Let's take our drinks outside. I thought we'd eat there too.

You're very lucky, having a garden, Phyllis said. You're very lucky, having a landlady like Frieda.

I occupied the ground floor and basement of Frieda's small terraced house, while she lived on the top two floors. In exchange for a rent well below market rates I tended the garden, cleaned Frieda's rooms, did decorating and repairs. *Clear areas of fallen leaves, repaint windowsills, unclog drain, tidy shed.* According to our initial arrangement Frieda had sole use of the garden at weekends, but in practice I used it at whim and she never minded. Frieda was the daughter of a Jewish mother packed off from Austria as a child. She ran a reading group for refugees in the public library where I worked. We had exchanged smiles and she eventually invited me out for coffee. She was non-religious, long-widowed, her children both working abroad. She introduced me to Viennese cookery and to lieder, accompanied me to theatre matinees.

Once, over a drink, I asked her what it was like being a parent. Tough, she said. You ever wanted children, Denis? Yes, I said. But it felt too complicated. Frieda swigged her gin. Lucky for me that you stuck to gardening.

Phyllis and I trod down the short iron staircase. Heat simmered between the grey-blue-yellow brick walls. We made for the trellised arbour at the little courtyard's far end. Climbing roses and clematis I'd planted at each side when I first moved in, ten years back, bent to intertwine and form a canopy. Now the climbers twisted and looped in all directions, and needed close, regular pruning. Similar to Phyllis and myself, old friends who'd practically grown up together, who snipped at each other when necessary, kept each other in neat moral shape.

This Merlot ought to breathe for a bit, really, Phyllis said, but never mind.

Funny, isn't it, I said, people used to refer to wines by the vineyards they came from. Nowadays it's just by grape. First time I was offered a glass of Chardonnay, thirty years ago, I didn't know what it was.

Phyllis said: those French vineyard names were tricky. Much less scary ordering wine in restaurants if the name's just one word. It's all clever marketing. People buy New World wines because they can say the names.

Lots of those new reds are too fruity for my taste, I said. Too rich. Not your Merlot, of course. I'm sure it will be delicious.

Half under the arbour's green roof stood a round table I'd spread with a pink-checked cloth, and two café armchairs plumped with the cushions, printed with roses, that I'd brought out earlier from the kitchen. The pink of the cloth and the cushion covers matched the pink of the clematis blossoms above. Phyllis made no comment, perhaps thinking my decorative touch too pretty-pretty, but simply sat down on the sunny side of the table. She said: I went to a wine-tasting recently, with my friend Angela. The woman giving the talk said there was far too much fuss made about *terroir*. It's just snobbery, a lot of the time.

Would Dad have known what *terroir* meant? He and Mum drank wine at weekends sometimes, and always at Christmas lunch, Bénédictine or cognac with their coffee after the French-style chocolate-sculpted Christmas log, weak orange squash the rest of the year. Dad did his regular drinking outside the house, in the pub. Trying to be a good Englishwoman, Mum had a sherry on Sundays, an occasional gin and tonic.

Clem couldn't afford decent wine, so mixed cheap, rough stuff with water to make it palatable. Her thin brown fingers worked the corkscrew, twisted out the stub, which she lifted to her nose, sniffed. On my annual summer visits she allowed me a finger of red or rosé, much diluted. We clinked: *santé*! Clem enjoyed such gestures, such rituals. When she picked up her fork, she said: *bon appétit*! When she'd had enough she laid her knife across her plate: that's it! She reminded me to sit up straight, hold my cutlery properly, not speak with my mouth full, and so on. When the doctor came to lunch with us of a Sunday, times when she'd open a bottle of Médoc, she wanted me to do her credit. If the two of us ate by ourselves, she allowed me to pick up my chicken bones to bite at the last of the meat, to wipe my bread crust around the emptied bowl of green beans in anchovy sauce, to sail my boats made of walnut half-shells over the round pond of my plate.

It's awfully hot out here, Phyllis said. There's not enough shade.

She tugged off her grey cardigan, hung it over the back of her chair. You ought to get a sun umbrella. But then you like the sun, don't you.

My skin stayed brown from all the gardening and walking and running I did. I'd inherited my French mother's colouring. She darkened at the first hint of sun in summer. In old age, still considering herself a beauty, rightly so in my opinion, she wore sleeveless dresses to show off her tan, not caring that the flesh of her upper arms hung slack and lined, and I loved her for it. She remained the Queen, upright, shoulders back. Head up, crowned by smartly cut white hair. Her keen eyes would survey the supper table I'd laid. You've forgotten the pepper. No, no salt. I don't eat salt, remember.

Phyllis pushed her chair back into the shade under the climbing rose. How pretty she looked. Her white linen shirt billowed loose over skinny grey trousers. A grey, green and white striped silk scarf looped her shoulders. She was wearing little green ankle boots with Cuban heels. Normally her boots were flat and black.

Here's to forty years of having known you, I said, and to many more of renewing that knowledge. Deepening it. Happy anniversary!

She looked wry. Some speech!

My darling Phyllis, I said, my very best friend.

My dear D., Phyllis said. She glanced down. She fidgeted with the stem of her glass, then looked up again, smiled. She bit into an almond.

We sipped our red wine, rich and full-bodied as I'd expected.

I'm thinking of going to France sometime soon, I said. Mid-June, perhaps.

On your own? Phyllis asked.

Over the past ten years, ever since her husband John had died, Phyllis and I had occasionally taken short holidays to France together. We stayed in cheap hotels, ate picnic snack lunches, dined in no-frills backstreet brasseries. Phyllis was easy to travel with. I'd look up hotels, museum opening hours, and she'd take charge of itineraries and budgets. It simplified things if you didn't have to try and make joint decisions every moment of every day.

I said: I was wondering whether you'd like to come with me. If you've some time free?

We hadn't gone away together for a year or so. I waited for her to jump at the offer and suggest a date. She smoothed out a wrinkle in the tablecloth and smiled. Not quite sure, darling. It all depends. I may have some time free, and I may not.

I felt taken aback but determined not to show it. The rules of friendship dictated recognising the other's need for reserve, respecting it. What was I, a child, to feel snubbed by my oldest friend? Yes. Clem opening the back door after Sunday lunch, shooing me into the yard: run out and amuse yourself, my dear, and stay there until I call you back in. Then we'll all have tea together.

I got up. Let's eat.

The narrow boats of red-tipped chicory leaves, each filled with a line of crab, pleased Phyllis, though she pushed away the bowl of mayonnaise, smiling, shaking her head. The next course dismayed her. Frowningly she surveyed the dish of roasted vegetables. A bit too blackened, darling, surely? She eyed her portion of chicken, the little hillock of mushrooms alongside, prodded them with her fork. I hardly eat meat at all these days. This is organic, yes?

I picked up the wine bottle. More wine, darling?

Perhaps Phyllis was upset about something. She'd reveal it in time. Or not. I had my own thoughts to share with her, but the moment did not yet feel quite right.

I cleared our plates, fetched the green salad and the cheese. I opened a second bottle of wine. Médoc this time. Homage to the doctor, with his close-cropped grey hair, his full-lipped mouth, his clean, blunt fingernails. Clem interrupting him, disagreeing. Their talk flowed above me, around me.

Phyllis cut herself a thin wedge of Camembert, a sliver of Comté, a scrape of *chèvre*, tasted each in turn. She smiled at me. Always French cheese for you, D. You don't eat much English cheese, do you? You're a bit stuck in your ways, aren't you, darling?

I pushed the bowl of salad towards her. Well, I am half-French, don't forget. To me it seems normal to like French cheese.

She lifted a couple of leaves, dropped them onto her plate.

36

Why do people automatically think everything French is better? They don't, I said. French food hasn't been fashionable on the high street for a long time. Most people think it's elitist. Too fussy. Too time-consuming to cook.

In the food supplement photograph of cassoulet, the cement tiles' pattern of blue and yellow triangle-formed stars blazed out like the stars on the page of a book. Golden stars representing gunfire, bullets exploding. An artist's book called *Jazz*. Matisse's book.

D'you remember the Matisse cut-outs show we went to see at the Tate? I asked Phyllis.

She nodded. Sure. Of course I do.

I'd gone back alone, several times. Those vast, bright pictures humbled the onlookers. Matisse manipulated our vision, directed it to flash right and left, to spiral, to steady. Part of his material, we squiggled like spurts of paint or glue. When I emerged from the last room of the exhibition, pushing through the enormous black door, took the escalator down, wandered out onto the South Bank, the world shook a fist at me. It clapped and jigged and shouted. It jolted, broken up, transformed into Matisse's shapes and colours: chopped triangles of green-grey waves, abrupt cherry-red flat arches of bridges, beads and chains of bright neon swinging and slapping.

In one room, live footage showed the artist himself. Clips seeming cut from a longer film. The cardigan-clad, slack-bellied old man trapped in an invalid chair gesticulated imperatively with a long stick at his two assistants as they struggled to pin up the paper shapes in the precise positions on the wall that he indicated. An inch to the left. Two inches to the right. The young women stood on almost the top rungs of stepladders, tilted forwards precariously, shifted their arms this way and that, gesturing like figures in La Danse. Those red figures. My dream surfaced, sank back. Matisse choreographed his ardent girls. They stretched out their fingertips, patting the cut-outs into place, knocked and tapped with slender hammers at thin nails.

The camera panned back. A high-ceilinged, corniced space. Half-closed shutters seemed to keep out much of the light. The darkness of early ciné-film, perhaps. A home movie: flickering, shadowy. The intent, serious young women dressed in glowing, jewel-like colours. A sleeveless amber frock. A broad violet satin headband binding shoulder-length black hair. Bare brown legs. High-heeled wedge sandals with open toes. It must have been high summer. They could have been out swimming with their friends in the blue-gold-green sea but instead they swam around this imperious old man, netted by his need. Just a few minutes and the stream of images ended. The loop began again. The man in the wheelchair raised his magician's wand. The young women bent forwards, pivoted, reached out their arms.

He was living in a hotel in Nice, I reminded Phyllis, renting a suite of rooms. He'd been ill, unable to go out. He turned one of the rooms into his studio. Then all of them. No separation between work life and domestic life. He fused them. That was revolutionary, at the time.

Yes, Phyllis said, yes, I remember, of course I do.

She sipped her wine. This is very dry.

She took another sip. Plenty of women artists, once they got married and had children, worked at home, didn't they? A corner of the kitchen table, if they were lucky. That's when lots of them gave up.

Yes, I said: but I'm talking about a male artist.

Matisse never had to cook or clean or look after his children, once he married, Phyllis said. There was always a woman for that. And there in that hotel, he had that secretary-housekeeper who took care of everything. Completely devoted to him. All right for some!

His cut-outs brought the outside inside, I said, paper leaves and branches on every wall surrounding him like a forest. He lived in his imagination too, he pushed the inside to the outside. You could say that the pinned-up shapes on his walls were his daytime dreams embodied and transformed in carved-out pieces of paper. His memories as well, of his travels abroad. Ajaccio. Tangiers. Oceania.

I suppose the housekeeper-woman felt flattered, Phyllis said, serving a genius. Like his models. They were supposed to feel flattered too. It's a real skill being a model, very hard work, but no one ever thinks of that.

That's not true, I said. Some of us do.

I didn't mean you, Phyllis said. I meant other people.

In her early twenties Phyllis had worked as an artist's model, at a college of further education in central London. I had an admin job in the same place: processing the staff's weekly claim sheets, booking the teaching rooms, answering queries. The art studio drew me, with its racks of canvases, its half-circles of easels, its glass jars stuck with brushes smelling of turps. Sometimes I'd find an excuse to visit the top floor while teaching was going on, to witness the magic close-up. Did the students have enough pencils, erasers, rags? I'd linger just a few moments, so as not to annoy anyone, then leave.

Officially I went home at six, but one night, staying late to catch up on filing, I got bored even sooner than I expected, and so to pass the time I wandered out, climbed three flights of bare stone stairs and strolled to and fro along the top-floor corridor, glancing through the panes of glass set in the classroom doors. In the art studio fifteen beginners were struggling to master charcoal, to sweep it across the blank sheet of paper the way the teacher in front of them was doing. A young woman, pale all over, perched on a wide, high stool set on a dais. She gripped its edges with both hands. Chin up, gaze distant. Long, wavy, golden-red hair. The matching muff between her legs. Long straight toes. The students, clutching their thin black sticks, were concentrating raptly on her. Such will and resolution of her muscles. Her commitment tensed along my spine, in my fingertips.

I returned to my cubbyhole-office downstairs, got on with opening and shutting metal drawers. A sudden flow of voices. Students chattering as they streamed past marked the start of the break, people making for the basement cafeteria. I waited until they'd passed, been swallowed by the stairwell, then wandered out, climbed to the top floor. The model stood just outside the studio door, her back to me. She'd thrown on a wrap, was yawning and stretching. Free. Returned to her private self. I shouldn't disturb her.

She began pacing towards the end of the corridor. I followed her. She reached the window, leaned against the sill, took out a packet of cigarettes, swivelled. She watched me approach. She inclined her head to take my light, gazed at me through a grey-blue cloud. I saw you peeping, earlier on. What have you got to say for yourself? I felt myself blush. I took off my jacket and placed it around her shoulders. It's freezing up here. Don't catch cold.

Over the following weeks we established a routine. She sat for the students in the art class, and I caught up with my backlog of filing and typing. Cigarettes and easy, complicit silence in the break, then later we'd lounge in the pub, making halves of beer stretch to an hour or so. She was training as a ballet dancer, posing at night to pay the fees, renting a room in a communal flat, living on apples and tinned sardines. I ended up taking classes held on the same nights as her modelling sessions. European literature, then later on gay history. Afterwards we'd meet on the college front steps, plot the rest of the evening, if not the pub then a mooch along the river. At weekends, if we had the cash we went to the cinema, or to rock gigs. Sometimes we watched TV in Phyllis's shared sitting-room, or put on records and danced.

When Phyllis was told that she would never make it as a classical dancer, too tall, she withdrew from ballet school. She began to starve herself. I formed part of a band of friends who tried to help, taking it in turns to visit, to coax her to eat. I think she wanted to die, at one point. She dwindled close to it. Finally she went into hospital and submitted to treatment. She decided to survive. Something in her had struggled out, fought back. The life force. The Phyllis force.

Dear Phyllis. The sunlight reached under the canopy of clematis and glossed the clear outlines of her face, marked and shaped by her life. What was a line or two, a wrinkle or two? They only deepened her appeal.

Modelling's demanding, Phyllis said, it's really tiring. But you hardly ever get to know the model's name. Unless she's the painter's mistress of course. Then you might. If he's famous enough.

Scissors as big as shears grasped in Matisse's hands. Pain drove him and he drove it back, controlled it. The young woman assistant stood by, held the big painted paper sheet, swivelled and twisted it as Matisse cut, instructed her on turns and angles and curves, cut again. Yes, a joint project. A collaboration. He couldn't have done it without her. Matisse and his pain. Matisse and the girl. The thick paper alive, tense and taut between them. He carved into it.

Not completely true, I said. Matisse named some of his paintings after the women who modelled for them, didn't he? Usually just their first names, I grant you. Unless they were portraits of course.

He liked painting luscious female flesh, said Phyllis, beautiful young women. But these days people don't only want to look at young women. Some people find older women beautiful too.

Yes, of course they do, I said. Like my mother.

Berthe's so slim and elegant, her neighbours would tell me, so chic, one can tell she's French.

Upright and eagle-faced. Everybody admired her. My eyes wetted. Quickly I blew my nose.

Clem's neighbours, on the other hand, wouldn't have called her beautiful. Her childlike hairstyle, lack of make-up. Her odd, old-fashioned clothes. The doctor taking off his wire-rimmed spectacles, regarding her quietly as she poured black coffee into small turquoise cups.

Not as old as your mother, Phyllis said. I didn't mean that.

I cleared our plates. Phyllis was so jumpy today. What was up with her?

Pudding distressed her all over again. Oh, D., I'm so sorry. But that looks much too rich for me.

Meringue interleaved with thinly sliced pears poached in wine, the whole topped with whipped cream and toasted flaked almonds. Frothy and absurd as an Edwardian hat.

I'd made the pavlova for Freddy, hadn't I? Freddy who loved

food and drink. A fantasy of his not scarpering but staying for lunch, sharing a bottle of wine, coming back to bed, making love all afternoon.

Phyllis scraped up a spoonful of pear, nibbled it. D., darling, it's kind of you to invite me to come away with you. But I can't, that's all. And don't you think you ought to go somewhere else, for a change? You're always going to France. Don't you think you've got stuck in a bit of a rut?

I like France, that's all, I said: I was hoping you'd come too. But if you can't, you can't.

I'm in the middle of something, she said: and so I'm not sure whether I can get away. Actually, I'm just at the beginning. But it feels like the middle already.

A sweet shot of sherbet fizzed and twisted inside me. I hadn't got that far with Freddy and I never would. Ah. I see. You've met someone, haven't you? Of course. I should have guessed.

Internet dating. The time before last that we'd seen each other, six weeks back, she'd mentioned it. I miss having a special person so much, darling. I miss having a companion. I've done my mourning. Johnny wouldn't mind. He'd take it as a compliment to our time together. We were happy, he'd want me to be happy again. That's how it works.

The sainted John had cooked for her, understood her need for close women friends, cheerfully escorted her to the ballet performances he couldn't comprehend. Why else had she chosen him? He was kind, willing to do his share of housework, tolerated her eccentric male pals such as myself. Once I demanded of Phyllis: I thought you'd decided marriage was a patriarchal trap to control women? Phyllis had said: I'll try anything once. And we wanted children, it was a way of making a commitment to be parents. The children hadn't happened, but the marriage had lasted. Typical John to die without causing any trouble, keeling over while watching football on TV.

When Phyllis had told me about trawling the websites I'd admired her. She was willing to make herself vulnerable, admit her need for sex, for love. Being Phyllis, she'd gone about it in business-like fashion. All her years of managing a shoe shop: she'd learned to sum people up. Some of her customers, without realising it, wanted Cinderella's ballroom slippers, some desired to walk on air, some demanded seven-league boots. Phyllis knelt before them, opened boxes, pulled aside tissue paper, extracted dreams, possibilities, refined these down to specifics. Choice! You tried on several pairs, you necessarily discriminated between brogues, ballet shoes, high heels, trainers. You found what truly suited you. Often a surprise. Lovers could be approached in the same experimental spirit. Try them on for fit. See whether they pinch, give you blisters.

The idea of advertising dismayed me. I'd tried to explain to her: I know I'm much too romantic. But I can't bear the thought of going to meet someone knowing we're going to judge each other on whether we're fanciable or not. I prefer to meet someone by chance. Phyllis had said: how long will you have to wait for that chance to happen, though?

I'd had many lovers. Several long-term love affairs. Then I'd met Freddy at that launch party. Much younger than I, gym-muscled, slyly handsome. Phyllis had hardly noticed him. He remained a secret I guarded. Now his departure was a secret too.

Phyllis drained her glass. Sunlight glittered on its rim. She set it back on the tablecloth in a puddle of pink petals fallen from the roses overhead. It's amazing, she said: I thought I might get some sex but I didn't expect to fall in love. I didn't think it would ever happen to me again. But it has.

She paused. Her face soft. Eyes half-veiled.

I said: so what's his name?

Her name, Phyllis said. Her name is Angela.

Oh, I said, Angela.

Phyllis began smiling. She's the most intriguing person. I've been wanting to tell you for weeks. But I didn't know how. I knew you'd be pleased for me. But I felt shy as well.

Perhaps she had feared I'd be jealous and so had been nervous. Yes, I was jealous. I knew I shouldn't be. Another rule of friendship: rejoice in your friend's happiness and don't reveal the tiniest hint of envy.

What's she like? I asked. Let me guess. She prefers New World wine to French, she doesn't like prosecco.

She's a film-maker, Phyllis said. She makes arts documentaries for TV. You've probably seen some of her work without realising it. People often give the presenter credit rather than her. You have to look carefully at the titles to find her name.

She's a part-time vegetarian, I continued. She likes colourful clothes.

On Phyllis, not on herself. She'd wear black, of course. A Japanese-style tunic, with a slanted hem, over baggy pleated trousers.

Don't be mean, Phyllis said. You know I'd be thrilled if something this wonderful happened to you.

Sorry, I said.

I looked down at my glass, then back at her. That outfit really suits you.

From a charity shop in King's Road, Phyllis said. All the rich women dump their clothes there.

She stroked the grey cardigan hanging over the arm of her chair. Cashmere. But it cost hardly anything. Oops. I'm not supposed to explain. Angela says I should just accept the compliment.

I made coffee and brought it outside. I served it in the yellow espresso cups from Monoprix Phyllis had given me for Christmas years back. She recognised them and smiled. In fact, she said, sipping, Angela and I are going to France too. To Paris, actually. There's a street art exhibition opening at a new gallery up in the 19th. Angela's been invited to the press view. Young artists from the *banlieue*.

I said: putting street art into a gallery negates it, surely.

Phyllis said: Angela says so too. But she wants to go and see for herself. Just in case it would make material for a film.

You're going by train? I asked.

As far as Paris, Phyllis said, then after that we'll fly down to Cannes. Angela's idea is to hire a car there, so that we can make more of a holiday of it, go wherever we like. For a start I want to go to Le Cannet and visit the Bonnard museum. You can't get into his actual house, apparently. But you can stand in the street and look at it, imagine Marthe in her bath.

I fired sugar lumps at Phyllis. So, a model who did have a name, a wife who was also a model. A model wife?

Phyllis chucked the sugar lumps back. Angela's interested in how knowing about their relationship might make you look at the paintings in a particular way, or not. Whether we feel intimate with Marthe, or whether we feel like voyeurs. Whether that matters.

Angela this. Angela that. She'd be showing Angela our favourite Parisian bars, our favourite backstreet routes. Together they'd discover new cafés, new bistros. They'd create joint memories. Doubtless they'd stay in our favourite hotel, with its creaking wooden staircase. One room not two. Don't be a creep, I berated myself. Here's your oldest friend fallen in love and full of hope. Be kind. Be generous. Behave.

Well, I said, it's definitely Paris for me again. So if we're all there at the same time, and if it suits, perhaps we could meet up for lunch. Only if you and Angela would like that, of course. Only if you want to introduce me.

Phyllis finished my speech for me. Only I don't want to intrude. I don't want to be a nuisance. D., you are ridiculous.

She left at teatime. She hugged me. Take care, darling.

She loitered on the front path, looking back, hand on the latch of the gate. D. Don't become a D.W., will you? Remember how we used to play dares? You used to be up for anything, in those days.

I pretended not to hear and lifted a hand in farewell. She raised her voice. I dare you to do something a bit different. See how it feels.

Don't patronise me, I called. She stepped out briskly, flapped aside a skateboarding youth, skirted a dog turd. She unchained her bicycle, disappeared up the street.

Dreadful Warning. One of Phyllis's youthful code terms. Applied to any of our contemporaries who steered clear of challenges, who aimed at bourgeois comfort, bourgeois certainty. Not her idea of a life. Yes, darling, I know, lots of people don't have the choice. I'm privileged even to be thinking about it. But still. Since I can, I shall. Accordingly, after leaving hospital she'd taken a clerical job like mine to pay for evening classes in applied arts, then joined a female design group, sharing ideas, work and wages, all of them living together, against the rules of the lease, in the rented workshop-studio. She supported me

47

to come out, she pushed me to open up to new adventures, just as she had.

I used to let that happen. When had I changed? I'd always thought that I'd keep on relishing life just as long as I kept on encountering new possibilities, I swore I'd only start to feel old when life stopped throwing new chances at me. I didn't want to know in advance what was round the corner. I sprinted towards the corner to find out. Now, in my sixties, I knew that death lay waiting there. Fuck off, death, I'm not ready. Phyllis was right. I could do with another adventure or two. Not another lover. Freddy had finished me off. I'd never find another lover now. Too old. No more erotic love. But the love of friends: yes, I had that.

In the kitchen Phyllis's hyacinths in their dark yellow jug were releasing their scent. Rich as the smell of warm naked bodies after sex. I wanted to ring Freddy, ask if he fancied meeting up for a drink, discover whether we could move into simply being friends. Was it too soon?

First of all, though, I should clear up. Then we'd see. He probably wouldn't be free. He probably had a date already. Presumably he'd been seeing other people besides me. I didn't know. On the other hand I knew that he used verveine eau de toilette, his sweat too smelled green and fresh, he cut his hair short to subdue its curls, he supported Arsenal, his tastes in music were eclectic and wide-ranging enough to overlap with mine.

Of course he wouldn't want to see me again. He'd made that pretty clear. He wouldn't return any message I left. He'd have deleted my number from his phone. Leave him alone.

Someone knocked on my kitchen door. It could only be Frieda. I glanced around. Had Phyllis left something behind in the hall?

My landlady cut a dashing figure in a low-necked fuchsia-pink angora sweater, narrow purple trousers, silver high-heeled mules, purple and pink feather earrings. She thrust an envelope at me. Denis, my love, this came yesterday, got mixed up with a whole bunch of my mail. I forgot to bring it back down for you. Only remembered just now.

Cup of tea? I said: I'm in the middle of clearing up, but you could come in anyway. Just ignore the mess.

No worries, Frieda said. Another time, dearie.

She departed. I looked at my letter. A second one from France, also forwarded by the undertaker. My name typed this time. I tore open the envelope, pulled out a single sheet.

Sister Marie-Lucile of the Sisters of Notre Dame de Bon Secour addressed to me her polite greetings. As Director of the care home in La Ciotat, near Marseilles, where my godmother Clémence was now living, she wished me to know that my godmother, having belatedly seen the notice in *The Times* of my mother's recent death, sent her sincere condolences. She ardently desired me to visit her at my earliest convenience, should such a visit be possible. If I would email, write or telephone, all could be arranged. My godmother was in reasonably good health, though her increasing years saw her becoming more fragile than formerly. A sprained wrist prevented her from writing to me herself. Sister Marie-Lucile signed off *yours in Christ*. Under her signature: the letters ONDBS surmounted with a black shield topped with a black cross.

Back in the kitchen the litter on the table waited: a pile of smeared plates and serving dishes, a tumble of crumpled tea towels, a heap of vegetable peelings and sauce-smeared wooden spoons flanking used saucepans and frying pans. Matisse painted the *before*: four shining pink-skinned onions sprouting little green horns, or two intact purple aubergines, or a clean coffee pot. He played with their shapes; he made them almost abstract. He didn't paint the *after*; that didn't interest him. Too ugly? Well, he wasn't thinking about cooking at all, was he. Just about colours. He wasn't thinking about eating. Once, I'd read, while working at the seaside he painted a turbot from the morning's catch then threw it back into the sea. The anecdote supposedly showed he wasn't possessive or greedy. But surely from the turbot's point of view that didn't matter. The turbot was presumably dead by that point. *Nature très morte.*

I took out my phone and photographed the dirty pots and utensils, the disorder. Why? I didn't know.

Then I opened my laptop, found the French railways website, and began checking fares.

6. Black-and-white photograph (place and date unknown) by Yvette Martin of Henri and Amélie Matisse

The corner of a dining-room. The couple sit at opposite ends of a table covered by a white cloth. Twisted table legs show underneath the tablecloth's white fringe, and a strip of Turkish rug. The ruins of a lunch fill the distance between the man and the woman. The table bears a wine bottle, a platter of disarranged fruit, half a baguette, two coffee cups. Spilled coffee stains the white cloth. A fallen empty wine glass, dribbling wine, nudges a split open peach. Pushed to one side: a pile of used crockery, two napkins flung down. A second wine glass lies broken on the rug.

Close behind them, four paintings, two on each wall, depict voluptuous women, their limbs contorted like plaits of dough referencing the plump baguette beneath them, the twisted table legs; one woman sitting and the others reclining; three sumptuously nude and two in harem costumes. Bellies swelling like choux buns. Impassive faces.

Moustached and bearded, Matisse scowls at the camera, one clenched fist resting on the tablecloth. In his other hand he clasps a serrated-edged fruit knife, pointing it like a weapon at the viewer. He wears a thick suit, the jacket open over a waistcoat; white collar subduing a tightly knotted tie. The characteristic heavy outfit of the bourgeois, urged upon him by Amélie, according to his biographer, Hilary Spurling. It's hard to imagine him with his clothes off; frolicking naked. Yet during the times when he lives apart from Amélie, so Spurling records, when he stays down south and Amélie remains in the north, he dutifully visits the local brothel once a month. It's not much fun, he tells a friend in a letter.

Amélie, in a black cardigan, a low-collared white blouse, leans forwards, frowning at her husband. Silvery hair drawn back. Dark arching eyebrows wriggle above big dark eyes. Her raised forefinger points at Matisse.

7. Odalisque Reclining

CLÉMENCE

The bakery smelled of warm bread. The baker's white-aproned wife was fitting a batch of loaves into the baskets on the half-empty shelf behind the counter. She turned, glum as usual. She nodded towards the back of the shop, the door open onto a brown-tiled corridor. Through there and up two flights. First door on the right. You can fetch down the breakfast things, see what madam wants for lunch. Nothing too fancy, tell her. We can't manage it.

I trod up the steep twists of stairs. Slippery, wedge-shaped brown boards. On the landing I hovered, then knocked. A pause. I knocked again, more sharply. A woman's voice murmured come in.

The room smelled sour. Ten o'clock, and she hadn't yet got up. Or she'd begun to, then lost heart. She was lying slumped on the divan set in the corner, a couple of cushions under her head. Downturned mouth. Black hair tangling around her shoulders. She wore a white dressing-gown with frilled edges, open over a pale orange petticoat trimmed with matching orange ribbon. A pair of mauve stockings floated across the back of a chair. Feather-topped mules lay on their side nearby.

She moved her head. The slightest of nods. She looked list-less. Winded, somehow. What was wrong with her? Was she feeling ill? Or was she just lazy? Women here did not lounge about like queens, only half-dressed, refusing to speak. Even when they were pregnant they got up every day. They greeted you when they met you. They got on with their work like anyone else. Ah. So that was it.

Someone had emptied the bucket by the divan, but the smell of sick lingered. Her hands clasped her belly, as though it hurt.

I began tidying. I collected a pair of men's sturdy boots, the soles clotted with earth, a pair of blue high-heeled shoes, the toes dusty, and set them by the door to take down for cleaning. On the table in the middle of the room crusts of bread lay on green-rimmed plates, next to a couple of flat beige books with hard covers, a coffee cup with brown dregs. A second coffee cup held a floating cigarette stub. A tray leaned against a straw-seated chair. I leaned down for it, then moved the books and newspaper aside, began to stack the dirty crockery. I put the crusts in a saucer, for the bakery hens.

She clicked her tongue. Careful with those sketchbooks. He doesn't like anyone touching them. Leave them alone.

She sat up, resting on her spread hands. I ought to finish getting dressed. Brush my hair for me, would you?

She heaved herself off the divan and moved to the chair by the window. A small table bore a hand mirror, a leather case like a tiny hatbox, with a black silk loop on top. A jumble of combs and clips.

I tied her lace cape round her shoulders. She grunted and muttered as I lifted the black mass of her hair. Then she calmed. My brush stroked her into submission.

Coil it up into a chignon, she said: make sure you fix it securely in place.

She clasped the mirror by its handle, grimaced. Well. That will have to do.

54

I handed her the silk blouse. Did she only have the one? So she wasn't as well off as she'd first seemed. I dropped the long skirt over her head and buttoned it at the side. The top two buttons wouldn't do up.

I said: what would you and Monsieur like for lunch?

She frowned, rolling on her stockings. She pointed to her feathered mules. I crouched in front of her, slid them onto her feet. Oh, Monsieur will take care of himself. He's got bread in his bag, a bottle of water, some fruit, he'll be fine. He does what he pleases, that one. I've got to stifle here all day in this poky room while he sits at his ease in the sunshine.

Her fingers pleated folds in her lap. Catching my glance, she placed her right hand over her left, spread them as though to admire her shiny nails.

If you'd like to take the air, I said, I could show you the square. It's got a very fine fountain, with a dolphin. There's a nice place to sit, on one of the benches under the plane trees.

And be stared at by all the old tabbies of the village, she said. No, thank you.

She pushed back the lid of the leather case, dipped her fingers in, pulled out an array of tiny pots. She unscrewed their tops, considered their contents. Mirror in hand, she began smudging rouge across her cheeks. One colour following the curve of her cheekbones, another defining the hollow under them. She worked busily, staring at her reflection. I stared too. My mother never painted her face. She said only tarts did.

Or if you prefer, I said, we could walk up the hill towards the vineyards.

No, she said, he'll be there, working, and he won't want to be disturbed. In any case, I'm too tired.

Well then, I said, I'll leave you to it. I'll take down the

breakfast dishes, then, if you'll give me a few francs, I'll go out to the vegetable stalls and buy something for your lunch.

I made her a potato salad, with a hardboiled egg, and olives on top. She merely picked at it. More leftovers for the hens. With her coffee she smoked a cigarette, then kicked off her mules and lay on the divan again, on her side, one hand beneath her head, the other cupping her belly. While she slept I drew her with the pencil I found on the mantelpiece. She curved like the letter S. I used the back of an envelope I fished out of the wastepaper basket. When I'd finished I folded the envelope and slid it into my pocket.

I ran home, borrowed our draughts board, a pack of cards. When she woke up, I'd have games all ready to amuse her with. I assembled a *tian* of courgettes I picked from the baker's vegetable patch, carried it back to the bakery, to cook in the cooling oven there, ready for her supper, whenever she wanted it, hot or cold.

Upstairs I found her still asleep. I went over to the table and leafed through the sketchbooks. Drawings of pots, dishes, seashells. Drawings of a woman with no clothes on: Mrs Camille standing, sitting, lying down.

The artist returned in the late afternoon, just as the light began to turn golden, the start of that lovely time when out in the street the air would grow chilly, somehow making a music like a struck bronze bell, and the sky would deepen purer blue as the sun slipped behind the mountain. He looked tired, dreamy. Twisting his hat in his hand. His hair standing up. Yes, just like a brush. He wasn't properly back yet. His mind had stayed behind, among the red and purple of the vines. She and I were simply part of the room. Shapes. Table, armchair, divan, two women. He didn't really see us.

She sat up, tears in her eyes. Oh, I've missed you so much.

What was his first name? I didn't know his surname either. The Parisians, Dad had called them. Did she have a nickname for him? I'd call him the Brush.

Sweetheart! He dropped his bag on the table, shrugged off his big coat. He nodded at me, dismissing me, crossed the room to her, kissed her forehead. She tried to turn her face away but he held her by the chin in his brown fingers. He spoke to her in a coaxing tone. Almost before I'd shut the door behind me I heard her complaints begin. It's so dull here. I've nothing to do. How can you expect me to endure this?

I loitered on the narrow landing, listening. His voice bore hers down. She needed to rest, she was in good hands here, he wasn't leaving her all alone at all, she had company. Such a good little country girl, one can see she only wants to make herself useful. A sob or two. Don't be silly, now. Come, we'll go out to the bar, have an aperitif, that will make you feel better, come along.

I left them to it. If they wanted their supper later on they could fetch it themselves. I walked home, got to work in the kitchen. While I chopped onions Mum prodded me for details. You worked hard? They were nice to you?

The day belonged to me, not to my mother. Yes, I said, yes, everything was fine.

The bang of shutters being closed in the shop. The shutters safeguarding the windows, the street entry. The squeak of their flat iron bolts. Mother and I were fastened in for the night, like the chickens and rabbits. Dad slammed the yard gate behind him. His back way out to the bar.

Mum nodded towards the mantelpiece. Look up there. A postcard came for you, from your friend Monique. She's working at the Hotel Regina in Nice. Very swish. Lucky girl.

Why had she read it? It was my post, not hers. She'd propped it against the brass candlestick, near the photo of my brother. A picture of a spray of yellow-flowered gladioli. Monique's message written in pencil. *I've got a new temp job, night work, looking after one of the guests. Lovely sunny weather, but much too cold to swim! Wish you were here! Meilleurs voeux.* Under her signature she'd put a lacy flourish. A twirl. Like someone dancing.

Dad returned in time for supper, and reported on the newcomers. Perfectly polite, I suppose, greeting everyone when they first came in then sitting over in the corner, not talking much, keeping themselves to themselves. That young woman was bold, though. Hard-faced. When people stared at her she stared right back.

He leaned across the table and stroked my hair. And how's my little girl? All right with you, were they?

Of course, I said.

After supper, in my room, I took out from my pocket the envelope with my drawing on it. No good. I would keep it, though, to remind myself how much I had to learn. I slipped the envelope into the drawer of the washstand. I put Monique's postcard in with it.

The following morning, once my parents had gone next door to open up the shop, I lifted the lid of my mother's workbasket, took out a paper of needles, a reel of dark blue thread. They went into my pocket, wrapped in a handkerchief. I added in a pair of nail scissors.

When I arrived at the bakery, the baker's wife told me that the artist had already left for the vineyard. He'd left instructions: I was to stay with Madame, as I'd done yesterday, see she had all she needed.

Upstairs, Mrs Camille didn't seem to hear my knock. Too quiet? I knocked again. No reply. I twisted the knob, opened the door, went in. She was pacing to and fro, hair twisted up untidily, hands in the pockets of her dressing-gown. Her nightdress lay flung on the floor, the sleeves stretched out. Like a woman face down, weeping.

She turned, nodded. Her eyelids swollen, pale mauve. I drew the chair to the table, got her to sit. She asked for coffee, and some bread and jam. Or I should say chicory, sawdust and mashed marrow. The café over the road will provide them, the landlady won't, she says she hasn't got time to wait on me. She does on *him*, though. She fetched him coffee before he left.

She pointed at the table. There's my purse. Take some money. Take that bucket away with you too, while you're at it.

I came back upstairs with a little tray, and served her. She said: I wasn't very friendly to you yesterday. I was feeling unwell. But today I am better.

I mumbled something. She said: use my name, will you? When you call me *madame* it makes me feel old.

Using her Christian name felt too familiar. Rude. I stayed silent. She lit a cigarette. You want one? I shook my head. She said: smoking helps my nerves. It helps me keep calm.

Her long fingers tapped ash. She'd forgotten to hide her lack of a wedding ring. Her nails gleamed like mother-of-pearl.

She caught me looking. She said: I like to take care of my hands. Massage them with almond oil, if I can get hold of it. Something else I forgot to bring with me to this godforsaken place.

My mother makes her own hand cream, I said. She mixes lanolin and beeswax, and lavender. I'm sure she'd give you some, if you wanted.

In Paris, said Camille, you just buy such things. Well, you

did, before the war. They've come back again, but much more costly. Some people call them luxuries but for me they're essential, given the work I do.

She paused. Inhaling. Blowing out harsh-smelling smoke. I fed her the question. What work's that?

I'm a model, she said. Now that the clothes shops have opened up again, they need girls like me to show the new clothes to the clientele. I have to be very well groomed. It all costs a fortune, I can tell you. The hairdresser, the manicures, the make-up. All my salary goes on them. There's no end to it.

She was boasting, just like we used to do at school, returning after the holidays, displaying a new skirt, a new bracelet.

I said: my mother runs a dressmaking business but she doesn't have models showing the clothes. She just fits them straight onto the customers.

My mother kept her tape measure slung around her neck. A narrow strip of waxed cloth, marked with lines and black numbers, with metal tips at either end. Piece of tailor's chalk, round and smooth, in one pocket, box of pins in the other. Gently she took hold of the client's shoulders, turned her to face the long mirror, smoothing out a tuck here, shortening a cuff there. She unpicked, re-pinned, re-sewed.

Camille lit another cigarette. Smoking kills the appetite, she explained. For the dress shop, you have to stay thin. Whereas with the artists, that's not so. They like to paint women with real bodies.

Not pregnant ones so much, surely. Would the Brush paint Mrs Camille now? He wanted her to hide herself away.

She yawned and stretched. I suppose I should get dressed. Give me a hand, there's a good child. Wait, there's a button off my skirt. That wretched waistband's too tight.

I said: I'll stitch it back on for you, if you want. I've got my sewing things with me. And I could let out the waist a bit, too. It's easy, as long as there's enough of a seam. It won't take more than a few minutes.

Well, she said, I see you understand the situation. So, since you're offering. Yes.

The Brush returned at dusk. He burst in to the stuffy room where I sat reading aloud to Camille. She was lying back, eyes closed, one hand thrown up above her head, the other spread on her belly. He banged the door behind him. Hello hello hello! He pushed past me to kiss her. I shut the magazine, got up. What a clatter! Bag dumped onto one chair, coat discarded, slung over the back of another. Boots pulled off thrown across the floor. Hat following. Rubbing his hands together. Sweetheart. It went so well today.

She gave him a cold glance he didn't notice. He thrust his feet into leather slippers, he stretched out his arms, flexing them, he strode back and forth across the room. I willed her to respond. He was doing his best, wasn't he? Cajoling her to let his mood cover them both, like a nice warm blanket. Was she punishing him, by refusing to speak? Perhaps she didn't dare allow herself to get angry. In case she exploded, flew into bits, killed him. Or in case he hit her.

She lay still. Stony-faced and silent. I bent over the table, tidying my sewing. He crossed towards me, smiled, pulled my plait. You like drawing, don't you? I remember now. I'll give you a lesson, one of these days. Would you like that?

Yes, please, I said. I heard myself sounding like a good little country girl. Camille heard me too. Being nice to him, I was betraying her. She lowered her eyelids, huddled even more into herself.

He patted my cheek. Not this evening, though. I'm too tired. Skip off home now, there's a good child.

As I closed the door, he began talking to Camille. Interesting face, she has. Not as plain as you make out. I should draw her some time.

Camille protested. No. She's as ugly as sin.

Next morning brought pale sun, an icy blue sky. At the top of the hill I turned the corner, looked towards the bakery just as the Brush emerged. He moved awkwardly, lugging a tripod, a black canvas duffel bag, a smaller bag, also his folding stool. I met him where our paths crossed in the street. He greeted me with a nod, a grunt. He was wrestling with his unwieldy load. I turned away, turned back. Can I help you, monsieur?

He said: you're early. Madame is still fast asleep.

I said: so there's time for me to give you a hand. That all looks very heavy.

I took the stool and the smaller bag from him. He fitted the duffel bag over one shoulder, the tripod over another. There. I'm laden like a donkey. Sure you can manage those? Lead on.

We batted our way into the cold wind funnelling between the houses. The Brush began gasping, protesting. I said: there's always a wind blowing in Provence. You'll get used to it.

At the edge of the village the wind changed direction and blew us up the steep path. At the vineyard we stopped. He clambered over the low stone wall. I handed him his things, piece by piece.

He said: don't go just yet. Would you like to watch me set up? Today I'm going to take photographs.

I climbed across. I didn't want to look too keen so I found myself something to do. I picked some sprigs of thyme from the low bush nearby, rolled them between my fingers, sniffing their harsh fragrance. Flavouring for tonight's leftovers soup. He took out a black box out of the duffel bag, unstrapped it. You know what these are? Specialist lenses.

He named all his bits of equipment as he took them out, one by one. You're not the only person in the world with a camera, I told him: my father's had one for years. Not like this one, said the Brush. I doubt that very much.

He reached over my shoulder, took hold of my plait, pulling it forward. He lifted it, dipped it into an invisible paint pot, made a series of crosses in the air. Thanks for your help. My dear little creature. I really owe you a lesson now, don't I?

He took my hand. Later today, perhaps. If I've time. He squeezed my fingers. This will have to do for now, by way of thanks.

He gave me a swift kiss. Just a graze of the lips. He dropped my hand. Now you must be off.

He stuck his hands in his pockets, smiled. White teeth in his brown face. Posing for his picture. Pleased with himself and the frosty day and the clear light.

Wait. There's something else you can do for me. I can trust you, sweetie, can't I?

Of course, I said.

He rubbed a hand over his nose and mouth. His voice was airy. It's nothing much. Just that I've suddenly remembered, I've left some papers on the table back there. Put them away for me, will you? Put them behind the clock. No need to tell Madame once she's up. No need for her to see them. I don't want her to be worried by anything.

He gave me a second brief kiss. Away with you.

Upstairs at the baker's, the door into the bedroom was closed. Camille was clattering about behind it. Among his clutter of breakfast things I found an open bottle of ink, a couple of sheets of scribbled writing held down at one corner by the milk jug. Looping lines in blue. A fountain pen marbled in green and black, with a steel nib. *Mon enfant, ma soeur,* he had written: *thinking of you, I remember Baudelaire's poem. Mainly because here I encounter its opposite. No luxe, calme et volupté. Nothing like that among the peasants. Just a hard bed, freezing cold weather, poor food and bad wine. But I'm getting plenty of work done, and that was the whole point of coming away, wasn't it?*

My eye jumped down the page. *The peasants and village people are dark, sturdy as planks of oak, impossible to know, toughened by their constricted, harsh lives, with their own very particular ideas and ways. They scarcely speak. To each other they grunt in dialect. The older women all wear black. You'd have shocked them, my dear, if you had arrived, with your colourful, unconventional clothes, your lovely curly hair falling down out of its pins, your free and easy ways. Much better you have stayed where you are. Give my love to Paris, and to any of our friends you run across. Our separation makes me sad, but in any case we'll see each other very soon. I've had a telegram from Mme Lydia on behalf of Matisse – as you know I asked her to write to me here poste restante, to keep me informed about his health. So now Mme Lydia is suggesting I visit them in Nice after I finish in Cannes. He's much better, apparently, and eager to take up where we left off, and as*

White paper, thin and light as tissue. Spoiled by ink blots and coffee stains. A smear of grease. Perhaps it was just a rough draft, such as we'd learned to make at school, for a fair copy later. I folded the letter, put it behind the clock. I stuck the pen and the inkpot on the mantelpiece, to one side of the mirror.

I addressed the person frowning back at me. Hard to speak much, you know, to people like you. With your bitter, limping tongue, your peculiar accent, your plain face turning away. Your ugliness.

I didn't see the artist that evening. I left before he returned. Next morning, when I arrived, the baker's wife told me that he had packed up and gone away. He had caught the early bus down to Marseilles. Presumably from there he'd be taking the train. Where to? How should I know? She shrugged. He had paid for the rooms in advance, so if he wanted to dash about the country it was nothing to do with her. And Madame? She's upstairs. In a fair old taking, I might add.

I climbed the stairs. The door to the room stood open. I peered through the gap. Camille, in her white dressing-gown, her hair loose, was sitting at the table. Upright, straight-backed. Her right hand moved steadily, rhythmically. Her fingers gripped a white edge of paper, lifted it, pulled it. She was ripping the pages out of his sketchbook, flinging them down one by one.

She tore up each drawing. In half then in half again. She swept all the white fragments together, lifted them, dropped them into the wastepaper basket. She threw the sketchbook in after them.

Why had he left one of his sketchbooks behind? Why hadn't he protected it better? Like a precious bird. And she was tearing its wings off. Too late to stop her. Too late to stop him, either. A tiny figure jumping onto the bus. Escaping.

I knocked, hesitated. She got up, pushed back her chair. Walked out of view. Footsteps clicked across the wooden floor. I pushed the door wide, went in. She was sitting on the divan, legs crossed, smoking. She looked clenched, like a fist. She'd shoved the wastepaper basket under the table. Torn white pieces pushed down and the sketchbook with outspread covers a dead bird indeed.

She drew on her cigarette. I waited.

She said: you're a kind person, aren't you? You sympathise with me, I can feel it. You've been helping me these last few days. You'd help me again, if I needed more help, wouldn't you?

She made kind sound like an insult. It meant weak. Dutiful. I nodded. I put on my good girl voice. Yes, I said.

She spoke fast, in a high voice. My husband received a telegram yesterday. His mother has been taken ill and he has had to leave in a hurry to go and visit her in the hospital in Cannes. He has gone on ahead, and the plan is for me to join him as soon as possible. I wasn't feeling well enough earlier to catch the bus with him. Mornings can be a bad time for me. I couldn't face that long journey. But tomorrow I'm sure I'll feel strong enough to travel. If you would come early and give me a hand with my packing, I'll catch the late-morning bus. The baker's wife told me the times.

She recited this speech with her eyes half-lowered. She darted a sly sideways glance at me through her eyelashes, to check how I was taking her tale. I kept a straight face, nodded.

So, she said, how shall we amuse ourselves today?

We played Lotto. We played two-handed *belote*. After her lunch she took a nap as usual. When she woke, she looked livelier. She decided to do my hair for me. It's a mess.

She took up brush and comb. You've got nice hair. You should look after it better. Arrange it properly.

Not completely ugly, then. Perhaps I should try to draw my self-portrait. Had the Brush ever drawn himself? Painted himself? Presumably he preferred looking at Camille.

First of all we stimulate the scalp, Camille said. Good for hair growth.

I leaned back in my chair. Camille's hands shook out my plait, rummaged my hair loose. They massaged, stroked. Warmth tingled and fizzed, sweetness washed up and down me, from my head to my toes. Next, the bristles of a brush had the same effect.

Camille said: we've only got these nail scissors, but they're sharp enough. You'll look so smart, just wait and see.

Snip, snip, snip. She smoothed lotion on, combed it through. The back of my neck felt cool. Most of my hair seemed to be lying on the floor.

Wait, I haven't finished. Don't get up yet. You need a touch of colour. Close your eyes.

The tip of a brush soft as fur went back and forth over my eyelids, my cheeks, my mouth. A different brush worked along my eyelashes, swept my eyebrows. A soft pad dabbed my nose, cheeks, chin.

You can look now.

I was a portrait of a girl with chin-length hair. A hairstyle similar to the one I'd had as a small child, but now I looked adult, because of the make-up. Shadowed hollows under my cheekbones. Eyebrows tidied to curving dark lines. Eyes made vivid with blue shadow, black mascara. Lips re-shaped, their plumpness magically thinned, formed into a scarlet bow.

Camille cocked her head on one side. How pretty I've made you, little one. You could be seen in Paris, looking like this.

Time I went home, I said. I'll take the rubbish down with me.

I carried the washstand slop-pail in one hand, and the wastepaper basket in the other. I emptied the dirty water over the potted plants in the yard behind the bakery. I transferred all the white torn-up pieces of drawings to my apron pockets. The sketchbook still had quite a few pages left in it. All blank except one right at the end: a nude sketch in pen and ink of Camille. Finders keepers. I tore out the page and stuck it with the sketchbook in my satchel.

When I stepped into our kitchen, Mum turned from the sink and cried out. My father stared, rose from his chair. His hand lifted, slapped my cheek. He grabbed my satchel from my shoulder, slung it across the floor. His fingers pincering my ear, he marched me to the kitchen tap, went at me with a harsh sponge, cold water. He swabbed my skin until it felt raw. Let go, don't touch me! He pinched my neck: just shut up! He bent my head down over the chilly hard edge of the sink, he scraped my jawline. My mother turned away: your lovely long hair, I loved that hair. She came back with a towel and handed it to me. I covered my face, blotting tears.

Dad said: that's it. You can go back there tomorrow morning, collect the wages they owe you, then come straight home. I'd go in your place to give that young madam a piece of my mind, but I can't leave the shop, and nor can your mother.

You just do as you're told, Clem, Mum said.

I mopped myself. Dampness all around the top of my dress. I wouldn't look at either of them.

Mum said: we have to tell you when you've done wrong. It's for your own good. She was making fun of you, can't you see that? She was mocking you. And she made you late home, you should have been here to cook, I had to do it myself.

I threw the towel at her. In my room I lay on my bed and cried. A soaked pillowcase. A wet patch on the cotton bedcover. After a while I stopped. I blew my nose, wiped my eyes. What was the point of crying?

Mum called that supper was ready. I wasn't brave enough to refuse to go down, to reject her food. And in fact I was hungry. I joined my parents at the table. I picked up my soup spoon, kept my head bent over my plate. Grey-green sludge. What a rotten cook she was.

Dad talked to Mum about shop stuff. He finished his tumbler of wine, got up, stood behind me, squeezed my shoulders. Hey, little one. You've learned your lesson, now cheer up. Just say sorry and that's the end of it.

I copied Camille, and said nothing. He stroked the side of my neck. Hey, come on. I jerked away. Reply when I speak to you! Don't be rude! I kept my mouth shut. He banged out to the bar.

Mum turned in her chair to face me. He only punishes you because he cares about you so much. He wants to protect you. People try to take advantage of you and you don't see it.

She began coughing, fished for her handkerchief. She looked at me pleadingly over its pale blue folds. Clem. He adores you. He only wants the best for you.

I got up and made her a cup of peppermint tea. As I handed it to her she clasped my arm. The saucer wobbled between us. She said: in a couple of days it'll have blown over. He'll have forgotten all about it and so will you.

She gazed at the photo of my brother on the mantelpiece, sighed. Don't look at me like that, Clem. You can't imagine what a mother feels, losing her child. I hope you'll never have to know.

You're not the only one, I said. Millions of mothers lost their children in the war. We should think about them too.

How do you know I don't think about them? Mum asked. Of course I do. You're too young to remember the war properly. You were in school, you didn't know what was happening.

I said: didn't I?

Palm trees cut down, to make better sightlines for the German soldiers. The port reduced to rubble. Blockhouses thrown up at corners. Heaped sandbags. The rumble of black trucks.

Mum said: you're all I've got.

No. She had my brother still. He lay on her bowed shoulders like a wooden cape. Stiff and aching, she'd carry him for ever.

I took my satchel upstairs with me. I emptied my pockets onto my bed. Flurry of white fragments. I scooped them up and put them in the drawer where I kept my drawings and Monique's postcard. What would Monique do? She wouldn't get into trouble in the first place. What would Berthe say? In her letters from Paris she stressed doing what you wanted but on the sly. For her that had turned out well. She and Roger had got engaged and planned to marry at Christmas. He's a real gentleman, Clem, he never tries to take advantage.

I climbed into bed, wondering. Had the Brush taken advantage of Camille or was it the other way round?

In the morning golden plane leaves rocked down in the cold breeze. The end of autumn. I put on two jumpers and a thick skirt, the woollen coat I'd worn in my last year at school. I wrapped my scarf around my head, pulling it forwards over my cheeks to hide my puffy red eyes. Don't forget to check the money she gives you, Dad said. Bring back the board games you've lent her, Mum said, and my sewing things.

I slung on my satchel, pulled my gloves over my cold hands. My parents watched me from the shop door as I set out. Mum lifted a hand, let it drop again. Fallen crinkled fans of leaves crackled underfoot.

Camille was twisting up her hair, stabbing hairpins into it. Here you are at last.

She glanced at me. That's a well-scrubbed face you've got there. A touch of powder, that's what you need. Get rid of the shine.

You wanted me to help you pack, I said: shall I fetch your suitcase?

I haven't got a suitcase, she said: just that cloth bag and my hatbox.

I folded her night things, her under-things. I fetched her pots of make-up, her hand mirror, her little drawstring spongebag. She threw off her dressing-gown, so that I could pack that too. She put on the skirt I'd altered, the white blouse, the blue jacket.

She opened her purse. I've enough money to buy your bus ticket, as well as my own. You'll come with me to Marseilles, won't you? You'll accompany me to the station? See me onto the train to Cannes? You'll be back again in no time, I'm sure. There must be plenty of buses.

Certainly, I said.

Camille checked her wristwatch. There's not time for you to go home and talk to your mother and get her permission. We should be off. You'd better write her a note. Leave it here on the table, and the baker's wife will find it, she'll give it to her.

That's a good idea, I said.

The bus trundled us past orchards and vineyards. Camille pulled up her collar, put her head on my shoulder and dozed. She smelled of musky scent. I clasped my satchel on my lap and stared out of the window at the turned earth of ploughed fields, the long flanks of the mountain crouching behind. My mother would be seated at her sewing machine, feet working the treadle as she guided cloth to flow under the jumping

71

needle. She'd be expecting me home well before lunchtime. She'd be expecting me to bring back a half-loaf, to set the table, to prepare the vegetables. At what point would she arrive at the baker's, to check my whereabouts? The baker's wife would tell her I'd accompanied Camille to the bus station, to carry her bags. Mum would go upstairs. She would find my note. Later, when she checked her handbag, she would discover I'd walked off with the contents of her purse: a week's housekeeping money.

Countryside gave way to suburbs, then to massed buildings, boulevards. The station in Marseilles rose up like a palace, with a huge forecourt and fine statues. I parked Camille on a bench, just inside the entrance to the main concourse, took the velvet wallet she handed me. The ticket office is over there, look. Hurry up, silly, I don't want to miss the train.

I went off to the *guichet* to join the queue. Returning, I picked up her bag and hatbox, escorted her to the platform, showed my platform ticket to the attendant manning the barrier. He waved us through.

We found an empty second-class carriage, stowed Camille's luggage on the overhead rack. I settled her on the leather-covered seat, then sat down opposite. Above Camille's head, a line of framed photographs showed views of snow-capped peaks. From the bottom edge of the brown blind half-covering the window dangled a string, finished with a wooden acorn. Another blind, a pleated one, shut off the corridor. A notice instructed us: do not lean out. Do not cry when hit do not hit back do not hate him do not tear yourself away from them like a long strip of raw red flayed meat do not feel afraid do not tell anyone you feel afraid.

Camille kicked off her blue high heels and put up her feet.

She hugged her arms around herself. Why didn't I bring a coat? Even colder in here than in your godforsaken village. I'm going to freeze.

She stretched out, leaning her head on the leather armrest that looked as hard as a policeman's truncheon. Whack. Whack. Don't think you've got away with it. Please don't let me get away with it. Come back home. Don't you ever dare come back home. Camille shifted on the seat. One hand flung up under her blue turban. She had collapsed, like a half-cooked soufflé. She closed her eyes and shivered.

I could give you one of my jumpers, I said. I'm wearing two. Or my coat. Monsieur wouldn't want you to be cold.

How would I get it back to you? she asked. I don't suppose you can spare it.

Doors began slamming all along the train. A whistle blew, skewered my ears.

You'd better get off now, she said: you'd better hurry.

I dug into my pocket and showed her the second single ticket I'd bought.

The whistle shrieked again. The train began to move.

I'm coming too, I said. I'm sure your husband wouldn't like you to be travelling alone.

Camille swung her legs down. She sat up straight, put her hands on her knees and stared at me. I leaned forwards and released the blind. It clattered up. Plumes of smoke streamed past the window. The train gathered speed.

In that case, you owe me for your train ticket, she said.

You can take it out of the wages you owe me, I replied.

She pouted. He was supposed to pay you, not me. She fished out her wallet. There. Now I'm almost cleaned out.

She took up a miniature mirror. A round black frame, with

a black handle dotted with flakes of pearl. She peeled off her glove, squinted, licked a finger. She smoothed an eyebrow. So what did you write in the message to your mother? I suppose you said it was all my fault?

No, I said, I didn't say that. I told her I was accompanying you to Cannes, to join your husband, and that I'd write to her as soon as we arrived, to let her know I was safe.

Good little country girls always told the truth. Or pretended they did. Complete truthfulness was impossible. You'd hurt other people too much, or annoy them. So I'd stopped short of telling my mother all the facts. I hadn't exactly lied. I hadn't told her I was running away, that was all.

Camille drooped her neck, looked down at her lap, spoke in a rush. You know perfectly well he's not my husband. Not yet, anyway. First of all he's got to get his family to agree, and so far they don't. However, they don't know about the baby. They'll agree to our marriage once they do. Four months until it's due. Plenty of time.

So has he gone to tell them? I asked. He's gone to see his mother, I thought you said, hasn't he?

Or had he gone to see his sister? From the way he addressed her in his letter, she seemed the tolerant sort. Or would she look down on a bride who worked as a model in a clothes shop?

Of course he hasn't gone to see his mother, Camille said, and of course she's not in hospital. I just made that up, to persuade you to help me. No, he's gone off to look at some artist's house near Cannes. To take photographs or something.

She opened a tiny paper book, tore off a leaf of powder, pressed it to one cheek, then the other. Her voice tuned itself to a whine. He actually planned to leave me in the country, all on my own, to wait until the baby was due. Can you imagine that?

He was going to come and visit me at the weekends. So he said.

Haven't you got family to help you? I asked.

They wouldn't want to help, Camille said, not with something like this. They'd throw me out if they knew.

She was like a wireless set. She was turning a knob inside herself, setting her voice to an even higher, whinier pitch. Well, I know where his mother lives. If necessary I shall go and see her myself. And if that fails, well, I'll think of something.

8. A man remembering his youth. Street scene, Camden Town

DENIS

The sunshine turned Phyllis's hair bright red-gold. For her twenty-fourth birthday the previous month she'd had her waist-length tresses cut shorter, to shoulder-length, finished with a fringe. I'd gone with her to the hairdresser, to give her courage for the chop, and then for her treat we'd taken a bus into the West End and had tea at Maison Bertaud. In the cramped space smelling of hot sugar and vanilla we perched on spindly chairs and ordered tiny choux filled with coffee cream, tiny strawberry tarts. Phyllis ate one of each. I knew she'd skip supper later, to make up for this indulgence. But at least she was eating. She'd brought her cut locks away with her from the hairdresser's, stowed in her bag. She sat the clump of hair on the chair next to her: meet my pet poodle.

On that occasion she'd worn a dark red 1940s crepe frock, the yoke embroidered with tiny coral beads. Today she was wearing indigo jeans, a dark blue T-shirt and matching cotton scarf. The smell of hot dust mingled with that of sandalwood joss sticks burning. The dryness and sweetness caught in my throat, made me cough. I turned, scanning the openings between tented counters for a way through into fresher air.

Stop a moment, D., Phyllis said. Let's have a look in here.

She was keeping an eye out for possible costumes for her street-theatre group's next play. A knockabout pantomime sending up women's roles as mothers and wives. As a sympathetic male I was allowed to help as wardrobe advisor and assistant props manager. I'd found an old pram for the group at a jumble sale. It would hold the actress playing the baby, plus a megaphone for her to yell through. For the moment it squatted in my bedsit like a broody black cow. A pair of fringed purple and yellow plush curtains, looped back, framed a dark opening. Phyllis peered inside.

Haven't you had enough yet? I said. I want to go to the pub.

Yet another tin-roofed warehouse selling second-hand clothes and furnishings. Camden Market on a Saturday afternoon. Goths and punks crammed the canvas-covered alleys between stalls, posters advertised a forthcoming Rock Against Racism gig, crew-cut young women arm in arm sauntered in ballgowns and Doc Martens. Phyllis and I had been scanning racks of moth-eaten velvet and chiffon, shelves laden with art deco vases, paper-sleeved 78s, yellowing lace-edged pillowcases. For her play she had picked up a man's dress-suit, a queenly hat in swathed pink nylon. For herself she had bought a pair of purple lace mittens, a paste brooch and a Biba mini dress, only slightly torn, patterned in green and orange whorls, with cloth-covered buttons all down the front. She wanted to buy something for me too, but so far nothing had taken my fancy.

Just this one, Phyllis said, and then I'll give up.

Church candles on black iron stands made starry pinpoints of light, lit up the dark, musty space just enough. An open trunk, its lid lined with flowered paper, its interior crammed with books, sat on the earth floor. Dog-eared orange Penguins. Blue Pelicans. Pink Barbara Cartland romances. Edwardian poetry in limp purple suede stamped in gilt. The librarian's training I'd started was teaching me to classify books by content, but I couldn't resist, on a day off, doing it by the colour of covers. Red for atlases. Black for Bibles.

Phyllis leafed through a stack of 1950s women's magazines. Oh, look at this, D. Look at these clothes.

Exuberant skirts with cinched waists, impossibly small. Wide boat necks. Tiny ankles. Tiny feet.

Super-feminine, Phyllis said. Men adore women who look like that. Confident but mysterious. Cool and distant, therefore alluring.

Had my father felt that, courting my mother? To my mother's English neighbours, Frenchness spelled ooh-la-la, the cancan, Maurice Chevalier huskily chanting "Thank Heaven for Little Girls". My mother played along with the cliché at drinks parties, bending forwards to have her cigarette lit, thick scarlet lipstick pout, showing cleavage, glancing up from under her eyelashes. She hid her strength and authority under her bouffant frocks. She laughed charmingly at the men's jokes. A relief from having to take charge at school, drive sullen pupils through their irregular verbs? Or her way of signalling that sometimes she wanted to be cosseted? Did my father understand her flirty messages? The men didn't actually talk to her much. Cigarette lit, compliment proffered, they retreated to their tight little group. Cars, football.

Men dislike women like me, Phyllis said. We're too independent. They think we're too masculine. Too like them. They like women who are everything they're not.

I put my arm around her. I adore you. You know I do. I may not be what those magazines think a man is, but I love you.

I'm hopeless, Phyllis said. I want to rebel, yet I still care what people think about me. One minute I'm saying fuck the bourgeoisie and the next I'm wanting them to like me.

It's called a contradiction, I said. It's normal. Marx would have understood.

It's the same with my parents, she said. I fight with them, all the time, yet I still want them to love me.

It'll get better eventually, I said. By the time you're ninety you'll have sorted it all out. And so will I.

A white cover printed in green and black. Typography like graceful handwriting. *The Guide for Girls*. I pulled out the little book, turned over the pages. Matchbox-sized illustrations of sharp-bosomed sylphs in foaming gathered skirts. Here, I said to Phyllis, look at this. You can buy me this.

The sub-title read *How to Become a Real Woman*. A magazine-style directory from the mid-fifties. A list, a lovely list, of alphabetically arranged subjects: you looked up a problem, read five lines of snappy advice. Semi-serious under all the froth. Employing the sort of self-protecting English irony Phyllis resisted: saying one thing while suggesting its opposite.

Phyllis took the book from me, flicked through it. It's kind of kitsch. You really want it?

She gave my shoulder a friendly shove. Let's leave it. You're right. Let's go and have a drink.

Wait a second. I took the book back. Phyllis rolled her eyes, wandered across to a rack of clothes, pulled out a black beaded cocktail frock. I went on reading. *Boyfriends, cookery, diets, etiquette, getting engaged, going out, hobbies, keep fit, tennis.* The book was proposing tongue-in-cheek rules for behaviour, certainly, but underneath the baroque iron grid of its instructions I glimpsed a chasm of the forbidden, a deep drop into what could not be said or spelled out, what must not be imagined.

On pain of what? Madness, presumably. Social ostracism at least. Punishment. And yet what could not be said or spelled out danced at the bottom of the chasm and when I lay at its edge and peered down I could see tiny figures embracing one another.

Phyllis paid for the book and I stuck it in my back pocket. We went to the pub overlooking the Canal lock. We took our beers outside. Packed around us people lay back in the sun. We found an uninhabited patch of yellowing grass, inspected it for dogshit and sat down. Phyllis produced neatly rolled spliffs from her shoulder bag, handed one over. She didn't need to be discreet. Everyone else nearby was smoking, the air thick with that woody, sweetish scent of weed.

I turned the pages of *The Guide for Girls* and read Phyllis extracts. Getting stoned had softened and relaxed her. She listened languidly. She had taken off her cotton scarf, rolled it up and put it under her head, on top of her shoulder bag she was using as a pillow. Her skin flushed pink. Eyes half closed as she inhaled.

Suppose I tried to act out some of this advice? I asked Phyllis. Could I, d'you think? What would happen? She tapped the end of her spliff against the edge of the empty matchbox she was using as an ashtray. Well, if you try, you'll find out. I went on flicking through the pages. *How to deal with spots. How to encourage a man to propose. How to make a nightdress-case. How to make scones.*

Choose a subject, I said, any subject. She hesitated. Then pronounced: going out to a dance. How to prepare. How to dress.

We'll have to do this properly, I warned her. If I'm going to be the woman, I think you should be the man.

Fine, she said, I'm always the man in the street-theatre plays, anyway, because I'm tall. I'll wear this dress-suit I've just bought.

The dope sang in my blood. We weaved along the baking street. Back in her warehouse-home we stripped down to our underclothes. She slung her dark jeans and dark T-shirt over the back of a chair. Those are too unisex, I said. I want something a bit more glamorous. Do you mind? She shrugged. Suppose not. Have a look through the street-theatre costumes. There's bound to be something there you could use. She leaned her shoulders forward, easing the dress-suit jacket over them.

In the mirror a gawky debutante scooped up her mauve-pink skirts, swished them this way and that. Too flat-chested, so I stuffed the bodice with a pair of tights. Scarlet mouth. Feet crammed into pearl leather slingbacks. I took a few steps. Had my mother wobbled like this as a girl in Paris, going out to a dance? Well, I would do. Phyllis was greasing her hair flat, pinning back a front flap to form a quiff, twisting the rest into a ponytail flattened under a cap. In her black and white she made a creditable boy. An urchin out of Dickens. Certainly thin enough. Too thin. But you couldn't say so.

I curtsied to her: my name is Denise. She bowed: and I'm Phil. Off we paraded to the Lyceum. People on the bus clocked us. Some stared, frowned. Others smiled.

The gilded ballroom's floor beckoned you to swoop across it. I kept dancing forwards when I should have been dancing back. No, Phyllis kept protesting, you're the girl. We did better once the band switched to rock 'n' roll; we twirled and threw each other and no one watching seemed to care.

9. Black-and-white photograph (precise date unknown) of Matisse by Yvette Martin, in the salon of his suite at the Hotel Regina, Nice

A white-haired, white-bearded Matisse sits propped against cushions in an armchair set close to the salon's tall window. He wears a white dressing-gown and slippers. Sun striking in makes a pattern of lace on the carpet. The window is veiled by two long, diaphanous curtains dangling pinned to the pelmet.

One of these lengths of see-through lace is all twisted, a column of spiralling whiteness. A naked fair-haired woman stands semi-concealed inside it. She seems to have posed in front of the curtain, grasped it, twirled herself round and round in it. Now she presents herself, half concealed and half revealed, a wrapped present, to the smiling painter. He can look, but not touch. She'll choose the moment to untwist herself, step free of the binding falls of whiteness.

10. Train carriage interior

CLÉMENCE

The telegraph wires flew backwards in long repeating loops. Hills of sheer rock pressed up close then fell away again. We plunged in and of tunnels. The sea appeared, vanished, reappeared.

More passengers got on. Camille and I shoved up to make room for them. A woman in a green coat, a matching green hat, holding on her knee a wicker basket with a small smelly dog inside it. A family of mother, father and two children, the man in a hairy brown suit, the wife in an embroidered wool smock and a gaberdine, the boy and girl in sailor outfits. Two nuns in grey habits and black veils. Grey cloaks, grey worsted stockings and sturdy black lace-up shoes. They smiled graciously, nodding, settling themselves.

Bon Secour sisters. The Order that ran my school, and the hospital next door to it where Monique had trained for a year, and the hostel for the homeless in the next street.

The nuns didn't seem to recognise me. I didn't recognise them, either. I kept my head down, my face turned away, just in case. Not teaching nuns. Social worker nuns, presumably. Patrolling the back streets of the towns along the coast, trying to rescue people with no jobs, no homes and no money, some of them on drugs. City streets were full of foreigners and criminals, my father droned: vicious people. Cities were no place for his innocent daughter, I wasn't to stray near them. Too late for your advice, now, Papa.

The older nun unwrapped a couple of buns. She gave one to her companion, who began to munch it. Stuffed with over-ripe cheese, to judge by the stink.

Camille frowned, turned her face away. She'd gone pale. I asked: do you need some air? Shall I open the window? The woman in green poked her lizard neck forward, spat out her words. Certainly not. Sitting in a draught is the worst possible thing. The mother of the sailor-suited children added: it's nearly winter! It's freezing out there! The older nun peered at Camille. Perhaps at the next station, when we stop, we could let in a little fresh air. Just for a moment. Madame certainly does not look well.

Camille closed her eyes. The two children sucked their thumbs and stared at her. Going far? the father of the family asked. To Cannes, I replied.

The younger nun had small, almost lashless eyes set in a pasty face. We're going past Cannes, to Nice, she said: back to our convent, our Mother House. Notre Dame de Bon Secour.

She managed to look both smug and severe as she pronounced this name. Our Order is renowned all along this coast. You may have heard of us. All through the war we held up the beacon of faith. Now it's the Communists we must resist.

I never have anything to do with nuns, said the father of the family, if I can possibly help it. His wife tugged the corner of his jacket. Ssssh.

Try to sleep, I said to Camille. That will make the journey go faster.

11. Eurostar interior

DENIS

I packed just my small red cloth rucksack: I liked travelling light. Shirt, T-shirt, boxers, socks, espadrilles, swimming trunks, swimming towel, shaving gear, eau de cologne, sunglasses, toothbrush, toothpaste. I'd picked up a special offer when booking: a seat in First Class. Exactly the same price as Standard Class, the clerk cooed down the phone, a special promotion we're running this week. Luxury breakfast included.

Free glossy magazines at the entrance to the carriage. A snug, solo niche. Room to lean back on the padded seat, stretch my legs, empty my jacket pockets, spread out my belongings. I remembered my first visit to Paris on my own, in my twenties, to visit galleries: subsisting for a week on bread and butter bought in cafés. Drinking red wine out of the bottle under a bridge. Falling asleep on a park bench, being woken by a gendarme and chased away.

The passengers surrounding me were snappily dressed, ready for business. Sleek haircuts. Well-shaven chins on the men, decorous make-up on the women. One or two swivelled their eyes over me, scanning my difference. My jeans and shirt: clean, though not ironed. My brogues: polished but old. My leather jacket: worn. Good morning, I said. They flinched, nodded. Hastily they began studying their phones.

The train entered the Tunnel. Two cabin managers appeared

at the far end of the carriage with a service cart, making their way along the narrow aisle. They wore well-cut grey trouser suits. The one with a glistening black flat-top, whose name tag read Maurice, handed me my airline-style tray. A varnished apple on a white paper doily. A tiny croissant and roll. A matching packet of foil-wrapped butter, a mini pot of jam. A tub of porridge. Stainless steel cutlery wrapped in a white polyester napkin.

Maurice returned with a coffee pot. His elegant brown hands, with short, polished fingernails, tilted the silvery spout above the doll-sized cup I held out to him. Porridge, I said. Not very French, that, surely?

Maurice's deep voice sounded amused. Porridge is currently fashionable, monsieur. It's what the passengers like. The management tries to take that into account. He set the coffee pot back onto his little tray.

I asked: do you eat porridge in the mornings, monsieur?

His eyes sparkled amber. No, monsieur, I certainly do not. I'm not much of a one for breakfast, in any case, I just have coffee. And then a cigarette. The first one of the day. The best.

I used to think so, too, I said, in my smoker days. Gitanes, I used to smoke.

Maurice said: very strong tobacco. Surely no one smokes those any more. Actually, I'm trying to give up, but it's hard.

I started once I left school, I said. I felt very nervous at parties and so I used to lean against the wall smoking a Gitane and trying to look cool. I'm sure I didn't.

A bark of protest. An invisible passenger two seats in front of me began exclaiming that he wanted eggs and bacon, a proper English breakfast not this continental crap. Maurice nodded at me, swung round and stepped away. I sipped my coffee. The train slid out of the dark Tunnel into sunshine and I slid into happiness, as I did every time I arrived in France. My French self surfaced. I'd spoken French to Maurice without realising it. I was at home with him in that language.

The meat-deprived passenger carried on blustering. Maurice, standing in the gangway, spoke to him politely and regretfully, offered him more coffee, more croissants. A woman's voice piped up: oh, Ted, don't get upset, please don't. We can get you a BLT or something from the bar, I'm sure we can.

Be quiet, will you? Let me handle this. He continued his harangue. I've paid good money for these seats and that includes being served decent food!

People on the other side of the aisle shrank into themselves, hunched over their trays. Maurice simply stood patiently, hearing Ted out. He half-turned in my direction, caught my eye. I said loudly in English: the service on this train is excellent, thank you, monsieur, and we are all much obliged to you. He shrugged, gave me a half-smile, as though to say, it's OK, I'm used to such boors.

The bully's grumbling dwindled, now that he'd alerted us all to his importance, and finally he shut up. Maurice walked onwards, towards the end of the carriage, where his fellow manager waited with the service cart. I bit into my croissant.

Barns, farms, wide fields flowed by. I glanced through the *TLS*, found the arts section, Angela's review of a recent TV documentary on western culinary fashions; nouvelle cuisine onwards. Phyllis had alerted me to the piece the day before, when she rang to say that she and Angela had already arrived in Paris. Bon voyage, D. Oh, and what are you taking to read on the train?

Angela wrote wittily, elegantly. She clearly relished food. She probably knew nice places to eat in Paris, different from my old favourites. Smarter. Cooler. I texted Phyllis to suggest meeting for lunch. She texted back: OK, I've got a plan, I'll make a booking, just confirm your arrival time. I duly did so.

Maurice reappeared with the coffee pot and refilled my cup. He leaned against the edge of the seat in front, balancing his tray, watched me pour milk. You're on holiday? You know Paris well?

I said: I don't know Paris all that well. I did go to the hammam once, also the catacombs. And to the vineyard in Montmartre.

Nothing wrong with being a tourist, he said. We're all tourists in each other's cities. I am when I come to visit my friends in London. Last time we went dog-racing, we went to a flute concert by candlelight in a church, we went to a pop-up restaurant in the East End.

His soft-looking mouth. His warm brown eyes. My eyes level with his hip. Any moment now he'd be straightening up, swinging back along the carriage to his galley at the far end, in the direction of the bar. That's it! You've had your two minutes. I've got other passengers to attend to. You're not the only one, *tu sais*.

My mother was French, I told Maurice: not Parisian, though. From the south.

He tapped a finger against the coffee pot. French? That's nice. So you like French food?

I said: Mum only cooked French dishes she thought my English father would tolerate. Also they were badly off, and she had to be thrifty. She made cheap versions of the real thing. Quiche Lorraine with white sauce and cocktail sausages. No eggs or cream. Even as a kid I knew that was wrong.

Well, Maurice said, some of the tourist restaurants in Paris have similar ideas. You'll need to steer clear of them.

He took me for an ignoramus. Part of me resented that; part of me wanted him to go on offering advice. In the past, I told him, I've always stayed near the Sorbonne. Good restaurants round there, I've found. I wanted him to realise I knew Paris just a bit more than I'd let on. No, I wanted him to know me. But this time, I said: I've booked myself into an Airbnb on the border of the 10ième and the 11ième, quite near the Canal. Maurice took back the little milk jug. That's a district very fashionable with tourists, certainly. At least I'd dragged myself away from my old haunts with Phyllis. Our unmodernised little hotel just behind the quay on the south bank facing Notre Dame. Dim, cramped, oddly shaped bedrooms, beamed ceilings and uneven tiled floors, framed prints of illustrations from the *Kama Sutra* hung above the bed, a sliver of bathroom boxed into one corner, and breakfast you ate in the small dark bar downstairs, sunlight lancing through the mullioned windows set in the panelling. The white-capped chef leaned forward out of the kitchen hatch, chatting, and a ginger cat slept under a brass pot of ferns.

Mauricet softened his snub with a half-smile. You're staying long?

I'm not sure, I replied. It all depends.

He departed, saying over his shoulder: well, I wish you a *bon séjour*.

I drank my coffee, read the on-board magazine. It proposed smart new bars and teashops in neighbourhoods I didn't know, fusion dishes I'd never tasted, glitzy cocktails I'd never heard of. Right. Take Angela and Phyllis on a tour. Impress them with my knowledge of French hipsterdom. I dozed, woke to hear the overhead announcement of our approach to Paris, our imminent arrival at Gare du Nord. My fellow passengers began flustering out of their seats, pulling down bags from the overhead racks. The bullyboy two seats in front rose up and straddled the gangway. He loomed, solidly built. Red face, a fleshy jowl, thin silvery hair. He began buttoning his navy overcoat and announcing that he'd be putting in a complaint about the food, make no mistake about it. I shan't forget this! Nor the lack of concern shown by the catering staff! People like that, I suppose you can't expect them to know what's what. But it's a disgrace, nonetheless.

I spoke to the air. The cabin managers have been so tolerant, so kind. How well they kept their tempers when provoked. Such courteous people, the French.

He glared at me. He's not French, that fellow, he's a foreigner.

You're being crass, I told him. We're the foreigners here, not him.

Pansy, he said. Fairy.

You're so deliciously old-fashioned, I said.

His companion, a tiny, sharp-faced blonde in a pink suit and pink beret, her quilted shoulder bag on its gold chain slung across her front, now joined him in the aisle. Pinch-mouthed, she nudged him. Oh, Ted, don't work yourself up. You mustn't stress. You know how bad it is for your heart. He interrupted her. Come on, for God's sake. We've got a taxi waiting. He pushed her ahead of him, shouldered past my seat, barged into the queue making for the end of the carriage. The Pink Lady's clipped voice issued in squeaks. Excuse me, excuse me, my husband has heart trouble, he needs fresh air, so sorry. People raised their eyebrows, muttered, but let them through.

I picked up my rucksack, joined the throng battling towards the luggage racks. Traffic jam; we remained immobile. The glass door slid open, slid shut. Ahead of me I could hear Ted barking that this was his suitcase, thank you very much, just move a bit, just let me get at it, will you?

A tap on my shoulder. Maurice had squeezed through the tangle of people. This must be yours, monsieur. You left it on your seat.

Elbows and backs corralled us. He thrust out a folded square of newsprint. The *TLS*. No time to explain I'd deliberately discarded it. Willy-nilly I accepted it, jammed it into my pocket. A smile, a discreet little wave. The glass door at the end of the carriage slid open again. The throng of passengers pressed forward and I was swept towards the luggage racks, away from Maurice, off the train.

One difference since my last visit: gun-toting police in bulky dark blue vests patrolling in pairs. Calm, blank-faced, they surveyed the travellers surging this way and that. The hurrying mass parted immediately on their approach. Their pathways were in fact the main ones. The crowd constructed itself around their steady progress, adapting its flow to them, falling away, making openings, closing up again.

I paused ahead of the entrance to the metro, fished for my phone. Where was Phyllis? Where did she want us to meet?

Ahead of me, the escalator rose towards the lobby of the Eurostar departure lounge. Soon the hall up above would disgorge the next body of passengers, to glide down the travelator, board the sharp-nosed train. Would Maurice be working that shift, or did he have a break? How many trips constituted his working day?

A pair of arms encircled me. Darling! Surprise!

A shot of carnation scent. I turned in Phyllis's embrace. Padded, silky texture of her green parka. Her lips on my cheek.

Her soft hair. I hugged her back. She held me away, smiling. Beam of her green eyes. How was your journey? Where shall we go? Angela's going to meet us later for lunch, this nice little café I've discovered near the Tuileries. You've got metro tickets, or d'you want one of mine?

When I patted my jacket pocket for my wallet, my fingers encountered edges of newspaper. I pulled out the *TLS* Maurice had handed me. Scribbled in black felt-tip on the front page, above the masthead, was a set of figures. Beginning with 06. A French phone number. Next to it Maurice had written his name.

Let's walk, I said, let's work up an appetite.

12. Black-and-white photograph (precise date unknown) of Henri Matisse by Yvette Martin, in the Hotel Regina, Nice

Matisse, dressed in a white dressing-gown and white slippers, sits, shoulders bowed, in an armchair set in the centre of the shadowy salon of his suite of rooms. His hands clutch a white handkerchief to his face. Blowing his nose? Crying? Impossible to tell.

13. Train carriage interior

CLÉMENCE

The train rattled and rocked, clattering over the tracks. Clackety clack. Clackety clack. The last stretch before Cannes. A cube of pressed heat and smells: sweating bodies, the dog in the basket, cheese. The drawn-down blinds filtered the light. Someone opened the compartment door and peered in from the corridor. A young soldier in uniform. He spotted Camille, and grinned. He clocked the two nuns, grimaced, shut the door again.

Camille began shifting to and fro on the seat. She concentrated, frowned. She clasped her hands.

What is it? I asked. Are you all right?

She whispered: I need to go and have a wee.

Well then, I said, it's along there, to the right, isn't it. I'll take care of your bags while you're gone.

Everyone in the compartment seemed to be dozing, apart from the two nuns, who were reading small black books marked with crosses on the cover. They looked up. Camille hesitated. Then whispered again. I don't want to go there alone. It's too embarrassing. People will know where I'm going. They'll know what I'm going to do. Come with me.

I opened the carriage door, onto the narrow corridor. The train jolted and swayed. Brown hills were flashing past. We staggered like drunks, knocking from side to side. Further along, a group of young soldiers blocked our way. Heavy khaki kitbags leaning against their legs. Caps stuffed under cloth straps on their shoulders. Close-cropped hair. Smoking and chatting. Perhaps on their way home from military service. That was it, over and done with, and now what? Or perhaps they were going the other way, back from leave, for more drills, marches, rifle practice. How would it feel to kill someone? Did they yet know? One of them turned his head and stared: ah, it's the beauty travelling with the black crows. Don't give up on us just yet, darling. I gripped Camille's arm and squeezed us both past. The young men pressed back with exaggerated politeness. After you! A button scraped my cheek. Fierce wool of a tunic. Excuse me, excuse me. I was her shepherd, her sheepdog, herding her.

Camille opened the lavatory door. Tiny cubicle, like a cupboard. An open grating, simply, on the floor, cold wind whistling up, the rails visible below as we sped along over them. Camille folded herself into the cramped space, vanished. The bolt grated across.

I leaned against the window frame giving onto the rocky landscape fleeing past. Clackety clack. The soldiers surged nearer, surrounded me. What's your name, pet? Where are you off to? Who's your gorgeous friend? You want a cigarette? No, I said, no, thank you. One of them, short, with sticking-out ears, reminded me of the baker's son. This boy looked as glum as the baker's wife always did. Another soldier clapped him on the shoulder. Hey, cheer up, we're not dead yet. He swore, and the other man shoved him. None of that, not in front of a lady.

Just a group of lads. I wasn't their enemy. Someone else was. Out in North Africa somewhere. *Les arabes. Les noirs.* Troublemakers, the lot of them, grunted my father. My mother said timidly: but they fought for us in the war, at any rate.

Camille emerged set-faced. Was she feeling sick again? She

said nothing, but leaned on my arm. I led her back through the bunched soldiers. They grinned at us. Make way, make way.

In the carriage Camille opened her handbag, unstoppered a tiny bottle, shook drops of lavender water onto her fingers. Brrr. That was horrible. She folded her arms over her belly and stared down at the floor. She seemed to be gritting her teeth. I whispered: are you all right? She whispered back: no. I took her cold hand in mine and chafed it.

The elder nun stared at Camille's ringless left hand. She sucked in air through her teeth. Where is your husband, madame? He ought to be here with you, to help you.

The woman in green, holding tight to her dog-basket, began muttering. Just loud enough for Camille to hear. No better than she should be. The girls of today. Little madam. I wanted to pin her lips closed with her own hatpin. If Berthe were here she'd mouth blah blah blah.

Sweat beaded Camille's forehead. She laced her arm through mine, leaned against me. Under the edge of the blind, beyond the window, the railway lines changed from a single track to a broad tangle that spread out lacily. The train slowed. Hang on, I said: we're nearly there. We'll be arriving any minute.

The man in the brown suit turned to his wife. Is there any water left in the bottle? Give her some water.

He spoke to me directly. You're getting off here? You must take your friend to a hospital. Do you understand? Can you manage that?

Camille's head dropped on my shoulder, sweat pouring down her face. I put my arm around her. Where were you thinking of going in Cannes? Do you really know?

No, Camille whispered, not really. He didn't tell me. He didn't want me following him.

The younger nun looked up, glanced at Camille. She addressed her companion. She could come with us to Nice. Wouldn't that be best? We're being met at the station. We'll take her in the taxi with us.

Where to? I asked: where do you want to take her?

To the delivery ward in our clinic, the nun replied. That's where she needs to go.

14. Street scene, Paris

DENIS

The café looked onto a cobbled square dominated by a Colonne Morris covered with film posters. We sat outside on the terrasse on aluminium chairs with woven plastic seats, our aperitifs on the round aluminium table in front of us. A Kir for me, a Campari for Phyllis.

Phyllis's phone bleeped. She turned to me. That's Angela, she's running half an hour late.

No problem, I said, we'll just people-watch.

The slender young Parisiennes idling past wore delicate flat leather sandals studded with glass jewels. They wore clingy tops, mini-skirts. Their shining hair swung from side to side. Suntanned arms. Long suntanned legs. From time to time one of these nymphs would perch at a nearby table and order an espresso. The well-dressed middle-aged men loitering nearby over their own cups of coffee would sit up, eye breasts, thighs, ankles. The young women smoked their cigarettes, chatted into their phones. They leaned back in carefully casual poses, ran their hands through their glossy locks. They seemed to take a certain pleasure in ignoring their admirers. They tossed down their coffee, wandered away again, and the men sank back into their seats.

You're not here just to be idle, D., are you? Phyllis said: what's the real reason?

I said: I don't suppose I've ever talked much about my godmother, have I? Probably not.

Surely, though, I had told Phyllis that Clem was an artist. That she flattened cardboard boxes, used their square brown sides as canvases. That the art teacher, in the school where Clem taught domestic science, gave her old paint brushes, almost empty tubes of paint. Clem carried them home and spent her evenings and weekends painting. My father, on one of our summer visits, looked through the works stacked against the kitchen wall. He shook his head, murmured. That's not proper art. My mother nudged him. Don't discourage her, it consoles her. Aged twelve, on one of my solo visits, I helped Clem re-hang some of her pictures. This way you see them freshly, *mon chéri*. If you don't re-hang them in different places from time to time you stop looking at them, you don't really see them. Delicately she adjusted the brown cardboard edges with her fingertips, stepped back to make sure the works hung evenly. One was abstract: a ground of pinkish-brown, striped diagonally with thin red streaks. The second, figurative, showed a large peach, cut open and split in half, lined up with the lower half of a face. A wide-open mouth.

I know she's French, Phyllis said, I remember you telling me that. She was a friend of your mother's, right? They were at school together. You used to go and see her when you were a child. She's still alive, I take it.

A troop of holidaymakers in sun hats and see-through raincoats, heavy trainers, surged past, shouting at one another. More policemen wandered by in pairs, hefting large guns, their gazes raking back and forth. Some swaggered, stiff-legged, self-conscious. Some looked gloomy. Inside their padded outfits they were the merest boys.

I told Phyllis about the summons from the care home to visit Clem. I took out of the inside pocket of my jacket the cut-into piece of blue paper I'd folded up and brought with me. I'm pretty sure Clem sent me this. Why she sent it anonymously I'm not sure. Perhaps she was just being forgetful. Anyway, I've taken it as her personal invitation to me, to find out.

Phyllis put down her glass, examined the blue shape. This is like a leftover from one of Matisse's cut-outs. You mentioned them the day we had lunch. Was that in connection with Clem?

I said: I think she knew him, or at least met him. Once, when she'd had a bit to drink, she hinted as much. As a child, I didn't take too much notice. I made little of it. But now, I wonder.

One of those Sunday lunches when the doctor came. A couple of glasses of Médoc with the piece of roast veal; Clem's mind unbuttoned. Home-made coffee ice-cream. Clem pink-cheeked, fiddling with her filled liqueur glass, a whole cherry swimming in it. She bottled cherries in eau de vie every year, creating cherry brandy she brought out on Sundays, feast days. She began to reminisce about her time working in the hotel in Nice. First time I drank fruit brandies was there, at the Regina. We never had anything like that at home. She turned to me. And of course, all through the war, everybody kept their wine and spirits hidden, if they had any at all. She turned back to the doctor: Matisse lived in the hotel at that time, you know, oh yes. Peach brandies for him. Not that he drank much. He'd been very ill. Most of the time he was in a wheelchair. He used to wear white slippers and white socks. The doctor listening. Really? Did you talk to him? What was he like?

Then she shut up like a clam, I said, like a Clem. Of course I didn't know who Matisse was. I only remembered the episode because she let me eat one of the brandied cherries, to try the taste.

Did your mother never mention Clem and Matisse? Phyllis asked. She must have known that story.

You'd think so, I said, but I can't be sure now how close she and Clémence really were. They drifted apart when I was eighteen or so. I stopped going to visit Clem at about that time, as well.

I'd needed to put some space between myself and my parents, myself and their friends. Near to them, I acted a cheery part, like a clown behind glass, encased in glass, didn't know who I was, who I might become. Breaking my glass carapace I shattered too, self-shards whirling. Scared I'd hurt my parents, cut them. I left home, left school, got a job, moved into a rented bedsit. In my holidays I went hitch-hiking abroad. Looking at art, looking for sex, for love. In Paris: first sex with another man. Tiny *chambre de bonne* with sage green walls, rattan armchair, red-painted bedstead. Fake-Tiffany lampshade of coloured glass. Years before I came out to my parents. Much later, my mother accepted me.

Too late to ask Mum now, in any case, I said.

Yellow ribbons knotting bunches of forget-me-nots looped her sky-blue wicker coffin. In the hearse Phyllis and I sat on either side of it, resting our joined hands on its lid. Inside her basket Mum was a clutch of bones. Going to her grave garlanded with spring blooms. Like Persephone, dragged down into the underworld, then crowned with pomegranate blossoms rising again. Mum believed in heaven, the resurrection of the dead. I didn't. I believed we'd rot down, become compost, dissolve into the cycle of seasons. Perhaps I'd return as a good sturdy weed. A dandelion. I'd seed into the wind, I'd scatter and drift away.

I still miss her, you know, I said. It feels so recent still.

Phyllis patted my arm. Well, it is. Probably you always will miss her. I think that's how it is.

I said: people are always telling me to move on. To get over it. But to forget her seems such a betrayal.

This time Phyllis patted my hand. Poor D.

I said: let's talk about something else.

Sure, Phyllis said.

She gripped the arms of her chair and advanced a foot. You see what I'm wearing?

I had indeed noticed when we met on the concourse at the Gare du Nord. Thick-soled sports sandals: bands of plasticised grey cloth striped with pale blue; prominent Velcro fastenings, like patches of Elastoplast, at ankle and toes. Their uncompromising design suggested rugged hikers scaling muddy hills. They suggested herring boxes without topses. Oh my darling Clementine. No, my darling was Clem, my erstwhile darling, and her dark blue espadrilles tied at the ankle with thin blue ribbons.

They're a bit different from what you normally wear, certainly, I said. But presumably they're just the thing for pounding the streets of Paris. Perfect for sightseeing.

Phyllis winced. Normcore sandals are fashionable this season. In London, that is. But here in Paris no one knows that. I mean, to Parisians I must look so dowdy. If they bother noticing me at all. I can't bear it.

Think of the ladies of Cranford, I said: when they were at home they didn't care what they wore, because everyone knew them, and when they were away they didn't care what they wore because no one knew them.

Phyllis said: I'll go shopping for shoes this afternoon. I was going to wear these to the preview, I discussed it with Angela, she thought they'd be OK, but now I realise I can't, they don't go with my outfit at all.

Over a skinny white vest she wore a see-through little jacket, pale blue, made of what seemed stiffened paper, with yellow and pink pressed flowers caught in its transparent layers. She shook out a fold of her calf-length skirt of pleated grey net. She said: Angela bought me this outfit. Nice, isn't it?

Her green silk parka flopped bundled over the arm of her chair. She picked it up and pulled it around her shoulders. There's a breeze getting up. At this rate I'll be needing fur-lined boots.

She needn't have worried about the judgement of Paris. Passing men of our own age seemed not to notice her footwear, flicked her appreciative glances. She was thin enough, *soignée* enough. She would do. Me they ignored.

A big woman in blue, advancing across the little square, was scrutinising the men in return. Head swivelling alertly this way and that. Coolly taking in their faces, shoes, clothes. Pursing her lips. She broke through another line of tourists, strode closer.

There's Angela, Phyllis said. At last!

Angela put down a glossy white carrier bag fastened with scarlet ribbon, leaned over Phyllis. The two women gently took hold of each other's elbows. Their lips pushed forwards, met.

Angela said: sorry I'm so late, dearest. Sorry I've kept you waiting.

Her curly dark chestnut hair was cut short around her rosy, sun-browned face. She wore a blue Chinese coat, fastened with twists of black braid, over wide trousers in heavy indigo linen. A necklace of yellow ceramic beads fat as plums. Grey suede lace-ups. She was solid, broad-shouldered. She shook my hand. Hello. How do you do?

She hesitated. Oh, for heaven's sake. You're Phyl's oldest

friend. She kissed me on both cheeks. I look forward to getting to know you. Now let's have some lunch.

It's a bit chilly, Phyllis said. Let's eat inside.

Our bentwood chairs scraped on the red-tiled floor. Just two other clients: a young man and a young woman, he in white shirt and black jeans and she in a tight Lycra mini dress striped black and white. Both had shiny black hair, his long and hers short. They were leaning their heads together over the menu, murmuring, discussing.

Phyllis turned to Angela. I came across it yesterday, on my walk, while you were doing your emails. Charming, don't you think?

Angela said: blimey, darling. It's so old-fashioned. There can't be many like it left. Or is it a fake, d'you think?

Brown wooden tables, octopus-armed hat-stand, posters of jovial vignerons holding up clusters of grapes, *plats du jour* chalked on a blackboard, a pink neon sign curving along the wall behind the bar. On the *zinc* stood a wire basket of eggs.

Artfully fashionable seediness? I said to Phyllis. Nostalgia for a vanished France?

She didn't respond. Apparently too busy discussing with Angela whether to try *boudin noir* or *côtelettes de porc*. The dishes matched the retro décor. No rocket salads. Nothing marked V.

So you'll be staying in the eleventh? Angela asked me. Nice. Quite a few new galleries opening up near the Canal. We've been to a couple of them, haven't we?

She smiled at Phyllis, then turned back to me. And we've found a cute little hotel, just across the river from Notre Dame. Beamed ceilings, funny old prints, breakfast in the tiny dark bar. There's even a ginger cat.

Phyllis picked up the carafe. Water, anyone?

My slice of calf's liver topped with fried sage leaves and moated with onion puree arrived. With it I drank a glass of earthy red Côtes du Luberon. Phyllis and Angela, who had opted in the end for *salade de lentilles*, drank mineral water. The press view's at four, Angela explained, and I don't want to be feeling sleepy. The *vernissage* is at six. There'll be drinks at that. I'll have a drink then.

No time for a siesta, anyway, Phyllis said: we've got to go and buy me some new shoes.

Angela picked up the brimming bread basket, lined with a blue-checked napkin, and offered it to me. Yes, darling, so you said. But we don't have to rush, do we? What's the hurry?

Phyllis bit her lip. I saw the vulnerability of someone newly in love, alert to the slightest hint of rejection, helpless, unable to control the situation, unsure, like catching on your skin a rain of pollen, sweet-smelling yellow drifts that yet could whirl up in your face, scratch your eyes, make you sneeze, weep. Darling Phyllis.

Sorry we can't take you in with us, Angela said to me, but you know how it is.

I speared a fried sage leaf, wrinkled and dark green. Just crisp enough. Oh, I wouldn't expect that. You're here to work. I'm here just to play.

I wouldn't call being en route to visit your long-lost godmother something as simple as playing, Phyllis said. It seems quite complicated to me. Going all the way down to La Ciotat to see her means there's something at stake for you, surely, though I'm not quite sure what.

She was trying to make me sound more than just a loafing tourist. Someone Angela would have to take seriously. Dear Phyllis. I lifted my glass to her. She gave me a nod.

Angela said: godmother? Still alive? Lucky you.

I said: godmothers, a species of aunt, prickly, evergreen, winter-hardy, dislikes waterlogged soil, prefers a sunny aspect. Needs regular feeding. At least, she used to.

So what's her connection with Paris? Angela asked. Why have you stopped off here? Phyllis didn't say. She just suggested we meet up.

I was being discreet, Phyllis said. I thought it was up to D. to tell us. If he wanted to.

Clem lived here for a while, I said, at a certain moment. A few years after the end of the war. So I thought I'd break my journey, try to trace her footsteps.

Such a fascinating time to have been here, Angela said. That ferocious surge of energy, creativity. There must be very few people left who can remember it.

Depends whom she knew, I said, depends how good her memory still is. I'm not sure she was lounging around at the Café de Flore with the existentialists, if that's what you're thinking. I don't think that was quite her scene.

I'd love to meet her in any case, Phyllis said, if that were possible, at some point. She was important to you as a child. I'd like to meet someone who knew you then.

On this trip? I'll have to see how it goes, I said.

After Le Cannet and Cannes, Angela said, we were thinking of driving west along the coast. Possibly as far as Marseilles. So we could easily drop in to La Ciotat.

If Clémence doesn't want more visitors that's fine, Phyllis said, but we could meet you anyway. We could go out to dinner.

Well, I said, we'll keep in touch about it. I'll ring you.

Phyllis forked up cubes of bacon, but left her lentils half-finished. Angela ate her lentils, but picked out the bits of meat, pushing them aside. She coaxed Phyllis to a *crème brulée*. If you like, we can order just one, and share it. We'll ask for two spoons.

You, D.? Angela asked. Shall we ask for three spoons?

Not for me, I said. I'm going to have a piece of cheese. The thin lid of burnt sugar tilted, and cracked like glass. The *patronne* behind the bar began joking with two regulars who'd wandered in. She'd brought me an entire platter of cheeses to choose from. I cut a wedge of Camembert. It sat, lonely, in the middle of my white plate.

My godmother taught me to like Camembert, I said to Angela. Despite being a southerner she ate certain northern cheeses. One of my mother's stories of the two of them in Paris was about how they sometimes went for cheap meals. Canteen-type places. So my godmother got a taste for Parisian bistro dishes. When they were broke they just had soup.

Phyllis touched Angela's wrist. So, darling, what's in the carrier bag? What've you been buying?

Shoes, Angela said. I've bought you a pair of shoes. I was passing this shop near the Palais Royale, and they jumped out at me.

Up-to-date slingbacks. Pale blue leather uppers covering the whole surface of each foot; peep-toed, on flat, thick rubber soles.

Phyllis unstrapped her normcore sandals, put on the new shoes. They're perfect. They match my outfit. She kissed Angela. Clever you.

Time for a siesta after all, Angela said.

They scrambled away, leaving me to finish my wine. Through the propped-open café door came white sunlight, a scorch of heat, flashes of passers-by, bicycles and cars, as the street came to life again after the lunch hour. Smell of hot oil and lilies. The young couple at the next table held hands, turned their faces towards each other, kissed.

I took out my phone. Not much larger than a playing card, it balanced on my palm. Poker game. Take a risk. Be bold. Be brave. He can only say no. I pulled the folded *TLS* out of my pocket.

His voice sounded warm, amused. Oh, it's you.

15. Black-and-white photograph (precise date unknown) by Yvette Martin, of Matisse drawing at the Hotel Regina, Nice

Matisse wears a black jacket with a white handkerchief tucked into the breast pocket, a collar and tie, a waistcoat, black-and-white checked trousers with turn-ups. Incongruously, he sports a pair of white open-toed flat platform sandals. Seated on a spoon-backed armchair, a board propped on the solid white chest in front of him, he is looking down, wielding a brush. An open bottle of ink stands nearby.

Leaning in the doorway to one side, a fair-haired woman watches him with an air of affectionate amusement. She's in her mid-thirties, perhaps. She wears a white overall, white plimsolls. She carries a tray set with a folded towel, a round lidded pot, a roll of bandages, a pair of scissors, various small tools. Presumably she has come in to treat his hurts, dress his swollen feet. Perhaps give him a pedicure too. She will have to wait. He is not ready to stop.

16. Interior, the Regina Hotel, Nice

CLÉMENCE

I worried Camille and I would be fined for travelling on beyond Cannes without having paid. On our arrival in Nice, however, the two nuns ignored the uniformed man at the barrier, waved aside his demand to look at my ticket. Can't you see this is a medical emergency? Let us pass, if you please. They took Camille away with them. They loaded her into their taxi like a piece of baggage. The nun who'd come to meet them was stooping, white-eyebrowed. She blinked, then took charge. To the clinic? Yes, of course.

I said goodbye to Camille but she didn't hear me. Bent over, arms folded across her stomach, eyes closed. The old nun turned. And you, child? Why is no one meeting you? You'd best make haste, wherever you're going. It's getting late. You shouldn't be out alone.

Should I ask for a bed at the homeless women's hostel that the nuns ran? Did the nun know the names of the probationer nurses in her hospital? Had she met Monique? She didn't give me a chance to gather my wits. The door slammed. The taxi revved and shot off into the twilight.

I bought myself a cup of coffee and a piece of baguette smeared with margarine, in the station bar, consumed them standing up, propped against the *zinc*. Then I parked myself at the far end of a bench in the Ladies' Waiting Room. A coal fire burned in the stove. Cold, greasy walls. Hours passed. I dozed.

Women passengers came and went. The door banged open and shut throughout the night. Every time I nodded off the clatter and crash of the door woke me up.

In the morning the mirror in the women's lavatory showed me my red eyes. I drank another cup of coffee at the station bar, then asked for directions to the Hotel Regina. Outside the city centre, up the hill, in a suburb called Cimiez. Take the bus or walk.

The Hotel Regina towered, many storeys high, a dark fortress ribbed with window-slits. I found a gate open at the back, the service door beyond it, knocked, asked for the housekeeper's office. I was in luck. One of the housemaids was down with the flu, there was a vacancy. Just temporary, mind. Normally I only take girls sent by the agency. You can start today and we'll see how you get on.

I changed into my uniform in the service cloakroom. Dark blue dress, black stockings and shoes, dark blue apron, blue cap covering my hair. On that first day the dingy clothes felt strange, like a disguise. A costume of shadows that turned us into shadows too as we clambered down the back stairs lugging canvas bags of dirty laundry. You counted out the sheets and towels before they went to the wash. You counted them back when they returned, stiff with starch, in long grey boxes with loose lids fastened with black tapes. You counted them onto the shelves in the big cupboard at the end of each corridor. The housekeeper hustled behind us, instructing, checking.

I was allotted to a workstation on the first floor. We cleaned the bedrooms after breakfast, when the guests departed for walks or went shopping. The season was over, but plenty of holidaymakers still lingered. For the sea air, the pale wintry sunshine, the casino. Kneeling with dustpan and brush in hand I wheedled grains of dust from corners, from the tops of skirting boards. The skin on my knees crinkled to red sores and my shoulders ached.

We rose at dawn. Short breaks for meals in the basement dining-room, each of us with her own napkin kept in our name-labelled pigeonholes by the service hatch. Breaths of fresh air snatched in the back yard, inside its high brick walls. Early to bed in the dormitory under the roof. After only a week I began feeling stuck. I hoped I might bump into Monique somehow, but I didn't. I lacked the nerve to roam the corridors, knocking on doors, to search for her. I didn't question the other maids; too soon to show myself a nosy parker. They might take against me, gang up on me. Nor did I present myself at the nuns' clinic, enquire after Camille. Going out to find her seemed impossibly difficult. I'd used up all my courage in getting this far. On my afternoon off I lay on my bed and slept.

One lunchtime, halfway through my second week, the house-keeper stood up in the servants' dining-room in the basement, asked for a volunteer to take over receiving the daily delivery of milk in the back yard. The kitchen maid whose job it was had gone off sick, no one else on the kitchen roster could be spared.

Stale air. Small, never-opened windows high up along the top of one wall leaked yellowish light onto our plates of macaroni. Nothing wrong with a change, a chance to spend some minutes outdoors. I stuck up my hand. Yes, you'll do, the housekeeper said: you're bright, you can count and add up, you'll have no difficulty.

On the first morning, she accompanied me out into the yard, and waited with me, to make sure I knew what was expected of me. If you get it wrong, I'm the one who'll be in trouble!

Pink streaks in the sky. Cool air on my face and neck. A toot on a horn. We unbolted the tall wooden gates, pulled them wide. The world rushed through. Sunlight slanting low across pavements. Feathery acacias, the stone facade of a house opposite. A woman with a poodle on a red lead.

In rumbled the truck over the cobbles. Down sprang the driver, a wiry man in blues. Thick black hair, a chipped front tooth. He shook hands with the housekeeper, nodded at me, clanged down the back of the truck.

Bring the crates into the storeroom as usual, the housekeeper directed, and she can count them as you go, and then count them again when they're all inside.

It seemed simple enough. The man stacked his trolley with crates of shining metal cans, wheeled it to the storeroom, deposited his load, filled the trolley again, trundled it back and forth until he'd emptied the truck, while we watched, and I counted. Only of medium height, he seemed very strong. The weight of the crates gave him no trouble. He lifted them airily as though they were plates of sponge cakes.

As he lugged each load into the storeroom I held the door open for him. When he finished, he chatted to the housekeeper while I went in and counted the stack inside a second time. He loaded yesterday's empty milk cans into the lorry. The housekeeper signed the chits. He tore them off his pad: a yellow one for her, a pink one for him.

Off went the man, whistling. The housekeeper and I pushed the gates shut, bolted them again.

Right, the housekeeper said, shooing me before her: so you see, there's nothing to it. I'll leave you to get on with it from now on.

Next morning the man said: oh, here's a nice little girl. Where did you spring from?

I said: we met yesterday. I work here. This is my job.

He smiled. You look too young to be out at work, petite. On your school holidays, are you?

Not at all, I said. I left school ages ago.

He let down the tailgate of the truck and leaned against it. Been around a bit, have you? Seen something of the world? Nice is the finest town in France, wouldn't you say?

I shrugged. I suppose so.

Well, he said, we're comrades now, you and I, so shake hands, and we'll get on.

He stepped close to me. He smelled of stale tobacco. I hesitated, stuck out my hand. He clasped it with warm, calloused fingers. Where's the old trout? Left you all alone, has she?

I pulled my hand away. I'm doing this job now. She told you so, yesterday.

He winked. So she did. Don't you worry. We'll get these crates sorted in no time. You hold the door for me, and I'll carry them through and you can count them as I go.

Yes, I said, I know what I have to do, thanks.

He lifted his hands. All right! Sorry. I was only trying to help. No need to bite my head off.

He'd wrong-footed me; I was being stand-offish, over-sensitive. He gave me a little sorrowful grimace. Well, let's get on, shall we? I haven't got all day.

Warmth began to slide in under the freshness of early morning. Outside in the street, palm tree branches rustled and clicked. Someone a few blocks away began playing a trumpet. Down the hill, down on the beach, hotel workmen would be sweeping the sand into long curls. Less labour for them at this time of year than in the summer. Fewer tourists about; fewer people scuffing up their handiwork.

The man shouted from inside the storeroom. Where are you? Come in and double-check! Come on, get a move on!

I hesitated. He was only doing his job. I should do mine. I've already checked out here, I called back: it's fine. Everything accounted for.

No, he cried, you're supposed to double-check, don't you remember? Then you can sign the chit and I can be off. Otherwise we're both in trouble. Me more than you. Come on, get on with it.

Stupid to make a fuss. As though I suspected him of something. Rude, too. I stepped across the threshold.

Once inside the storeroom I faced a wall of crates, glossy in the light slanting through the doorway. Yesterday he'd stacked them to one side, so that I could stand in the gap and count them easily.

He shouted from behind the wall he'd built. Give me a hand, would you? The trolley's stuck and I can't move it.

I edged round the stacked crates into the dark corner. His tobacco smell. The darkness moved, broke loose, lunged at me. Hands gripped me, an iron embrace, sour-smelling. Dry lips scraped mine.

There, my pretty! Now we're proper friends! He pushed past me with the trolley and went out, laughing.

I followed him into the yard. He folded my fingers over the signed chit. He said: just a spot of fun. Don't hold it against me. Oh, but I'd like to hold it against you! The cab door slammed. The engine coughed, roared. The lorry lurched forward, drove out of the yard. I pushed the heavy gates shut, slammed the bolt across.

The second time a man not my father had kissed me. I'd never kissed any of my playmates at home. Our games focussed more urgently, went straight to a certain point: undressing in the corners of dark sheds, standing on top of piled boxes, showing ourselves to each other, studying one another closely, hardly talking. Grubby little kids, stretching out curious hands. A bit of a scuffle in damp straw. Then giggling, fleeing. A secret to be kept from the grown-ups. Encounters cut out of ordinary life. No words for them.

Next morning I forced my feet to walk me into the yard. I put on an indifferent face, stuck my fists in my apron pockets.

He jumped down from his cab. Whistling. A chipped-tooth smile. Morning, doll. Shake hands.

I dodged to the far side of the trolley. He came round it, grabbed me. I tried to push him off. The kiss landed on my cheek. He aimed a second kiss at my mouth but I twisted away. He laughed at me. Scaredy-cat.

I did the second count of crates from the storeroom entrance. He'll be gone soon. Just stay calm.

Before leaving, he advanced with outstretched arms: say goodbye nicely, now, doll. I backed against the brick wall. He came closer. I ducked away, but I moved awkwardly, my hem caught on something and tore. As I ripped myself free he seized me again, thrust a hand under my dress. Oh, what a good little girl! Just like the fucking Brush. I bit him hard on the neck.

He let go of my waist, what the fuck, *putain bordel*, he pulled away, shouting, he let go of me, stood there stupid, his neck beading and running with red.

His face twisted. You little bitch! He lunged at me but I made a dash for the door to the kitchen quarters, threw myself inside.

I sped up the back stairs. Ground floor, first floor, second floor, I lost count, the flights repeated and repeated. Identical small landings, walls painted grey-green.

A stitch in my side halted me. I turned, pushed past a service lift into what seemed a cupboard, fell through it into a wide, carpeted passage lined with marble-framed doors. Tall arched mirrors stood between them.

I leaned against a gilded column, heart thudding. Hide for a bit. Calm down. Work out what to say to the housekeeper when I got hauled before her, as presumably I would. Would the man report me? Even if he didn't, I'd be for it. Hadn't signed the chit, hadn't closed the gates. Suppose he got blamed for that? Suppose I lost him his job? Suppose he had a wife and kids to support? They might become destitute, end up in the gutter. All my fault. What had I done? Presumably I'd get the sack too.

Wall lights twinkled in the greyness. The grand corridor stretched ahead, hushed and empty. Guests would be breakfasting downstairs. Early risers, having breakfasted already, would be back inside their rooms, dressing to go out. Any moment someone might emerge, notice me. Where was the workstation on this floor? I should hide there. Make a plan.

Something moved in the distance, startled me. A tall shape began to advance. I made off in the other direction. Around the corner I knocked into a cart of laundry parked next to the brocade-covered wall. A dustpan and brush. A broom. A pair of men's shoes, left out for cleaning. A half-open door. One of the chambermaids might be inside. Refuge. I slid in.

A sword of sunshine slashed at me, halted me. In the beam of light a woman stood with her back to me. She might have been cut from black cardboard, so still she was. Shoulders back, arms by her side; an upright soldier.

A woman's voice spoke from the darkness beyond her. Don't bother to wait for the day nurse. I'm here. We'll see you this evening, as usual.

A man's voice, fainter, more hesitant, joined in. I'm always sad when you have to go, my dear. Thank you for your company. You made my night bearable. I'll be back to work very soon, and it's all thanks to you.

You're welcome, maître. I'm glad I could help.

The shape switched round and faced me. My eyes adjusted. A young woman in nurse's uniform. Black stockings. Polished lace-ups. Starched wide head-dress.

Hello, Monique, I said.

She stared. A smile cracked her face. She ran forward and put her arms around me. Clem. You should have told me you were coming.

She kissed me on both cheeks. She pushed me back towards the door, whispering. We can't talk here. We mustn't disturb him. Come outside into the corridor. We'll talk there.

17. Two figures in a Parisian street

DENIS

You caught me at a good time, Maurice said, I'm on holiday as from today. Two whole weeks. He wore jeans, a loose coral-red shirt in thick, soft-looking cotton. Out of his crisp grey Eurostar uniform he didn't seem to require the formal distance you accord to an official. I felt less shy of him in one way, and more so in another. With the former code of politeness gone, we'd have to invent a new language. We smiled, shook hands. He said: so, let's walk.

He'd given me a rendezvous near the Canal. We paused on top of a green-painted iron bridge. Willows on the banks either side swept down long leafy branches that trailed in the green-scummed water.

The water here's a different colour, I said: at the Quai St Michel the river was grey-green. Here the Canal's just grey.

What took you to the Left Bank? Maurice asked. Surely you've been there before. What did you go to see?

Under the green shade of the trees we stood close together, leaning our elbows on the green iron parapet. His skin smelled fresh and sharp.

I said: I'm pursuing Matisse, in a way. The Quai St Michel was where he lived at a certain period, on and off, with his wife and children. Later, they had a flat on the Boulevard de Montparnasse. He lived in Vence, during the war, in the Villa le Rêve, and right at the end in a hotel in Nice. Since I'm on his track I thought I should start here in Paris.

Too much information? I paused. Was Maurice interested in Matisse?

Maurice moved a little away. He hooded his eyes, stuck out his lower lip. Sunlight glistened through the leaves overhead, spattered his brown cheeks. Yes, I have heard of him, I do know who Matisse was. He shook his head. You foolish man.

Sorry, I said, I don't know how to explain. I don't want to bore you.

Maurice said: my mother took us to exhibitions all the time in my childhood. Every time a show opened that was free, we went there. When I had to do an art project at school, she got me to choose Matisse, because he admired African art. I made a scrapbook with postcards. Pictures of little wooden statues. Cloths. He collected them, he put them in his paintings. He learned from them. New ways to see things.

He fiddled with his cigarette packet, then shoved it back in his pocket.

He said: I'd have liked to study art history. But it didn't work out. So I just go on going to exhibitions whenever I can.

I said: I'd a fancy to see where Matisse lived in Paris, that's all. And I wanted to break my journey, in any case. It's a long way down to the south.

Maurice turned his face towards me. His crossness had blown away like thistledown. His bright brown eyes asked me the question.

I said: I'm making for Marseilles, and then La Ciotat, to visit my godmother. Just a short stay.

A group of young people clattered up the iron steps, pushing past us. Careless, shoving. Coming the other way, a woman with a pushchair, laden with a toddler and various dangling shopping bags, braced herself for the descent. I went forward, took the chair from her, carried it down. Maurice followed me.

Let's keep walking, shall we? You're staying near here, you said. If you like, I'll show you a shop where you can buy good bread. Harder to find in Paris than it used to be.

The *boulangerie* queue spilled out onto the pavement. People stood patiently, chatting with each other, stopping their little dogs from jumping at each other, tangling their leads. The window's shelves displayed wheels of fruit tarts on stemmed glass dishes. Whorled pastries. Chocolate cakes cut into marbled cubes varnished with black icing. Small pale golden boats iced in white.

I said: *calissons de Provence*. My godmother used to buy me those.

We inched forwards under the shop awning striped green and cream. Ahead of us the bell tinkled as people went in, came out.

I said: she's pretty old now. She's getting on for, let's see, her late eighties, I'm not sure. Apparently her health is not too good. She wants me to go and see her, so I feel I must.

Maurice reached the shop threshold, held open the glass door for me. He said: as your godmother, she's part of your family, then. Family is important.

I said: to some extent I've had to find a family. A family of friends.

The queue in front of us moved on again. To one side: an array of open-faced baskets of different breads, seeded and plaited and twisted, brown crusts dusted with white. To the other, blue metal shelves bearing packets of flour arranged in pyramids, packets of spaghetti in bright paper wrappers, a jar of striped lollipops.

Maurice said: my family's been a stronghold, a refuge. We hold each other up. I've tried to provide that for my nephews and nieces. Life here is very hard, if you have no contacts, no one to help you. You have to make your own way.

He glanced at me. No, I'm not married. No children. You?

I'm single, I said. No children. They didn't happen. Too late now.

You don't have to have children of your own, Maurice said. My older sister's a widow. I love her kids, I'm like a dad to them.

Other people pressed in behind us. Again, the tinkle of the bell, the murmur of greetings. *Bonjour, m'sieur, 'dame.* The white-overalled assistants wrapped baguettes in twists of tissue paper, pushed forwards change on a small ceramic tray.

I said: to some extent, visiting the Quai St Michel was just an excuse for delay. I don't feel able to go directly to La Ciotat. I need to make the journey slowly. Step by step.

I knew why. I was afraid that Clem was dying and that I'd arrive in time to assist at her deathbed. Too soon after my mother's. Please please not another one. I was a selfish coward. What was there to be afraid of? That Clem'd be suffering and I wouldn't be able to help her. I'd witness her pain at close quarters but not be able to stop it. Anguish for her and anguish for me. How egotistical I was, just thinking of my own feelings.

Maurice read my mind. Doctors put people on morphine, so that they don't suffer. But if she's ill as you suppose, and if you want to talk to her, you should arrive before that happens. While she can still speak. Don't be afraid. She'll be so pleased to see you. It will be all right.

I said: you're being very kind to me. You're speaking to me as a friend would. Thank you.

Carrying paper bags of rolls, one for Maurice and one for me, we stepped out of the cool, shaded shop back into the street. We paused, adjusting our eyes to the sunshine. I said: and you, what are you going to do now you've got some leave? Maurice smiled. I'm going to go and visit my younger sister, north of here, she's a social worker, and then she's lending me her car so that I can drive to London, to visit my friends there. They've had to move flats, the rent went up so much, they've found a new one, so I'm going over with a flat-warming present or two. Bulky things, so I'll need the car.

I said: you'll be staying with your friends?

Maurice said: oh no. There won't be room. The new flat's tiny, apparently. But I'll do as you've done, I'll find an Airbnb. As soon as I get home now I'll sort it out. I've left it rather late, I realise.

We began to cross the road, weaving between slow-moving cars. On the far side we halted. Was this where Maurice would be leaving me? He was glancing to the left, as though checking his route. He was hovering, gathering himself, about to say goodbye.

I said: would you like to use my flat while I'm away? You'd be very welcome. My landlady won't mind a bit. I'll phone her to expect you. She'll be able to let you in and give you my spare keys.

Maurice stretched his eyes at me. But won't you be back soon yourself? I wouldn't want to be in your way.

I liked the way he didn't say: but you hardly know me. I liked the way he didn't ask for reassurance that I trusted him. I said: after visiting my godmother I'm thinking of travelling on for a while. Perhaps along to Bagnols, and then to Collioure. So the flat will be empty. And I can phone you to let you know when I'm due back.

Well, Maurice said, thank you. I should like that very much.

His graceful acceptance, his lack of fuss, charmed me. I said: I'll give you my address.

18. Black-and-white photograph (precise date unknown) by Yvette Martin, of Matisse in the Hotel Regina, Nice

Matisse, in three-quarter profile, reclines in an armchair with padded armrests. He wears a pale, long, loose coat, thick and soft-looking, open over a jacket, loose trousers, a flowing patterned scarf.

He looks tired, his head sunk on his chest, the fingers of one hand touching the side of his face, the fingers of the other hand curling lightly above his big patch pocket. Light reflects off his spectacles. Perhaps he's wondering about the drawing pinned up on the wall next to the window. About how to finish it. Whether he wants to. Whether he can.

The drawing shows a nude woman. She lies back on a couch with a striped cover, her arms and legs flopping. Head turned to one side, eyes directed at the viewer. She matters less in the composition than the huge, exuberant bunch of flowers sprouting from the vase on the *guéridon* beside her. Like a shout of pleasure. Matisse is drawing his desire; his hope of *jouissance*.

19. Hotel room, the Regina Hotel, Nice

CLÉMENCE

The Brush seized my hand, led me towards a grey marble doorframe. A grey curtain of mist. We pushed through it easily. Room led into room, a tunnel of rooms. In the furthest one, walled with yellow screens looped with strings of pearls, the enchanter sat in his wheeled chariot, his magician's wand in his hand. He wore a grey coat sewn with grey feathers.

The Brush propped a tall ladder against the wall, held it steady as I climbed up to get a better view. Welcome, Clem. Grey doves broke loose from the old man's coat, flew round his head, and brown nightingales, and white hummingbirds. He circled his wand in the air and colour erupted and the birds flared and flashed in brilliance: scarlet, purple, emerald, yellow, blue.

Dazzled, I took a step backwards, fell off the tall ladder. The air rescued me. I was flying, flying. Just concentrate. You can do it. I wavered, plummeted. I hit the ground and woke up. Thumping headache and dry mouth.

Last night we'd held a party in the maids' dormitory, perching on the sides of our beds. To say goodbye to Annette, who was leaving to have a baby. Sweetmeats were coming back into the shops: we shared out nougat and *calissons*, our crammed mouths crusting with sugar. We ate tinned apricots too, fishing them out of the syrup with our fingers, since someone had brought up a tin-opener but no spoons. Juice rolled down our chins that we mopped with our aprons. We toasted Annette in prune brandy collected late at night from dregs in the bar, passing the jug from hand to hand. I tipped it back. Harsh golden-brown liquid scorching my insides. Another swig. My stomach clung to my backbone, and the brandy carved round it like a golden knife. My head spun. Too heavy for my neck. I laughed loudly at everybody's jokes. You're drunk, old girl. The room heaved up and down in the candlelight. Poor little country mouse, she's falling over. Here, give us a hand with her. Arms lifted me and I toppled into bed and into sleep.

I had been celebrating my own release. Monique had taken charge. The Girl Guide captain squaring her shoulders, heartening the troops. Chin up, Clem. I know what to do. As soon as I'm back at the nurses' home I'll go to see Reverend Mother, ask her to write you a reference. Just in case. That will do the trick. You're an ex-pupil. She'll feel bound to help if you're in trouble.

Reverend Mother rallied to the call. Monique brought her letter back to the hotel straight away, in her own time, when she should have been catching up on her sleep. She slipped me a message to this effect via her chum, Félix the bellboy. He caught me in the corridor where I was pushing my trolley of laundry between rooms. Small, neat man, black-haired, with brown eyes in a brown face. He winked. She says you're not to fret, she's sorted it out, it will all be OK. She's cute, your friend, isn't she? Think she'd like to come out with me some time for a drink? You could come too. I'll bring a mate, we could make up a foursome.

The housekeeper sent for me mid-afternoon. I stood in her stuffy little office. She said: I don't know what you were up to with the milk delivery man and I don't want to. She droned through a ticking-off: I'd messed up on the job, hadn't closed the gates after the lorry, hadn't got the chit signed. Nonetheless she was giving me a second chance. I was to take over Annette's job on the third floor, cleaning three of the hired suites. Your friend the night nurse can keep an eye on you. You can start tomorrow morning. Do your work properly, don't be familiar with anyone, keep your head down. Understand? Yes, I said. Yes what? Yes, madame.

For the rest of the day she put me on cleaning the flights of back stairs. Bare, uncarpeted stone, the pockmarked surface clotted with dust and grit. On my knees with a dustpan and brush I laboured. Then a soapy rag to erase footprints. Each time another maid went up or down her shoes left black marks in the damp patches, oh, sorry, Clem dear, and I had to swab them away.

At supper, going into the servants' dining-room I found a note from Monique. Via the bellboy, presumably. He had tucked it into my pigeonhole. Hidden behind my rolled-up napkin. A message in brown crayon. You remember which suite I'm working in? Come and find me tomorrow morning, come and tell me how you are, we'll have a chance to say a quick hello before I go.

Her night duty, I would learn, ended when her admirer Félix wheeled in the Master's breakfast trolley: milky coffee and a bowl of pap to be served to him in bed. Always the same design of wide cup and bowl: pale blue porcelain, with a stripe in darker blue around the rims. Such rituals matter to him, Clem. Something he's got control over, d'you see? Likewise the starched white napkin folded alongside, neatly lined up with the silver spoon. And the clean white cloth on the silver tray, which stopped the breakfast sliding about as it was carried across the room.

Mme Lydia, his secretary-assistant, who had a small bedroom at the back of the suite, took over at that point. She breakfasted with him and discussed business, letters, visitors, timetables. The day nurse, sent like Monique from the agency, would arrive around the same time as the breakfast. The two would confer. Monique would hand over the notes she'd written on his state overnight. She was free to go.

On that first morning I tapped at the door, entered the suite as quietly as possible. Monique met me in the shadowy salon, the shutters still closed. She appeared from a corner beside the fireplace. A crack of light in the tall doorframe behind her. A click of the door closing, the line of light vanishing. Her white apron gleamed. Her winged cap sprang backwards from her head.

Her black eyebrows wrinkled. They forgot to tell you. You're supposed to use the service entrance, on the back corridor. She lifted a finger to her lips, cocked her head. He's still asleep through there. He'll wake at any moment.

Soft grey darkness walled the room, felted the edges of picture frames. Monique pushed the tall shutters apart, folded them back a little way in zigzag creases.

Sunlight stabbed and glittered in. Since two days ago someone had pinned up a pale, floor-length hanging over the window. A design of three steep arches patterned with shining cut holes, like petals or tears. The light pierced the thin cotton. The centre of the room felt formed by light. A corridor of light.

Monique stepped forwards, clasped my arms. We pecked each other on both cheeks. You're all right? Yes. You? Yes.

I explained that I was now one of the housemaids for this floor. Clem: at the Master's service. Responsible for this very suite. Monique and I would be able to see each other every single day. Monique folded her arms, said nothing. Yes, I know, I said, thanks to you. You got me out of a tight spot, all right.

She checked her watch. His breakfast should be here by now. This morning they're running late.

She began preparing to leave. Closing her little case, snapping its locks, putting her cloak round her shoulders, fastening it under her chin. Suddenly she collapsed limp as noodles, dropped onto an armchair. The cushion puffed up round her. She slumped, rubbed her eyes. I'm exhausted.

Didn't he sleep? I asked.

Hardly at all, she said, not until dawn. It's not just because he's been so ill. He told me early on that he's always been like this. He needs someone to stay with him, read to him, soothe him. Insomnia's a terrible affliction, Clem. It makes people very anxious. And then the anxiety makes falling asleep even harder. And so it goes on. It's a spiral.

What did he worry about? His painting? Not like the Brush, then, bounding into the room cheery at how well the day had gone, what he'd managed to achieve. Was the difference simply one of age? Perhaps the Brush had had his times of worry, too. Perhaps Camille had sat by him, night after night, waiting for sunrise, praying for him to cheer up. No wonder she'd been so cross, so tired, in the daytime following. No. In their case it had been the other way round. The Brush had tried to hearten her. Sometimes.

Monique said: but I mustn't complain.

She raised herself away from the cushion propping her, sat with a straighter back. The creases smoothed from her face, her cheeks plumped out again. Her efficient nurse self. Calm and controlled. The Master must have learned he could rely on her. His bed was a punt that she pulled across the lake of night. She waded through the dark waters and the old man lay against his pillows and floated along behind her. She'd stopped him panicking that he would not recover. She'd given him fresh heart.

Nursing's not like housework, is it, I said, the same every day. Something changes. You see people get better. If they don't die, that is.

Monique reached up, checking her veil, tugging out its edges. It's hard to explain, Clem, how blessed you feel, to know that you can help your patient survive such times of anguish, that you can bring them some comfort.

Anyone else spouting such words I'd have mocked for a goody-goody. Not Monique, though. She really did like to help. She liked to be the giver. Giving made her feel strong and in charge. Someone else could be the weak one.

In the night, she went on: when they can't sleep, that's when patients reveal their souls. That's when certain things get said. The nurse doesn't have to talk much. Mostly she just listens.

When I woke in the night I had no one with me. Often I dreamed that I was back at home, the house caught fire and was burning down with us in it, the kitchen stove exploded, the fire was leaping up the stairs on scarlet feet. Roaring and crackling it chased me, I snatched up my baby brother and escaped with him onto the roof. As the timbers sank under me I turned, tossed him into the flames' red mouth.

Monique began showing me around the room, pointing out the things to dust. On the mantelpiece stood a fat-bellied pot like a pregnant woman, two little wooden statues with similar curves. On a side table a painted pottery jug, a painted bowl with handles sprouting sideways like fanned leaves, a coffee pot in twisted silver.

No touching his ornaments, I said. Yes, I get it.

They're not ornaments, Monique said, they're *objets d'art*.

The beam of sunshine in the gap between the shutters shifted, reached a painting on the side wall. I walked over to it. A girl's head and shoulders in close-up, against a green background. Slanting brown eyes. She looked steadily out of the frame as though it were a window, though at the same time her thoughts were elsewhere, turned inwards. I must be standing where the painter had stood. He'd put out his hands, perhaps, and arranged her to sit just so. He'd pushed back her bobbed brown hair to reveal her sharply defined face. Bleak, and flat as a mask.

That belongs to one of the Master's younger friends, Monique said, another painter, he gave it to him a while ago. He's borrowed it back, to have it photographed for a catalogue. You see all those tiny holes? The young painter and his gang of men friends were using the painting as a dartboard.

Dabs of creamy, yellowy white patched the right side of the girl's forehead, her right cheek. She wore a red dress, its top edge scooping her collarbones; a wide black ribbon round her neck. Small, tucked-in red mouth. Dark shadows under her eyes. She was perhaps twelve or so. About the same age I'd been when my little brother died. She seemed full of experience, full of pain. The painting was pretending to be the sort of thing a child might do, but it wasn't childish at all: it concerned growing up. The paint spoke to me and told me so. Paint was alive, had its own voice. Created by the painter, a voice made of paint.

That's his daughter, Monique said. He told me about her. She was very ill as a child, she had to have an operation on her neck, a tracheotomy, to let her breathe, they had to cut open her windpipe, he had to hold her down on the kitchen table

132

while it was done, afterwards she wore the black ribbon to hide the scarred hole.

Perhaps the daughter had died, despite the operation to save her life, and the pain in the portrait belonged to her father painting her. He'd painted his beloved child after she'd died, in order to remember her.

She used to pose for him often, apparently, Monique said. She grew up in the studio, more or less. That was home. He'd placed her here, he'd placed her there. She'd liked standing, sitting, in the ways he chose. His eye directed her, made her feel she belonged, that she mattered. His need for her fitted her in to the world.

Of course she's grown-up now, Monique said, married. But she still helps him. She still works as his assistant in various ways. She's completely dedicated to him and to his work. She adores him, I think. Lucky her still to have a father.

I asked: how come you know so much about him and his family?

Monique said: he talks to me at night. He tells me things. I told you.

Darkness. Monique stationed on a chair next to his bed, bending forward to listen. Hands folded in her lap. His voice flung out towards her, winding round her, holding her fast. How could she leave him? Impossible. Love meant you had to stay. If you left you were hard, unloving.

Monique said: some of the things he tells me are truly terrible. He's haunted by them.

Part of me wanted to hear. Part of me didn't. Monique was holding some sharp spiky object. She was going to pass it on to me, let me carry it. I wanted to hurl it at the window, smash the pane.

In the war, Monique said, his daughter was in the Resistance, she was captured by the Gestapo and tortured, back in her cell she tried to kill herself with a piece of glass, she thought she wouldn't survive more torture, but she couldn't do it. The Red Cross rescued her. She came to see her father after she was freed, she told him what had been done to her.

He shouldn't have told you, I said, and you shouldn't tell me. You shouldn't repeat what he says to you, it's private.

The girl in the picture spoke to me in her words of paint. Now it's your turn. Now I'll listen to you.

How could anything I had to say possibly be of importance? My tiny life, other people's atrocious suffering. That day walking back to school after early Mass. Those black trucks, their black canvas backs laced down, crashing away over the sunlit cobbles, vanishing up the street. Shopkeepers inching open their doors, peeping from doorways. Policemen shouting at them to go back inside.

The girl's calm gaze drew words out of me. I told her about the nightmares. How wicked I was for dreaming such things. The girl spoke again in our shared language. You resented your brother because your parents preferred him to you, but you didn't harm him. It wasn't your fault he died.

How did she know this? Because she had survived, and she had forgiven herself for surviving when so many others had not.

Like feeling better after an illness, sitting up in bed, fresh clean sheets, the attic walls catching the glossy light, the fever gone and the window in the roof open, letting in cool air, the burble of pigeons.

Clem, what's the matter? Monique asked: why are you crying?

It's the picture, I said.

You'll be crying a lot, then, working here, Monique said: plenty of his pictures around the place.

I followed her back into the centre of the room. Right. Ready. I took up my dustpan, my brush, waved them. Lead on!

Monique read from an invisible notebook. After the Master has had his breakfast, Mme Lydia will bring out the breakfast trolley for you to wheel into the corridor, you just leave it there to be collected, then while the day nurse gives the Master his bed bath you can get on with cleaning in here, and then when she's finished you can clean his bedroom and the bathroom.

You sound just like the housekeeper, I said. For heaven's sake!

Sorry, Monique said, I shouldn't fuss. I'm sure you know what to do.

She hesitated. It's just that he's so special. In one way he's very strong but in another he's so fragile. He nearly died. He says himself that it's amazing he survived. He calls this his second life.

Hasn't he got a wife, then? I wanted to ask. Why isn't she here looking after him? Or is she dead?

And he's so generous, Monique said. During the evenings when he's on good form he's been teaching me to draw. He says I've got a vocation as an artist. No, I should say, as a graphic designer. He says I shouldn't marry, I should concentrate on painting. Learn how to paint, then move into design. Not do anything else.

Her harsh childhood had led her not to expect kindness. As a nurse she cared for others, and perhaps she turned that round somehow and secretly got enough caring for herself in the process. Not too much. She wouldn't know what to do with it. Now here was the man she called her Master showing her kindness, encouraging her to develop a talent she hadn't known she had. The Brush had promised to do that for me. Lucky Monique.

So how does he imagine you'll earn a living? I asked. You'll start selling your work straight away? And when d'you get time for painting? What do you paint? Portraits of your patients?

I heard the spite in my voice and felt ashamed.

I think the good Lord will help me, Monique said. I'll ask him to show me what to do.

For her, the door to God stood open. For me: shut. How could He possibly care about each and every one of His creatures? Surely there were far too many of us. Like those mothers back home with ten children, eleven children, exhausted and cross, forgetting which child was which, getting their names muddled up, hitting them to stop them crying. Those women would long for a shut door, with the children chucked away on the other side of it.

For Monique God was present, close. She did not doubt the word of the Gospel: God knew every one of the hairs on her head.

Did He equally know the hairs on Camille's head? Just in case He didn't, perhaps Monique could find out how she was. Whether she was still in hospital or had been discharged.

Wait, Monique. Don't go just yet.

I told her the story of Camille on the train being taken ill, being whisked off to the nuns' clinic.

Yes, of course, Monique said, I'll go in to the gynaecology ward and talk to the sister there.

We kissed each other goodbye. See you tomorrow. Yes, tomorrow.

I pushed back the shutters fully, lifted the hanging aside, opened the long windows to air the room. Colour blared and leapt out at me from every wall. Also black and white. Line drawings, enormous drawings of naked women lying as though flung down from a great height, such force in their simple lying down. Energy like bolts of lightning, bolts of darkening, forming them expressing them yet at the same time they did not lie still they shook and quivered they took up all the white space they could punch you soon as look at you their bunched fingers like roses unfurling. I bowed to them. I backed away.

20. Street scene, La Ciotat

DENIS

The sea glittered a couple of hundred yards to the left, beyond a stretch of pale yellow sand. I leaned forward and spoke to the back of the taxi driver's head. His black hair, sprinkled with silver-grey, crinkled above his sunburned neck. I've changed my mind. I've decided to walk the rest of the way. Put me down here, will you, please?

He took my note, counted out change. You'll find your way easily. Just follow the road round, and you'll reach the *vieux port*, and the old people's home is just beyond it, at the foot of the hill.

He had a gentle face, very lived-in. Peaceful and humorous. I wanted to sit and drink a cup of coffee with him, hear about his family, what his life was like. I wanted to tell him about mine. What was I doing, clutching at people on this journey? First trying to turn Maurice into a confidant, now this man. For years Phyllis had been my confidante, as I'd been hers. I'd hoped Freddy would become my new companion, but he had gone, and things between Phyllis and me had shifted, she'd moved away a little. Had I relied on her too much? With other friends I filtered intimacy through playing the game of humour, self-mockery. Since my mother's death I often felt sad, and it didn't do, with many people, to admit it. Tacit acknowledgement of sorrow, tacit sympathy. Keep bouncing the ball. Keep rising onto your toes, keep dancing.

The taxi door shone in the white sunlight. Hot air wrapped me. Sweat began flowing down the sides of my face. The driver said: I'll give you a card, in case you need a taxi back again. It's out of high season. Taxis are not plentiful. Here's my name, look. Gérard. Thank you, I said. He lifted a hand, drove away. I set off along the boulevard under the blue sky. Palm trees rustled overhead. The white pavement dazzled. Tiredness weighed me down. The Airbnb room in Paris had throbbed with the noise of next door's TV, then at dawn the roar of rubbish trucks. Two broken nights decided me. Changing my ticket, catching a dawn train out, felt like a blessed relief. At Marseilles a sprint between platforms let me board the branch line with five minutes to spare. Within half an hour we reached La Ciotat.

The air felt loaded with heat. To escape the brilliance and scorch I walked close to the line of shops and apartment blocks, keeping in the shade of their awnings. The villa-style frontage of the Eden Theatre reared up, a notice proclaiming it formerly the cinema where the Lumière Brothers showed their films. In front of the art deco facade, to honour the pioneers' memory indelible on celluloid, the tarmac surfacing the road had been laid in white with black edges and stripes resembling strips of film. I took a photo, sent it to Phyllis. Show this to Angela, she may like to see it. How are you getting on? Let's talk soon.

A horseshoe-shaped jetty enclosed the *vieux port*. I followed a paved path close to the boats. To my left, behind a row of bollards, the water jostled with masts. To my right curved a line of tall houses, Italianate blocks of pale yellow, pale blue, cream, pale salmon pink, with shutters in lavender blue and pale green. White umbrellas shaded the tables outside one quayside café, pale rose pink ones guarded another.

Past the port the road turned inland towards brown hills planted sparsely with pine trees. A salmon-pink apartment block stuck out its prow like a liner's, sported layers of port-holes and balconies. Next to it a high white-plastered wall held a metal gate. A metal nameplate read *La Maison du Rosaire*. I pressed a button, waited a moment, and the gate swung open.

Grey concrete walls enclosed a gravelled courtyard set with cement pots of begonias drooping waxy red and pink blooms. I trod across the noisy stones. On their far side jutted a glass verandah, its doors open.

A woman appeared in this entrance. She wore a calf-length grey tunic, in what looked like polyester, a bulky grey cardigan, black shoes. A grey veil, tied like a headscarf behind her head, revealed a line of her silver-brown hair. Hands clasped over a bundle of papers and what looked like a clipboard, she watched me approach.

Clem, reminiscing one evening on one of my childhood visits, recalling her schooldays, had described the habit worn by the nuns who taught her, modelled on the full-length, graceful and sweeping costume of the Foundress, a seventeenth-century widow who'd favoured a crisp white coif, a broad, starched white collar, a wisp of black muslin veil. At home, Clem had mused, the widow would leave off her veil. She'd wear it just for church. You could imagine her, *mon chéri*, looping her skirts over her arm to mount her horse, or striding out to feed her doves or prune her apple trees. In her deep pockets she'd keep a pair of gardening gloves, a prayer book, a pair of secateurs. Hands deep in those pockets she'd pace between her vegetable beds, swishing ample folds of gathered grey wool from side to side. Her spaniel would trot alongside. A door in the far wall would admit the friend bringing her a brace of partridge, a fresh cream cheese, a sheet of piano music. And then? And then? And then she'd obey her elders, *mon chéri*, and go to bed when she was told. Be off with you. We'll continue the story tomorrow.

The updated habit worn by the nun in front of me removed all that antique glamour. She was simply a dowdily dressed woman shifting her folder of papers to one hand and holding up the other. I was the traffic and she was halting me. She said: did you not hear me? We do not shout in this place.

I whispered: sorry.

I crunched over the gravel towards her. She rapped out: I said, monsieur, what can I do for you?

I mumbled. Certain French people had that effect on me. When I liked people and felt they liked me, when I felt easy in their company, I could speak French fluently. When they were brisk and brusque, like this woman, I became tongue-tied.

I fitted words awkwardly together. We've emailed each other. At least, I emailed a Sister Marie-Lucile. And I phoned earlier. You're expecting me, I hope. I'm here to visit my godmother. When I phoned, the sister I spoke to told me I could come at this time.

She consulted her clipboard. She gave me a softer look. So you're here to visit Clémence? Let's hope that cheers her up. She doesn't get many visitors.

I stuck out my hand. She merely nodded. She said: I am Sister Marie-Claude, the assistant to Sister Marie-Lucile. We haven't seen you before, have we? Follow me, please.

I trod after her into a cream-painted foyer. Three white plastic chairs surrounded a low coffee table with a veneer top. A desk opposite bore a computer, a plastic pot of fabric roses. The smell of synthetic-lemon air-freshener made me sneeze. Sister Marie-Claude marched through an archway into a wide corridor floored with shiny green vinyl. Pinned-up posters decorated the pale blue walls. Prints executed in pale blue, sludge green, yellow, black and white. Sheaves of corn, doves with olive branches in their beaks, suns rising over snowy mountains, sunflowers. Printed captions exhorted the people of God to have faith, to follow the uphill road.

Sister Marie-Claude slowed, looked over her shoulder. Those come from the Dominicans in Nice. One of their sisters was a gifted artist, she ran a poster workshop for a while. The posters sell to parishes all over southern France. We hang them in our retreat wing here, also. They're very popular with our visitors.

You have a large establishment, it seems, I remarked.

The nun said: people have need of us. Sometimes the retreatants like to visit our old people. It does both sides good.

She led me up two flights of stairs, along another green-floored corridor. She knocked on a door halfway down, opened it, thrust me inside. Here, Clémence, I've brought you a visitor.

She closed the door. Her footsteps squeaked away. The dim interior smelled of camomile. A propeller fan whirred in a corner. Small cube of humid air. The shape of a thin woman in an armchair by the darkened window materialised like a ghost. A frail outline. She turned her face, gave me a glance that took and held mine. I stood still.

The room became clearer. The dimness slithered like a curtain from its pole, crumpling in folds. Clem. A pink crocheted blanket swathed her from the waist downwards. Feet propped on a low stool. Hands clasped over a folded newspaper in her lap. Her white hair, swept to one side and fastened with a clip, exactly as years before, looked freshly washed.

She said: thank you for coming to see me. Thank you for coming all this way.

I remembered her voice as contralto. Now it had more of a silvery sound. I took a step further in. Then another. How are you?

As you see, she said, stuck in this chair, stuck in this room.

I leaned over her, and she tilted up her face so that I could kiss her soft cheeks.

How's your wrist? Your sprained wrist?

Oh, she said, much better. I can use both hands again.

The table beside her held a wide pink cup on a yellow-rimmed pink saucer. Rising steam, again that scent of camomile. She said: I can't stand the smell, can you? They don't like me drinking too much coffee at breakfast, so they bring me tisanes. They're supposed to be good for you.

Behind her hung a painting on cardboard. One of hers, presumably. I didn't recognise it. A tightly worked composition in gouache of a tilted black rectangle superimposed on parallel lines of small grey circles. A row of blue upright rectangles. Uncompromising. Not at all inviting. More like a sign saying Keep Away.

Clem turned her head. She said: it's a street scene. A memory from when I was young. Still at school.

I said: it's more abstract than some of your work. And a different colour palette.

Clem lifted a hand. Very likely. I painted it a while ago, in any case. Before coming here.

She had introduced the subject of time. What about the time before the before? Clem parting the straw in the hens' shed, slipping her hand in, drawing out an egg. She placed it in the wire basket I held. Another egg, and another. There. Now we've got supper. From the pots at the back step she picked tarragon, sorrel, parsley, chervil. *Omelette aux fines herbes* swirling yellow in the wide black pan. I asked: is the doctor coming again on Sunday? What will you cook for him? Oh, Clem said, something as delicious as this, I suppose. And you'll help me cook, won't you? After supper she folded back the blue cloth and we played cards, Clem slapping down the shiny oblongs as fiercely as I did, just as desperate to win as I was, shouting back at me when I accused her of cheating. Clem, as determined as my dear mother.

A hot tide was surging up into my throat, wanted to choke my words, burst from my eyes. I said: it's a beautiful day outside. Shall we go out? Would you like that? Do you think that would be a good idea?

Certainly, Clem said.

21. Black-and-white photograph (precise date unknown) of Matisse by Yvette Martin, in the room he uses as his studio in the Hotel Regina

To the left of the image Matisse, white-haired and white-bearded, sits in his wheelchair. Big round spectacles. Posed in three-quarter profile, half his face in shadow, he holds one end of a length of paper flung across the floor, unrolling, billowing out. A dark-haired young woman, with a vivid, sculpted face, stoops some distance away, holding the other end of the paper. She is bare-legged, casually chic in her pale sleeveless dress, her wedge-heeled sandals. A nearby table is loaded with jars of fat brushes, beakers of paint, scissors. Matisse gazes affectionately at the young woman, who does not return his smile. She looks bored. Willing herself to be patient.

Just behind Matisse gleam the elaborate twists and curlicues of glass framing an oval mirror, darkness in its depths. Placed there as an image of seeing, perhaps, of imagination. In the centre of the mirror: the blurry reflection of the photographer and her camera.

22. Figures in a salon

CLÉMENCE

Mme Lydia's grey back vanished from view beyond the door of the salon Monique was holding open. She disappeared into the dimness of the corridor.

She must have halted, and turned to speak over her shoulder. Her low, clear voice came distinctly towards us. Her words flew past Monique and reached me. I was balancing on top of the stepladder brought in from the studio, polishing the glass doors between the folded-back shutters. Mme Lydia's words perched on my stretched-out arms, pecked me. Oh, Clémence. I forgot to tell you, we're expecting visitors later on this morning, so you'll need to have finished your work and be out of the way by then.

Yes, madame, I said.

And if anyone should telephone while you're still here, please tell them we've gone out to buy materials, we should be back well before lunchtime.

I leaned forward so that the glass of the window nearly touched my forehead. Some people were like that. Keeping just enough cool distance. Glass armour you couldn't see but felt. No touching, in any case.

Had the Master ever touched Mme Lydia as a lover would? Certainly he had loved her face, her shape, re-composed them on paper. Once, Mme Lydia, with her tightly controlled hair, her business-like overalls, her plimsolls, had been that slender nude coiling across his drawings over and over again, a spiral held by their edges, she unwound herself, she was the outline and she was the body outlined, the pure thin black line. Now she was older and he no longer wanted her to pose for him naked. Other young women had taken over.

Now the artist sat on his crystal throne, and Mme Lydia whirled about him with her glass sword, repelling invaders, protecting him from nuisances, from servants who longed to speak to him. People who'd try to sneak his essence, as though he were paint you could squeeze from a tube. People who'd crowd about him as though he were a saint, whose touch could work miracles. I certainly wanted him to work one for me: please show me how to paint.

Mme Lydia's tone deepened, warmed. Monique, my dear, it's time you were going.

The Master's tones were fainter. Thank you again, my dear Monique. You know I'll never forget what you have done for me.

Mme Lydia had manoeuvred the Master, in his wheelchair, through the salon and out over the threshold into the corridor. She'd pushed him expertly, smoothly, though he pretended to be alarmed and cracked jokes about women drivers so that in turn she would pretend to be cross. They were both in a relieved, teasing mood, because he was so much better, and able to get on with his real life again.

Like him, his studio had revived. Now, most mornings, two young women, locals, arrived to help him with the new project he was working on. They lounged in, chatting with not a care in the world, knocking past my cleaning things. Sisters: dark-haired; very alike. Girls who'd left school but didn't have to work, Monique said, kicking their heels until they got married.

They'd vanish into the studio behind the salon, which was the last I'd see of them before I left mid-morning to clean the neighbouring suites.

The Master's work consumed everyone's energy. Every other day, it seemed, he ran out of paper and paint, and Mme Lydia had to take him down into town to get more. He didn't trust anyone else to buy them for him. About tools and materials he was very fussy, very precise. As you'd expect, Monique said, spreading her hands wide: he was a genius, he was chasing perfection. About privacy for his art he was fierce. I dusted and vacuumed everywhere in the suite but was not allowed in the studio. Forbidden, Mme Lydia said. You understand?

Monique shifted in the doorway. Just as she prepared to close the door behind them, Mme Lydia's voice rose up again. Monique, my dear, I know the doctor says we no longer need you to stay overnight, but are you going to drop in this evening? Just for a quick visit?

Just for half an hour, perhaps, Monique replied. My patient has improved so much that the doctor says you no longer need me at all. After the weekend the agency is transferring me back to daytime work.

Well, Mme Lydia called, that wasn't made quite clear. But never mind. I'm sure we'll manage.

I climbed back down the ladder. Monique pushed the heavy door shut, turned round, leaned against it. She yawned, shoved her hands into her apron pockets, watched me load the tray of used breakfast things onto the trolley. Madame Lydia's pleased. She'll have him all to herself again. She likes being the main one to take care of him.

That's obvious, I said.

From the tray I removed a scatter of pencils, a packet of

lozenges, a folded clean handkerchief, put them on a side table. Move, will you? I said. Let me put this lot out into the corridor.

With the messed-up trolley gone, the crumpled napkin and dirty crockery removed, the salon felt calm. I noticed the room so much because Mme Lydia, under the Master's instructions, kept rearranging the furniture, changing the pictures round, draping one exotic cloth after the other over tables and chairs. Today, a large trunk had propelled itself in, stood skew-whiff to the right of the window. Also a naked porcelain woman had arrived and knelt on all fours on the marble mantelpiece. She looked foreign, with that topknot. Was she pretending to be a dog? Was she saying sorry? For what?

We stood at the window, looking at the pale blue sky.

I'm sad I've got to leave here, Monique said. I thought he and I would have longer together, and I thought you and I would have longer together too.

So stay a bit longer now, I said. I know you've got to get back to the nurses' home to sleep, but the nuns won't fuss if you're half an hour late, surely.

Nurses have to obey their superiors, Monique said, discipline is discipline. You can't run a hospital without it. Nor a nurses' home. Rules are rules.

Yes, yes, Monique. Sometimes she did sound just like my father. I'd written twice to him and Mum but hadn't heard back from them. Perhaps they had cast me off. Assumed I was gone to the bad. Fat chance of that, with my dear Monique on hand to keep me on the straight and narrow. I wouldn't object to straying off it, with someone I fancied. Félix the bellboy, his neat hips, his lively glances shot from under his black eyebrows. No good, he preferred Monique to me.

Monique was reaching for her grey cloak, preparing to fling it round her shoulders. I felt suddenly sick with loneliness. Don't go yet, don't go. I managed to swallow the words back.

Any news of that lady I told you about? I asked. Did you have time to go and find out?

Monique said: that unfortunate person, yes.

My mother and her neighbours would huddle in the street, grating phrases off hardened opinions. I loafed nearby, collected their dropped expressions. *She lost it.* When that happened to a married woman it was very sad. *She's expecting.* When that happened to someone not yet married it was shameful, disgusting. A nod, a tightening of lips sufficed. Like that woman on the train, staring at Camille's ringless left hand, sneering and muttering. No better than animals.

Monique said: apparently she suffered a miscarriage. Apparently she refused to talk to the chaplain when he came in. On the other hand, she has recovered well. She's been discharged. Sister said it was all for the best.

She took a breath. Her voice changed. The poor girl. She's got no family here. For the moment she's in the hostel for homeless women. I didn't have time to go in and see her. I left her a note, telling her you were here in the hotel, that you'd got a job cleaning the Master's suite.

The Brush had mentioned the Master in that letter of his I'd read. Perhaps he'd introduced Camille to him. Perhaps she'd sat on the sofa here in the salon, drinking the lemonade brought in on a gilt tray by someone like me. She'd have crossed her long legs and the Master would have sat back and admired her curving shape. He'd have asked if he could draw her. She'd have stood up, shaken herself, shed her clothes, let them fall to the floor, and his pencil would have darted at her, its black tip tracing and caressing her flesh, her muscles, he surrounded her with himself his lines he pressed himself into her into the paper she resisted she pressed back she escaped him flew free he followed her tracking her with thin black marks she turned over and over a flashing fish in his net she'd have bitten free turned on him turned him inside out upside down finally exhausted he'd have laid down his pencil, exclaiming, calling a truce. The drawing done. Both of them lying back, smiling.

I picked up one of the pencils from the side table, tested its lead point against my finger. I've got tomorrow off, I said. I ought to go and see her. Invite her out for a stroll, perhaps.

Monique was hovering. She obviously did want to delay leaving but she couldn't admit it. I searched for an excuse she would accept.

Before you go, would you give me a hand tidying up?

I wanted to seize Camille like a piece of leftover cloth, roll her up and put her away. I was no better than the Brush. Clap her into a dark cupboard, close the door, pretend she'd never existed. What could I do for her? Nothing. Yet she was down and out. She was suffering. She pricked at me, she pulled at my hem, she pleaded for help. The nuns had rescued her so far, but after this what would happen to her? Surely she'd return to Paris, with her figure back, she'd find a new job in a dress shop, she would survive. She would crack jokes and laugh, toss her head, gallantly get on with life. Would she?

The phone began shrilling. Just a minute, Monique said, I'd better answer that.

She crossed to the bureau, a shiny walnut elephant, picked up the receiver. She listened, nodded, scribbled a note. Yes, yes, mademoiselle, I'll let Madame Lydia know. Of course you can't help it. Obviously. Not your fault.

151

She hung up. She smoothed the thick cord of the telephone into place. The two studio assistants can't come today, they've got to be with their family. Help make family lunch. For a christening party on Sunday.

What would the daughters cook, for such a feast? Could their family afford meat? The daughters would tie on aprons and separate eggs into bowls and peel garlic and chat to each other and wave their wooden spoons and sing. Kitchen magic. Kitchen art. Compliments all round. Someone like me would come in later and do the washing-up.

For my brother's christening I acted as his godmother. In church I held him out over the font. He yelled when the priest poured water on his forehead. That was the devil going out. If I didn't believe in God I didn't believe in the devil either. Pieces of my past life were falling, discarded fragments, onto the floor.

Monique said: the Master and Madame Lydia will be cross. They're both so dedicated to his art, they think everyone else should be too. They're really put out when the assistants don't turn up on time or when they ask for days off.

The Master is brilliant at getting other people to help him, isn't he? I said. He's got the services of a day nurse, a night nurse, a secretary, laundresses, cooks, waiters, but he hasn't quite managed it with those two girls.

Possibly they don't understand what he's doing, Monique said, working with bits of paper. Perhaps they see it as some kind of childish play, they don't take it seriously enough.

Slacking, the nuns would call it, I said, wouldn't they?

Art's a vocation, Monique said, same as being a nun is. You've got to be single-minded. Completely committed. Once you put your hand to the plough you must not turn back. You are pursuing perfection, day after day. Not many people are capable of such intensity.

I suppose not many people are geniuses, I said. I wonder if they know they are when they start out? It must be so hard to behave as though you know you're a genius when you're not sure.

You're just being catty, Monique said. You're envious. But you shouldn't be. He's so high above us that envy's pointless.

She hesitated. I admit that when I first saw his work, I didn't see its beauty. I liked the colours but I thought the painting was terrible. I told him so and he laughed, he said he liked my honesty. And in fact he doesn't swank about at all. He's an extremely modest man.

But does he think he is a genius? I persisted.

He's not concerned with that, Monique said, more with the enormous effort required for his work. The fear, the anxiety he has to conquer in order to push forward into the unknown, achieve something completely new. Most people are content with much less. The cost is too high.

What was it like, being a studio assistant working with the Master? At least those two girls were allowed to enter his studio. Behind its closed door they could witness his mysteries. He conjured new life out of paper and paint. Would I ever learn to do that? Monique had taken my sketchbook from me a couple of days back, promising to give it to Mme Lydia, ask her to show it to the Master, request his opinion. I just had to wait.

I pointed to the trunk lying to one side of the window. Madame Lydia had this brought in yesterday morning from the hotel storeroom, after you'd gone. I don't know what it's for. But where should I put it? It's in the way.

Of what? Of my being able to clean. I felt like a mother telling her child to put her toys in order, not leave things in a mess. I wanted to be the one making the mess, not the one clearing it up. I wanted to play, like the Master did.

Madame Lydia mentioned the trunk last night, Monique said. Some people are coming to take photographs of the Master at work. Apparently they began taking some quite a while ago, before he got so ill, then had to stop. Now that he's so much better they're ready to start again. This time they want to make a short film as well, to be shot in here. Madame Lydia was wondering about extra props. Whether to include some of these. Some of his treasures.

She lifted the lid of the trunk and pushed it back. Like a dark trapdoor banging open, packed-down colour jumping up, fireworks exploding from night back into day. Yellow gauze scarves with gilt fringes, purple beaded bodices, baggy trousers in red velvet, pink chiffon see-through blouses. We knelt, pulled out side-slit skirts, diamanté belts, headbands jingling with coins.

Harem outfits, so he told me, Monique said, fancy-dress outfits. He used to collect them for his models to wear, twenty, twenty-five years back, before the war, and he's kept them all this time. They were so sensual, he said, so exotic, that he couldn't bear to part with them. Wearing them, the girls were transformed.

When they wore just their flesh he transformed them too. The nudes on the walls had skin like tight satin. They looked like cooked prawns: curved shapes of rose and silver-pink.

Monique drew out a carved sandalwood box, opened it. Glass gems glittered and flashed. A thick rope of coral twigs. A string of red beads plump as cherries. She said: when I arrived yesterday evening, he was sitting in his armchair with his lap covered with costumes. He said they were memories of all the beautiful girls who'd modelled for him in those days, and all through the war, all the beautiful girls he'd ever wanted to have sitting in his lap, and then he gathered them up in his hands and hurled them into the air and they flew all over the floor. Madame Lydia wanted to take a photograph but he said no. He said just to put them away.

The spangled, slinky clothes: like the costumes heroines wore in certain silent films. I fished out a sequined brassiere and held it out to Monique. D'you remember?

That special season of Arabian Nights-type films from the 1920s, that Monique, Berthe and I had sneaked out to see one weekend in the backstreet cinema, when we'd told the nuns we were going to watch nature documentaries with the Girl Guide troop. The pleasure of the forbidden. No one in authority knowing where we were. Lounging secretly in the velvety darkness. Strangers moving and rustling close to us. The smell of ancient hot dust from the carpets, the seats. The rosy glow of a torch. Up above us on the lit screen prowled men, eyes outlined in gleaming black kohl, wearing jewelled turbans and sweeping robes, flourishing curved daggers. Girls glistened in silvery scales, flopping around like sardines and mullet on the fishmonger's stall at market. Mermaid girls, bare-breasted under see-through seaweed lace. Thickly mascaraed eyelashes. Bow mouths. Brazen hussies, my mother would have called them: tarts.

Monique was stroking a pink silken sash. She said: I expect everyone likes playing at dressing-up. Only I never had the chance. Nor did you.

Let's have a go now, I said, just a quick one. Come on. No one will know.

Monique hesitated. She sat back on her heels. All right. Why not?

She fingered a pair of flat turquoise satin mules sewn with amber chips. So. For example. If we were in a film, in a scene about going out for the evening, what would we wear?

Going out with your admirer? I asked. Taking me along?

I was going to tell you, she said. I was going to ask you if you'd like to come too. Tomorrow night. You're free, aren't you? Félix said he'd bring one of his pals if you want, we'll be a nice group.

Forget the pal, I said. Let's take Camille too, that'll cheer her up.

Monique chose a low-cut pink evening frock. Frills of chiffon. She unpinned her wide-winged cap and put it aside, rapidly undid her chignon, shook out her black curls. She stripped, stood poised like a diver, with hands joined and arms raised, showing her tufts of black hair, and I dropped the dress over her head. She vanished. There was a pink struggle. Then she rose out of the pink foaming waves and I pulled them down to fall in wide folds from her hips. Fake orchids I pinned in her hair. Pearls in a string I hung round her neck.

Come on. Take these off too. She sat on the edge of a chair and I knelt in front of her, while she bent forward, crinkled up her skirts. I removed her nurse's shoes, flat black lace-ups with sturdy soles. She unrolled her stockings down to her ankles. I pinched them off. Black woollen tubes with sweat-dampened ends. She wriggled her toes. That's more like it.

You ought to have gold slippers, I said, or at least painted toenails.

She stood up and twirled around. Her skirts ruffled and flared like a peony's petals. She said: once, in the holidays, some man wanted to paint my portrait. My family fell about laughing. You only paint beautiful women, and I'm not beautiful. I told the Master about it one evening and he said it wasn't true, there are many different styles of beauty.

She swished her frills from side to side then up and down. He told me that when he requested a *garde-malade* from the agency, he stressed that she had to be young and good-looking. He wants me to sit for him sometime, did I tell you? Madame Lydia's going to look me out a costume. Apparently he thinks something Grecian-style would suit me.

She stood on one leg, spread her arms, leaned forward in a fancy pose. D'you know how many bones there are in one foot? If ever I go back to training as a nurse I'll have to learn all their names. I've learned how to give a foot massage, at least. The Master says I've got a good touch.

She scrabbled deeper into the trunk, found a pair of black high heels. She stroked her round white neck. The Master said he admired my neck, it's like a white column.

If we were in a film, about to go out for the whole evening, I told her, dinner and dancing and so on, surely we'd start off at the bar. We'd have a drink. That's what the guests do here.

Mme Lydia kept the bottle of peach liqueur in the corner cupboard. A black-market present from a visitor. She'd grimaced at it, then put it away. She wasn't likely to notice if I helped myself. In any case, I'd top up the bottle with water later on. I poured yellow liquid into two tumblers, brought them across. I offered one to Monique. She said: but it's ten o'clock in the morning! She paused. She seized the tumbler. All right. A pick-me-up. Just what I need, actually, after being up half the night, listening to him fret. He seems so well in the daytime, but he still gets very anxious come evening. I calmed him down in the end, but it did take time.

She arranged herself on the divan, lifting one knee slightly, shaking back the hem of the dress, pointing her feet. She lay back. Now you, Clem. What are you going to choose?

To don the harem trousers I peeled off everything. Sturdy knickers, girdle and brassiere all got hurled onto the floor along with my maid's outfit. The low-slung brocaded waistband sat on my hips, drooped in front to show my belly button. On top I wore a white see-through filmy blouse. I draped a black net veil over my head, drawing it down over my face. I found a pair of embroidered high-heeled mules, practised stepping back and forth in them. Strange, how they tilted you, threw your weight back at you. Too tricky: I kicked them off. The trousers, loose and thin, freed me. I could stride. I could cartwheel. I could perform the splits.

Monique applauded. You'll do, show-off. Now come and sit down.

Just a minute, I said, I need some decoration.

From the box of jewellery I picked out a pair of gilt earrings strung with tiny golden beads, a chain anklet clinking with coins, and put them on.

Monique said: there's something I want to ask you. No, wait a minute.

She got up, crossed to the window, pulled the shutters across, almost closing them. A single line of bright gold light divided them. The room settled itself in semi-darkness. There. That's better.

She reclined at one end of the divan and I perched at the other, tucking one foot under me, twiddling my anklet.

Pull your veil right down, she said. I obeyed her. She said: now I can't see your face. Good. It's like being in the confessional.

I deepened my voice to a growl. I balanced my hands together, fingertips against fingertips. *So, my child, what have you come to tell me?*

A cough. A rustle. Then she blurted it out. *Have you ever kissed anyone? Do you know how it's done?*

I've been kissed, I answered, *but I haven't yet kissed anybody.*

Only in dreams. Kisses like slow electric shocks, my mouth buzzing and stinging, my insides turning over.

Let's have a go, Monique said, *I want to know how to do it. Just in case.*

What she meant was: after the evening in the café Félix the bellboy might walk her back to the nurses' home, and if kissing was going to be involved she needed not to feel caught out. Not to feel inexperienced and foolish.

I folded back my veil. She leaned forwards and I mirrored her and did likewise. I closed my eyes. She smelled heated, the fruity warmth of alcohol, the faint scent of salt-sour sweat. I opened my eyes. Her blue ones, staring into mine. Stubble of black eyelashes. Her strong, even white teeth. She took my face between her hands. *Right. Now. Over to you. You be the boy and I'll be the girl. So you start.*

Why? I said. *No. We both have to do it at the same time.*

A serious business: working out how not to bang our noses together. Her lips pressing mine felt dry as the delivery man's had been. She paused, wetted her lips with her tongue, kissed me again. Now she tasted of peaches and sugar. We tried working our mouths up and down over each other's, we licked each other, we opened our mouths, explored with tongues, tasted each other's saliva. It was all very active and practical and at the same time dull. Too much chopping and changing.

Monique sat up. That'll do. I think I've got the hang of it now.

I haven't, I said. Let's have another go, let's do just one sort. I took a second long swig of peach liqueur. Sticky, sweet. Monique lifted her tumbler, sipped.

All right, she said, another try.

We put our mouths together again, and just let them stay there, very gently. Of themselves they began to move. Slow, slow kissing. Idling. Not needing to stop. Like two animals finding each other, nuzzling, nipping, butting. Heat stirring and building inside me. Nothing but mouths. We were gone, dissolved like sugar in coffee.

A heavy click. Somehow part of the flow we were in, just the start of a different rhythm click clack click like dance music tap tap of dancers' heels on the polished floor just to change our tempo for a moment musical sounds that rearranged themselves into the door opening, people talking.

Mme Lydia's crisp voice. Go on ahead. Do. Monsieur Martin, Madame Martin, please just go in and sit down and we'll come in after you, the wheelchair is awkward and heavy, we need to take our time. Go on, we're following you. Oh well, if you insist on helping. Thank you.

We unstuck our lips. My mouth huge, swollen, a peach ready to burst with juice. I grabbed Monique's hand, pulled her up. I scooped our clothes from the floor, bundled them under my arm, dragged Monique over to the far door to the left of the mantelpiece. I shoved open the door. pushed Monique through into the studio-room beyond, pulled the door to behind us.

A shock of light. Inside a box of light. Pinned against the door by light. A block of light pressing us outwards, away, against the walls. Tall thin unshuttered windows. Walls breathing and flexing. Live creatures swarmed over them, shimmied all round us. Swirls of painted colour caught us up, paper edges curling and fluttering in the draught. Fronds of curling weeds. Fishes flicked past. An octopus. At the same time an aviary, filled with long-tailed birds, wings outspread. A trestle table to one side, big sheets of coloured paper scattered pink yellow blue green. Paint pots and brushes. Scissors and shears. Hammers. The floor underneath was littered with coloured scraps.

I turned, peeped through the crack at the intruders next door. Soft as a bolster Monique lolled against my arm.

On the far side of the salon the Brush stooped in the shadowy doorway giving onto the corridor. All right, Madame Lydia. There are too many of us. I'll leave it to you. He straightened up, dusted his hands together. Come on, darling, move out of the way. A woman carrying a coat over one arm. Fair curls toppling from a loosely pinned topknot. She wore a tight-waisted scarlet jacket, a calf-length gathered orange skirt, scarlet and black striped stockings, black high heels. Madame Martin. So who? Not his mother: too young. His sister? Oh, Clem, you stupid fool. She's his wife.

She was standing close to him, as though that was where she liked to stand. She was peering forward into the dim room. Peering towards us. Mme Lydia's voice spoke from just behind them. So fortunate that we have all arrived at the same time. Just a moment and I'll find you somewhere to sit, and we'll have something to drink.

Mme Martin said: too early for an aperitif. A glass of water will do. After our walk up the hill my throat is full of dust.

Just a minute, then, Mme Lydia called, and I'll ring for the waiter to fetch a bottle of soda water.

It's very dark in here, said the Brush. I'll open the shutters. And then may we take a look in the studio?

Mme Martin stepped further forwards, threw her coat onto a low stool. Don't be so impatient. Don't rush him.

The Brush said: I want to get going while the light is so good. I'd like to set up a few shots, check some angles. Then we'll be all ready for filming tomorrow.

Wait, wait, called Mme Lydia, here we come. Just a moment, I've caught my scarf in the door jamb.

Monique sagged against me, gave a giggle, a burp. Next door the shutters banged and creaked as they were folded back. I pinched Monique, to rouse her. She straightened up, one arm on my shoulder. There's only one thing for it, I said. Come on.

I lowered my veil to hide my face. I put my arm round Monique's waist, squeezed her hard, let go. I thrust open the door.

A performance. Like the school play when I mimed St Joan with a cardboard sword. Into a current of sunshine we made our entrance. Arm in arm, heads up, we paraded back into the room. We halted, bowed to our audience.

The Brush and his wife jerked with surprise. Then responded to our theatrics: smiles, hand claps. To the Brush I was obviously a stranger. Certainly not that country mouse. I was veiled, an actor dressed in men's clothes. I said to the stranger-myself: just say and do whatever you want.

And who may you young persons be? enquired Mme Martin.

I bowed again. We are the new studio assistants, madame. At your service.

23. On the beach, La Ciotat

DENIS

Clem resisted putting on a purple headscarf, a green woollen jacket. The colours don't go. I look a fright.

Suffragette colours, I said: you'll do.

Sister Marie-Claude spread the pale pink crocheted rug over her knees, tucked it in at the sides. If you don't wear them you can't go out. A wind may get up. I'm not having you catching a chill.

Clem glared. She sat upright, clasping the padded armrests of the wheelchair. I slung her pink-striped canvas bag from one handle, my red rucksack from the other. We glided out of her room and along the shiny-floored corridor, Sister Marie-Claude in front, squelching over the vinyl tiles in her rubber-soled shoes. Her shoulders bowed, as though she were tired. Perhaps she'd been up half the night, checking on her charges. Probably she'd be good at tending. Not too soft. Brisk enough to keep you going, inspire you not to fall over just yet.

Phyllis would respect her, understand her. I tuned into Radio Phyllis. Nuns live in sisterhoods, d'you see, D., in the past the Orders had to fight to get free of the authority of male bishops, they are proto-feminists, they live gender differently, that's fascinating, don't you think? On the other hand, I suppose they are still defined by men's ideas of gender. We're not yet free of those.

Thanks, darling, I said. That's enough.

Phyllis's voice still warmed and tickled my ear. I'd phoned

her earlier, from the train, to say hello, swap travel tales. She talked about the street art show in Paris, about *art brut*, about amateur artists, about who defined who was an artist and who wasn't and why. Perhaps I began feeling competitive. Perhaps that was why I ended up telling her I was convinced there was a real story to be uncovered about Clem's relationship with Matisse. Something must have happened there. I would find out whatever it was. Phyllis said: you didn't sound so sure when we talked before. Why have you changed your mind?

I said: blame it on a dream, I dreamed it a while ago, last night I dreamed it again.

I sketched for Phyllis the dancers in red, how I flew between them. She said: I don't see the connection between you and *La Danse*. But still. May I tell Angela all this? She'll be intrigued.

I said: sure. Tell her whatever you like.

Sister Marie-Claude yawned, straightened up. The lift doors clunked open in front of us. We trundled out. The ground floor, smelling greenly of nameless hot vegetables, seemed deserted. Everyone's at lunch, Clem said, so-called ratatouille today, I'm not missing much. They cook it in a pressure-cooker. No olive oil. Watery gloop.

She swerved her keen profile right and left as we passed between the rows of posters. Still the same old sentimental guff as a month ago. We could do with some new ones.

Sister Marie-Claude said: now, don't you start. Most people like them. Sister Jacques's work is greatly respected. You were a friend of hers, you shouldn't be unkind to her memory.

Clem flung words to me over her shoulder. I don't come along here usually. The way to the back garden is behind us.

There's a ramp at the far side of the house, Sister Marie-Claude explained to me, for retreatants in wheelchairs to use, but for us it's quicker and easier to go out here, the same way you came in.

Clem said: people like coming here on retreats, Denis. Nobody minds if you're old, or ugly, or fat, or unhappy. All those things people despise in the world outside, that they reject you for. Here you're just a person, as such you're taken seriously, you're accepted.

People coming here feel spiritually cherished, Sister Marie-Claude said, because God welcomes them just as they are.

Clem said: coming here makes them feel loved. That makes them feel beautiful.

We're all special to God, Sister Marie-Claude said, and you think too much about beauty, Clem. It's just a surface. It doesn't matter.

Yes it does, Clem said, and I like noticing it.

Sister Marie-Claude opened the glass doors of the verandah and stood back to let us pass, then followed us into the bright sunshine, the buzz of crickets. A lid of blue sky, heat simmering under it. I pushed Clem onto the narrow flagged path crossing the courtyard towards the outer gate. Sister Marie-Claude walked alongside, crunching over the grey-white gravel. She said: please be back in two hours' time at the latest. Clémence needs to conserve her strength. She must not get over-tired or over-excited.

We halted by a tub of pink-flowering begonias. She pressed the buzzer at the doorway in the outer wall, held it open for us. I pushed the wheelchair through. Careful, said Sister Marie-Claude, careful. Blah blah blah, remarked Clem. Sister Marie-Claude sighed. Now, Clem, now, Clem.

She lifted a hand, as though in blessing. Have a good time. See you later.

To me she said: I've had a word with our Sister Almoner. There are no retreatants booked in this week. So you are welcome to stay a couple of nights. More, if you so wish.

The door in the wall clanged shut behind us. The warm air smelled of petrol fumes and flowers.

I said to Clem: just now, you sounded like my mother. Blah blah blah. She always said that. Whenever my father or I annoyed her more than usual.

She used to say it to me sometimes too, Clem said, a long time ago. We were good friends, you know, when we were young.

Yes, I said, yes, I know.

I turned the chair to the right. We began passing the massive salmon-pink block of apartments pretending to be a sea-going liner. I glanced up at the curving prow set with big windows shaped like portholes. A movement stirred the air. High up on the sixth floor, two people were leaning over their balcony, waving at us. I waved back.

We tilted down the gentle slope, the narrow street lined with cars parked nose to tail. Ahead, in the distance, sparkled a line of blue sea. At the bottom of the hill, a wider road led away in two different directions between single-storey white shops, their open fronts spilling sports gear, souvenirs. I halted. Which way do you want to go?

Clem said: to the left. I'll give you the guided tour, shall I?

That's not what I've come for, I said.

Clem said: you don't want to know the history of the place?

What did I know of her own history? After her brief spells in Nice and Paris, another brief spell at home with her parents, she'd trained in domestic science then worked as a teaching assistant in a girls' school in Marseilles, renting a tiny flat.

Once her parents died, she'd moved back into their village house. Commuted in a 2CV.

Clem hadn't married and had children. She'd had lovers, obviously. The doctor, for one, that discreet widower popping in for lunchtime trysts. In her spare time she painted. Because she'd never made a fuss about it I hadn't seen it as important.

We reached the *vieux port*. The benches set along the cobbles fronting it had filled up with people idly surveying the moored fishing boats. Pet dogs had been tied to the bollards, looped with chains, on the harbour's edge.

Clem pointed. The fishermen land the catch just there. They work as a cooperative, they share what they make selling the fish.

How d'you know? I asked.

Those two people who waved at us from their balcony. They're British, they come to visit me sometimes, they bring me newspapers, French ones and English ones. They're interested in what goes on, they keep me informed. They give me a different viewpoint from what I hear on TV and from the nuns.

The air leaned in at us, salty and fresh. A gust of breeze whipped up Clem's hair around the edges of her purple headscarf.

She said: it was thanks to them I saw the notice of Berthe's death in the paper, in their copy. That was how I tracked you down.

She unknotted her headscarf. She held it in one hand, stretching her arm up high. The scarf flew out like a flag. Clem let go of it and it streamed away. Horrible thing, she said. Who needs to wear a scarf in this lovely weather?

Just a yard or two from the quay, families were eating outdoors at café tables in the shade of sun umbrellas. I slowed my pace, glanced at the menus displayed on boards. *Salade niçoise* with fresh tuna. Tagliatelle with clams. *Pissaladière* with onions, olives and anchovies.

You know Matisse lived here briefly, Clem said, before he moved further along the coast to Nice. That was some years before I met him. I want to tell you about that time. I will, later. Let's get to the sea first.

Did Matisse ever come to the quayside to buy fish, or did he send his wife Amélie? She would carry home red mullet wrapped in damp newspaper in a straw skip. He would paint them flopping on a plate, their silver and scarlet scales. She'd want to grill and eat them. Two lots of mullet. One for him and one for her.

We came to the start of the boulevard lined with palm trees. Restaurants and apartment blocks on our left, the modern harbour on our right, boat masts bobbing beyond the low cement wall.

Clem said: you see that green carousel in the distance, on the promontory? Just past there is a good place for swimming, I'm told. Let's make for that. Then you can have a swim and I'll sunbathe.

Why don't we take a picnic with us? I suggested: surely we'll be hungry in a little while.

Clem pointed. There are food shops just here. You go in, and I'll wait for you outside.

In a greengrocer's, its front shutters half drawn against the heat, the cool, dim interior scented with melons, I bought a couple of big, fat tomatoes, a bunch of grapes. From the *épicerie* next door I chose a chunk of white sheep's cheese, a bottle of mineral water, a bottle of local rosé. The shopkeeper opened it for me, and stuck the cork back in.

Outside, Clem balanced a baguette on top of her pink-striped canvas bag. I got a child to go up the street and buy this. Luckily I brought my purse out with me. She raised her golden baton. Right. Let's be off.

We wheeled between rustling palm trees and pink-flowering oleanders. The sea spread out in front of us, low waves tipped with points of light. They toppled, met land, spread forward, flat swirls scalloped with white froth.

A wooden boardwalk ran parallel to the beach, extended sideways a little way down onto the loose, dry sand. We halted at its end, near a breakwater of boulders. Beyond them the sea waited, a clear blue-green.

Go ahead, Clem said, I'll be fine here. Take as long as you want.

My swimming towel draped round me, I stripped off, pulled on my swimming trunks. I crossed a line of damp sand, waded in to the rippling water, then plunged forward.

Light glittered and danced on the tiny waves. For a while, I let go into the rhythm of movement, I let go of thinking. Nothing but light sparkling on water. Then I turned onto my side in the turquoise sea and looked back at the shore.

A green rectangle, a pale pink rectangle, against a patch of yellow. Two black circles. A square striped red and pink.

An abstract painting.

A figurative painting.

Clem in her wheelchair on the beach.

I swam towards her. I stood in the shallows, wiped and shook sea water drops off my face. I licked my lips, tasted salt.

Clem seemed to be dozing. I strolled along the tideline, letting the sun dry me. I picked up shells, small striped pebbles, worn, smoothed chips of bottle glass. Green, blue. Like bits of lost stained-glass windows. I threw them down in a heap by my rucksack.

Clem yawned, took off her sunglasses, rubbed her eyes. I'd like to dip my feet in the water. Will you give me a hand?

I knelt in front of her chair, removed her shoes and socks, rolled her loose cotton trousers up to her knees. I helped her shake off her woollen jacket, her blanket. I stood up again, held out my arms. She tipped herself forward, into them, and I lifted her and clasped her and walked half backwards half sideways across the band of shingle into the low waves breaking in frills at the water's edge. Shock of coolness on my sun-warmed feet. The flat sand of the shallows let me keep my balance easily. She weighed little. I dipped her up and down. The translucent green water rinsed her ankles.

Further out, she said, further out.

I hesitated.

Please. I'll dry off afterwards in the sun. It's so hot. I'll get dry in no time. I won't catch cold. I won't come to any harm, I swear I won't.

Once I was in up to my waist, carrying her, she could float. I stood behind her, my hands under her arms, and she lay back, stretched her legs out, reclined on the blue-green up and down. Her cotton shirt billowed out then soaked up water and sank back, clinging to her. Back and forth I paced, my feet on the sand under us, towing her, and she relaxed, half-closing her eyes. She sighed. The sun's roar above us. Tiny waves broke round us, crystalline, glittering.

Deeper, Clem said, deeper. I want to swim.

I launched into the light-tipped waves. I kicked out, holding her firmly in one arm, doing a sort of doggy-paddling back-stroke with the other.

I'm not too heavy, am I? she asked. I'm not weighing you down? I won't give you backache?

No, I said, you're light as a feather.

Light as a young child learning to swim. Clem was depending on me utterly not to let go of her. She lay against me, on me, so slight, her head on my chest. I drew us through the water. It flowed over my shoulders, over hers.

She said: I feel weightless. Birds must feel like this when they fly. If they think about it at all. I suppose they don't. They just do it. That's the trick. You just get on with it. My mother used to say that to me and it drove me crazy. Now I know what she meant. What I'm getting on with is being old, and it's very hard. Don't let anyone tell you it isn't.

I've been thinking that too, I said. I've begun to, at least.

Clem said: don't be so bloody stupid. You're young, compared to me.

A wave slopped towards us, broke under our chins. She turned her head, spat out a mouthful of seawater. When the Master was old, when he was infirm, trapped in his wheelchair, no one ever thought of taking him out for a swim. As far as I know. Yet he loved swimming. When he was living at Collioure, when he was a young man, he'd go swimming with his family, with friends. They'd row out into the bay in a boat, then dive off it. There was a photo of them that I saw, in the hotel in Nice, that he'd kept from that time. A tiny group of them, in the far distance, two of them standing up in the boat and the others in the water.

I asked: so you didn't just meet him, you knew him. How well did you know him?

Clem said: I worked for him, very briefly, at one point, surely I told you that.

171

No, I said: no, you didn't. Not explicitly, at any rate. You just said you worked in a hotel.

Anyway, Clem said, I found the photo in a drawer one day, when I was dusting his rooms.

When you were snooping, you mean, I said.

She went on dreamily. Stuck in that chair, he still felt free in his mind. He flew loop-di-loop through the skies, he dived loop-di-loop under the sea. He brought it all back indoors, the sky, the sea, the palm trees, the fishes. Art was his house, indoors, and also his world, outdoors. Both at once. Magical, I think.

My lunch in the garden with Phyllis: I'd thought something similar. Perhaps my thoughts had meshed somehow with Clem's. Our minds had overlapped, collapsing distance and time. Thanks, Monsieur Matisse.

I said: you mean the cut-outs, I suppose.

Clem said: the first time I saw some of them, before I understood how they had been made, they looked so easy, so effortless. As though he'd thrown up confetti and it had stuck. Later, I saw how difficult it must have been.

I said: I felt something like that too, when I saw the exhibition.

The tension between the pieces existing in controlled relation to each other: gaps that separated and that connected; powerful white gaps. The paper shapes vibrating with the effort of staying still not flying off scattering in the wind. Yet at the same time, yes, flying. Alive and intelligent as flocks of birds in close formation crossing the late summer sky.

We splashed on. A young man, bronzed and sleek-haired, powered towards us, striking out to deeper waters, his arms flailing in a flashy fast crawl. He suddenly slowed, met my eyes. He gave me a merman glance, plunged on again. A woman and two children followed him, doing a calmer breaststroke. They turned their heads to survey us. The children frisked forwards, kicking, turning over and over, buoyed up by puffed orange armbands. Clem's head lolled on my shoulder. So easy, she said. I could go on like this for ever. Just let the waves carry me right out to the horizon. Fall asleep, fall over the edge of the world.

I'm not coming with you, I said, and I'm not letting go of you. Time we got out.

I moved us further inland, back towards the shallows. Ruffles of white broke over us. As soon as I could touch the sand with one foot I heaved myself up, stood knee-deep, pulling Clem from the wavelets, then carried her across the strip of shingle, up the beach, to the tumbled heap of rocks.

Sitting on the sand, propped against the largest boulder, she moved her shoulders back and forth, got comfortable. A little lizard sunning herself.

She pushed back her dripping hair. I mopped her with my towel. She thrust it aside. I'm fine. I like feeling the heat of the sun on me.

She consented to sit on my towel. I chafed her feet, rolled her socks back on over her toes. She leaned forwards, head on her knees, to let the sun reach her back, dry her shirt. I sat down near her in the lovely scorch and dried off too, then pulled on my clothes. I left my feet bare. Shoes would have signified the intention to leave. The end of our chance to talk to one another.

I settled myself on the warm sand, facing Clem. I scooped up a handful of dry grains, let the bright grit trickle through my fingers. I sorted through my heap of pebbles, shells, tiny lumps of coloured glass, began to lay them out in a mosaic.

Clem nodded towards my arrangement. The past. It comes

back to me like that. In bits and pieces. Random scenes. I've tried writing some of them down, because I feel I need to, but I don't know how to do it. So far it's just a mess.

She stared at her knees. Perhaps she was scanning one of her scenes.

I think I'm writing it for you, she said. It's a bit like a confession, but not really. Not like the stuff we were taught to say to priests. In any case I never did tell them the truth about anything I felt or did.

Go on, Clem. Spit it out. I've come all this way to hear it. Whatever it is. I fisted sand, let it trickle out.

It's difficult, she said, knowing where to start. Knowing where to stop. *Devoirs* at school were easier. We were given the subject and off we went.

She paused again. I refused to help her, to say something comforting. Oh, you'll be fine. I'm sure you can do it. Pious banalities. Like the captions on the posters back in the care home.

She said: if I painted this seascape I'd have to simplify it. Just ripples of blue and green. Circles of indigo. Circles of purple. Writing is the same. You have to find a language. Invent one. She drew up her knees and clasped them in her thin hands. Sometimes an oval shape rises up inside my mind like a burst of coloured light. An intricate pattern. Like a mandala in a painting. Everything in it. All at once. All words, all images. Writing that out would mean breaking it up into bits, then laying the bits out in lines, like a shopping list. Anyway, not the same thing at all.

She cocked an eye at me. D'you think? Am I making sense? Tell me what you think.

What was wrong with lists? I'd kept some of my mother's

in my wallet. *Drycleaner's, shrimps, library books, Elastoplast, flour, birthday cards.*

You'd end up with a different sort of pattern, that's all, I said, that's how narrative works. It involves time, it reveals itself over time. If language is your material, you have to work within its constraints.

I leaned back, half shut my eyes. Flashes of red. The sun glared through the fine lattice of my hat brim. I was Matisse's fish, being grilled.

Clem said: my mind darts ahead faster than my fingers. Writing my memories down will take years. And I haven't got years, that's the point.

But you don't have to put down every memory, I said: you can pick and choose. I'd have thought there were particular moments you want to record. That's what this conversation is about, isn't it?

Yes, Clem said.

She looked at me. I am doing my best, but it's difficult.

Let's have some lunch, I said.

I opened my rucksack, extracted the bottle of water, the bottle of wine. I unfolded my handkerchief, put it on top of a nearby flat rock to serve as tablecloth. On top of it I laid the cheese, the bread.

Actually, Clem said, the moments seem to pick themselves. They cut themselves out of longer memories. They just arrive. Like someone throwing knives at me. I'm outlined by knives.

She considered for a moment. If I wrote them down on separate bits of paper then putting them in order is something I could do later, I suppose.

I uncorked the wine. No glasses, I'm sorry, we'll have to drink from the bottle.

Not at all, Clem said. See what I've got here.

She opened her canvas bag, drew out a small thermos flask. Sister Marie-Claude insisted I bring this. The prices in cafés horrify her.

She unscrewed the cup-shaped lid of the thermos. Under that stout one was another, smaller one. She unscrewed that too. She held them up. Sister Marie-Claude thought of everything. There's even a spoon, look. The drink is camomile tisane, of course. Remind me to pour it away later on.

I poured wine into the two plastic cups. I unwrapped the slab of cheese and put the fruit next to it. Clem fished in her bag again, produced a small, pearl-handled penknife. Here. The nuns don't know I've got it. But I always carry it with me. I've had it for ages.

I don't remember seeing it before, I said.

I kept it in a pocket, Clem said. I always hated handbags, never could be doing with them. I did have a satchel once. But I liked clothes with pockets. Now I have to carry a bag, all my pills and so on, and I hate it.

I sliced the cheese and tore the baguette into chunks. We sipped our wine. The sun-warmed, juicy tomatoes smelled and tasted earthy, sweet. Clem didn't eat much. She lost interest before I did, began stirring up the shells, the bits of glass, rearranging them into a new pattern. A seagull squawked, flapped down nearby, strutted towards our leftovers.

We have to use language, I said, if we want to survive we have to communicate with words, not just with images. If we want to understand each other, that is.

She glanced at the penknife. The Master once said to some art students that now they had decided to become painters they'd have to cut out their tongues, because it was only through their painting that they'd be communicating from now on.

In the shimmering heat her face seemed to dissolve. It re-formed, old and young at the same time. The young girl in her looked out. Something opened. A door in her heart. She said: being an artist means loving your materials and finding out what you can do with them. Great artists like the Master break through the limits of how painting was done before, they break the world up, then they put it back together again in new ways.

She looked down at the pieces of coloured glass balanced on her palm. All that matters is getting on with your work. It doesn't matter what the critics say, it doesn't matter if no one buys it, you've just got to get on and do it.

24. Black-and-white photograph (precise date unknown) by Yvette Martin, of Matisse at the Hôtel Regina

Matisse, propped by a fat white pillow, is sitting up in bed, covered from the waist down by a turned-back white sheet. Domed forehead. White moustache and beard. He looks loose-bodied, plump. Whiteness flows pleated across his belly, his slightly raised knees. He wears a flowing pale jacket.

He concentrates on the cut-out he is working on. He holds a smallish square of paper in his left hand and a big pair of scissors in his right. The lower blade of the scissors slants right across the sheet of paper.

Curved eyelids lowered, he looks intent, relaxed. Somehow light, almost floating, released from illness and old age by the act of making. He looks really happy. A hovering smile. A private delight. Not self-conscious, not, apparently, aware of the camera, not required to pose as The Master. He looks content as a child completely absorbed in arranging his treasures. Pleased to be working. To be creating something. Totally in control of his work. In that sense not like a child at all.

Tall mirrors catch the light and draw it in, make Matisse seem suspended in light, part of a delicate composition of light and shadow. Behind him, on the high white wall, the light creates a play of reflections of leaf shapes, pot shapes. Yes, like cut-outs.

25. A corridor, the Hotel Regina, Nice

CLÉMENCE

Brisk as a broom Mme Lydia swept us in front of her into the anteroom beside the salon. You're not in trouble, she assured us. You made the Master laugh. You delighted him.

She picked up the stocking fallen from the bundle of clothes I clutched, returned it to my arms. I must go and see to the guests. You two get changed. You haven't got your cloak, Monique? I'll find it and bring it through.

She tapped away. Neat, tightly wound blonde chignon. Narrow blue-cardiganed back, narrow cream-skirted hips. Clothed for business. In the Master's drawings of her naked she'd invented new poses: both free and precise. She was coiled and still, she was dancing lying down, she was snaking through the air, she was just a few thin curving lines dividing the white space. As his secretary-assistant she stood upright, she walked decorously. Did she remember how she had danced?

We peeled off our skimpy silk and chiffon costumes. We hauled on girdles and stockings. Fastened on petticoats, dark dresses, aprons. Monique became an *aide-soignante* again and I a maid. Monique fussed with her veil, drawing it down low over her forehead, tying it tightly behind so that it came down over her ears and cut into her cheeks.

Into the pocket of my work dress I tucked the earrings and anklet I'd been wearing. I was borrowing them just for the evening, so that I could draw them later. Mme Lydia wouldn't notice their absence. The Master wouldn't mind, surely. My apron pocket held the pencils I'd picked up earlier in the salon. The one I'd brought from home was worn to a stub. I'd slip the borrowed ones back tomorrow.

Mme Lydia returned with Monique's cloak, began to shoo us towards the service entrance. Since you have so kindly volunteered to help us out, we'll see you in the morning. Nine o'clock sharp. You do have some Saturdays off, Clémence? You're sure you're free tomorrow? I don't want to be let down a second time. And you, Monique? The sisters won't mind?

Monique said: on the contrary, they'll be pleased I've got something to do. They won't want me hanging around all weekend doing nothing. And you misunderstand, they're not in charge of my timetable, my working life, they let me stay in the nurses' home out of the goodness of their hearts.

Like as not they'd find you some horrible task, I said: you're much better off here with me.

Mme Lydia gave me a snippy look. Was I talking out of turn? I didn't care. I was still lit up with daring. Tomorrow I was going to watch the Master at work. To help him, even. And he might have had time to look at my drawings, and with luck he'd talk to me about them. And I'd learn how to improve.

Mme Lydia said: you deserve a rest, truly, Monique. You've given us heroic service.

She nodded, vanished. I hovered with Monique outside the service lift. It hid behind a door looking like a wall panel, just past the last of the mirrors on the corridor. Monique took my arm, wheeled us to face the shining glass.

I said: what should we wear tomorrow? Should we dress up a bit?

Monique said: we haven't got the clothes, have we? Though I

suppose we could borrow something. Don't bother about that now.

She stared at our joint reflection. Two shimmering apparitions held inside the gilded frame, wax-faced as the saints lying in the glass cases in the school chapel, under certain side altars, tip-tilted by some miracle, the saints surprised into standing on tiptoe. Resurrection of the dead. They'd break out in a shower of bright shards. In the mirror we looked as serious as saints. So stick out my tongue, send the saints packing.

Monique said: we'll have to go to Confession tomorrow evening, if we're to go to Mass on Sunday and take Holy Communion. What we did back there was wrong. And we were enjoying it and we shouldn't have.

Oh, Monique. For heaven's sake.

She lowered her voice. Two girls doing things together is disgusting.

She was quoting words I'd heard at school, in the village, in the hotel here. You were twisted and deformed, unnatural, neither a woman nor a man, you did not belong in the normal world.

Don't be upset, Clem, Monique said: it's OK, we're friends, we'll always be friends, but we must never do that again. It was all my fault. It was my idea. I led you astray.

She looked so serious I laughed. I said: you can go to Mass with the nuns if you want, but leave me to sort myself out. I may prefer a lie-in. Please don't preach at me! And you know I loathe going to Confession. I doubt if I'll go.

Monique said: I'll pray for us both, then.

I said: I'll confess to you, not the priest, here and now. I confess that I shall never be able to give up liking peach brandy. But I promise never to nick it from Madame Lydia's cupboard ever again. There. And now for my penance: I'll shake hands with you every time we meet, rather than kiss you.

Monique shook her head. Don't mock me.

She halted. Biting her lip shut as though words might leap out and shame her. They won the struggle, forced open her mouth. I want to tell you something. I've never told anybody this.

She kept her arm hooked inside mine. I stood still, looked straight ahead into the mirror. Her lips trembled, parted. When I'd kissed them they tasted sweetly of peach liqueur. Now every time I drank peach liqueur or ate a peach I'd remember kissing Monique.

She said: when I was confirmed, Clem, and the Bishop anointed me, I expected to feel something astonishing. The Holy Ghost coming down on me, into me. But I felt nothing at all.

Nor did I at my own Confirmation, I said. Nor did Berthe, perhaps. I don't know for sure. Berthe didn't say.

Monique rushed on. I was so disappointed that I was tempted to stop believing. In the end I went to Confession and explained I had doubts.

She let go of me, folded her arms. The priest said that feeling nothing was a test of my faith. It's like St Paul said: in life we see as in a mirror, darkly. Yet God's there. Beyond the door. You just have to step forwards through the darkness and believe you'll find Him. So d'you see, feelings like happiness or pleasure don't matter, this way or that. They're just sensuality. Spiritual truth is the important thing. Believing with the intellect, which connects to faith.

Monique of half an hour ago, sprawling in pink chiffon on silk cushions, had vanished. Someone had stepped forward with a knife. No more juicy flesh. Just a scraped canvas, curls of dry paint dropping to the floor.

I said: if the mirror is a door you can step through, into another world, I want to know for sure you can come back out again. I don't want to get stuck! She was staring ahead, through our reflection. I want to give myself to a perfect love. Sometimes I wonder whether I've got a vocation.

I jerked. Oh, Monique. Don't overdo it.

She said: God wants total commitment, He wants us to offer ourselves completely. That's the joy of it, you see. The risk. You hurl yourself at Him, you leap into the abyss. You trust that His hands will bear you up. No earthly husband could do that for you. No earthly husband could love you that much.

She stared at the glass. Shadowy forms moved in its depths. Like wings fluttering. God and His angels, for her. For me: shapes with no names. The priests taught that women looked in mirrors out of vanity. No. It was to make certain we existed. Sometimes it caught you off guard, who am I, you weren't quite sure, you nearly panicked.

Monique said: and it would be risky for me to have children. You know my father died of TB, I had a touch of it when I was young, I might pass it on. So I probably shouldn't marry. Yet I don't think I can spend the rest of my days sitting up all night with sick people. Even ones as lovely as the Master. Yes, it's all very well, he wants me to become a graphic artist, but I've got no money to pay for an art training. I've got to make a living somehow. I don't know what to do.

In the mirror one young woman, steady and composed, outlined, with edges made by her uniform, stood next to another. Part of Mme Lydia's army. Presumably, modelling for the Master, Mme Lydia had grown used to putting on a new self, taking it off. Easily she'd stepped back into her clothes. My own model self had gone; like Monique I'd put aside the person I'd been half an hour previously. She was folded up, shoved into the trunk, the lid slammed down on her.

Not quite gone. My fingers dived into my pocket, fiddled with clumps of tiny beads on wire hooks. My fingers searched further, stroked a chain circle strung with clinking metal discs. The anklet. An O like a mouth talking. It did happen, it was real.

A bell chimed at the far end of the corridor. Behind us the service lift creaked. A door near us began opening. We moved, we lost the conversation, we shook ourselves back into work mode.

Monique turned towards the service stairs. On my way back I'll drop in to the hostel and find your friend Camille. I'll bring her with me tomorrow evening, after I've been to Confession. Why don't you come with Félix?

I'd left my little cart of cleaning things back along the corridor, outside the service entrance to the Master's suite. I checked I had my tin of polish, my duster, my dustpan and brush. I took up the brush, dipped it into a crystal pot of gold paint, I swept it up and down, I whirled gold streamers across the dark air of the corridor, back and forth.

26. Boulevard scene, La Ciotat

DENIS

The sun was burning through my shirt. I was the shirt and the sun was ironing me. Blue sheet of sky overhead with not one cloud. Sweat dampened my back, my forehead.

Time to move, I said. We need more shade than this.

I haven't even begun saying what I meant to, Clem said, but you're staying the night, aren't you? We can go on talking tomorrow.

We tilted onto the boardwalk, away from the beach. Sunshine shifted through the rustling green branches of the palms, spots of brightness, patches of shade. I swung the wheelchair left, began to push it along the white pavement. Children on tricycles and bicycles wobbled past. Young people in sportswear strolled hand in hand. Making for their hotels. The siesta. Shutters drawn, semi-darkness, hands laid on each other's warm skin, mouths exploring.

The Italianate church flared on our right, a blank pink facade at the top of the wide flight of steps. Clem turned her head. Nothing worth seeing in there. Full of hideous modern religious art. Inauthentic, dishonest, weak. Completely disgraceful, fobbing that off on people. They deserve better.

They deserve someone like Matisse, you mean, I said, Matisse who'd lost his faith.

Certainly, Clem said. Matisse was able to design that chapel in Vence, right at the very end of his life, precisely because of that. He could imagine what the nuns might need because he'd been raised a Catholic, but he had to be free of Catholicism in order to invent their chapel in a truly modern way.

You've seen it? I asked. You've been there? I never have.

I went some years after it was inaugurated, Clem said. It's a work of astonishing purity, astonishing power. Photos of it can't begin to convey its beauty. You have to be inside it, that's the point. You're enclosed by four walls, two of them made of white tiles, the floor white tiles as well, opaque and hard and brilliant, but the whole thing's transparent too, the other two walls are made of glass, sea-blue and leaf-green and sour lemon yellow, the light pours through them, it pours at you, through you, you're inside and you're outside both at once, you're inside some kind of transparent body and also you're swimming in the sea, flying in the sky, the colour from the windows falls right across the white tiled floor.

Was Clem drunk? Two glasses of vin rosé and she seemed well away.

She raised both arms, letting the breeze flap the thin cotton of her loose shirt. To me the chapel hardly felt Catholic at all. Not in any traditional sense. No huge crucifix showing a man being tortured. Even the Stations of the Cross, they're all scratched high up at the back, yes, graffiti, almost abstract black marks on the white tiled wall, held in a single space above the entrance. You have to turn round and look up to see them. Suffering's there, but it's contained, not strung out round the walls as you get with traditional Stations. What matters is the light. And the huge image of the Madonna on the side wall, holding her child. She's faceless. You have to decide for yourself who she is, what she looks like.

I said: that was why you admired the image?

She said: I can't explain it, not at this moment.

She blew out her breath. Seeing the chapel, being in it, almost restored my childhood belief. If God existed, God was there, embodied in light. But Matisse summoned God, d'you see? It took an artist to make that happen, for God to arrive. It's the artist who creates the sacred. Through his use of materials. For the nuns, of course, the sacred already existed, and Matisse simply helped draw it down.

I said: perhaps both those views are true.

Pushing the wheelchair along, I tried to push my mind as well. Distracted by the growl of passing cars, the bright specks of sunlight dropping through the palms' shifting branches overhead, scattering on the pavement. I said: not that Matisse invented the sacred, perhaps, so much as collaborated with it? Thereby making something new?

Clem said: and perhaps, as well, he accepted ugliness as part of his inspiration. The Church's misogyny, for example. Catholicism damages women in ways most men never have to think about.

I don't think my mother felt that, I said. For her religion was simply an aspect of being French, woven in with it, it was normal, it was deeply part of her. I don't think she ever questioned her faith.

Mum shepherding me out of church after Sunday Mass, her hand on my shoulder. I looked up at her peaceful face. The ritual had fed her, nourished her. Renewed her strength for the week ahead. The church was her own place. My father scoffed at her religion: sentimental, hypocritical. Over Sunday lunch he'd try to pick a fight about the Pope, or indulgences, or miracles, but on Sundays my mother didn't rise to his needling, she remained serene.

My life made me question my faith, Clem said: and now my question is: why did I let myself end up in a care home run by Catholic nuns? But they had a room free, they offered it to me. At the time I was very grateful. I couldn't go on living on my own any more. It was Monique's idea. My friend Sister Jacques. The one who did the posters. She's dead now.

She was a friend of my mother's too, I said. I remember Mum mentioning her.

Seagulls wheeled and shrieked above the boats moored in the port. Behind us the church bells tolled two o'clock.

Clem said: Berthe was a very strong character. She wasn't the sort to change her mind. Not about her faith. Not about anything.

My phone beeped. Sorry, Clem, I said, d'you mind if I take this?

Phyllis's voice: a faint boom deep under water. We're arriving this evening, later than we thought, I'm afraid, have you got any ideas about hotels? Where are you staying? Nice place? Book us a room? Angela's wondering whether she could not just meet your godmother but interview her as well. It would fit in with some ideas she's got for a new documentary. What do you think? Would that be all right? Ask Clémence how she'd feel about being filmed.

27. Black-and-white photograph (precise date unknown) by Yvette Martin of Matisse in the Hotel Regina

Matisse, spectacles on, his white hair floppy and silky-looking on his collar, wears some sort of loose cardigan. Propped against a big pillow, he sits up in bed, the white sheet turned back. A bed table held by a stand swivels across his lap, holds notebooks and papers, an open sketchbook. A side table holds a paper model of the chapel at Vence. An easel and a ladder tuck into the corner of the room.

Matisse faces his outline image of St Dominic, in habit and scapular, which he has painted directly onto the wall and which dominates the room.

Matisse grips what seems a very long walking stick, presumably the one described by Lydia Delectoraskaya as characteristic of this time when he is confined to bed, bearing at its end a strapped-on brush dipped in dark ink. He has begun sketching onto the wall, next to the sparely sketched image of the saint, a series of curved lines: a woman's tall, sturdy body; strong arms; oval face.

Lydia, in her characteristic white overall and white plimsolls, hovers to one side of the bed, watching him tenderly, gravely. Like a mother. Her life devoted to him. All her creativity, all her intellect poured into making his life possible. Matisse's huge, powerful Madonna bears witness to that inspiration.

28. Café de l'Abeille, Nice

CLÉMENCE

We met at the agreed time at the café door, two and two, and piled in. We sat down at the back, near the stove, away from the groups of men playing cards and dominoes. I said: we should all pay for our own drinks, OK? We're all equal. We're all broke.

Monique clapped me on the shoulder. That's the spirit, Clem. We're all pals!

I hung my satchel over the back of my chair. Camille fished in her handbag. She drew out a handkerchief, her powder compact, a pearl-handled penknife, a packet of cigarettes. She shook out a cigarette, put everything else back. She caught my glance. What's up with you? What are you staring at?

How had Monique coaxed her out? She looked shrunken, clenched into herself. A line of brown showed at the parting of her peroxide waves. Her nail varnish was chipped. She turned to Félix. I had to hide my fags, back there in that hole they stuck me in. Luckily I've a few left.

Félix produced a matchbook, struck a light. Allow me, madame.

We should have yellow drinks, I said, to match the décor.

Walls mottled in dark yellow, yellow ceramic ashtrays advertising Ricard. Yellow checked curtains. A basket of lemons on the bar.

Monique had changed out of the green wool dress she'd worn earlier. Now she was in her usual weekend clothes: pale yellow blouse, pale blue skirt. She said: and I match it too. Part of me does, anyway.

Félix said: so who chose this crazy beeswax nest?

Monique said: I did. I asked the nuns a couple of days back. They said that this was a place where I could safely go. They know the patronne, she comes to their rosary group on Thursdays.

Félix said: so you always do what the nuns say? Hey, loosen up a little.

No, you've got it wrong, they care about me, Monique said. They're good people. They're very kind.

I flourished a hand at Camille. So what will you have to drink, mademoiselle?

She tensed. Sorry, I said, I mean madame, of course.

I still couldn't use her first name. Still too intimate. I felt hard as a yellow varnished chairback, and she looked it. She glanced at Monique. Monique beamed in jolly Girl Guide mode. Right! I'll choose for both of us.

Tipped ice cubes cracked and glittered, splashing into tumblers: marigold cordial for Camille, lemonade for Monique. Taller glasses of pastis for Félix and myself. Dad's tipple, when he could get it. The black-market bottle kept under the bar, produced for favoured customers. Now the war was over and I was spending Mum's housekeeping money on alcohol at post-war inflated prices. Cheers, Mum. Félix said to me: girls don't drink pastis. I said: now they do.

We chinked glasses. I took a swig of my yellow drink. Powerful smell and taste of aniseed. My tongue curled over.

Camille leaned back in her chair, frowned at the edge of the tabletop. Elbows well in. One arm pressed across her waist. Sucking in smoke, she looked hollow-cheeked. Pale, too. She was wearing a lumpy brown knitted coat with a tatty fur collar. Presumably from the nuns' second-hand store. They might as well have hung a label around her neck: poor creature.

Monique said to Camille: you'll warm up in a minute. Pull your chair nearer to the stove, look.

Camille scared me. Her distance. Talking to her felt like tapping on a glass screen, mouthing words she could only lipread. As though she were inside a glass box. A glass cot. Babies born too soon could sometimes be kept alive in incubators, Monique had once explained to me. Enclosed within glass walls. Camille's baby hadn't had that chance. Now Camille seemed dead too. She was cut off from us by what had happened, the death inside her that could not be mentioned.

Perhaps in their walk here from the hostel Camille had confided in Monique. Had she seen the baby when it was born dead or had it been quickly taken away? Had she felt sorry at first, then relieved and glad? Had someone sat with her, talked to her? I would have tried to, if she'd asked me. If I'd been there. Probably I'd have failed. We hadn't really made friends. The connection between us had snapped.

The jukebox began playing dance music. My voice came out scraping and false. A toast to art and artists!

Camille flinched. She stubbed out her cigarette in the yellow ashtray. I couldn't stop being stupid. I waved my glass. I blundered on. Here's to Christmas coming up, and to holidays, and to going out and having a good time.

Félix said: what's up? You're fizzing like a cricket. No, like lemon sherbet.

Félix had arranged to meet me in the hotel's back yard when he finished his shift, and to escort me to the café. He eyed my dress donated by Annette, too tight for her now, pale green broderie anglaise with a Peter Pan collar and pleats. A summer dress, her only spare. I was bare-legged, unwilling to wear the thick black stockings that belonged to work. Félix avoided looking at my clumpy black shoes. He pretended not to notice my schoolgirl's coat as I buttoned it up. He put a hand on my arm, steered me through the back yard towards the tall gate. He had on a clean blue shirt, narrow black trousers, a raincoat. He'd shaved, sleeked back his black hair. He kissed my cheek. You look very nice tonight. I said: so do you. He walked me down the hill into town.

Monique said: ah well, Clem's had a new experience today.

I tried to reach her foot with my own under the table. I frowned at her, trying to signal: be careful what you say in front of Camille.

Félix poured more water into his pastis, turning it cloudier. He picked up a wooden swizzle stick, tapped my knuckles. Go on. Let me into the secret.

Not a secret, Monique said, just a nice change of routine.

I jumped in. We were helping the Master, that's all.

He'd been unwell at the start of our nine a.m. session, so while he rested in bed, gathering his strength, we got to work next door in the studio. Instructed by Mme Lydia, stripped back for action in her white overall, hair in a tight twist, we set up two ladders. She picked up the Master's long stick and gestured with it. We can film these two pinning up the cut-outs, Monsieur Martin, and then bring the Master through later, when he's feeling better. We'll begin with the little scene featuring the girls and see how we get on.

The Brush, when we were introduced to him and his wife, had tightened his face, pretending not to know me. *Enchanté*, *mademoiselle.* He took my hand, gave me a fake smile. I'm immensely grateful to you both for standing in at such short notice for our absent assistants. I've already seen you know how to act a part. You were most professional. I can rely upon you, I'm sure. He gave my fingers a squeeze. Yes?

I nodded. I would not betray him. If necessary I would lie. To protect my chance of meeting the Master. No point provoking a scene. No point, either, upsetting the Brush's wife, this sweet-faced woman in a blue dress and jacket, orange stockings, busily unpacking the camera, setting up the tripod. From time to time she stopped to consult with the Brush, push her tumbling hair back into its pins. Why should she discover the truth about what her husband got up to? Why should she suffer? Camille had suffered, must still do so. Couldn't some of us be happy, just for one day? But. How could you be happy, knowing someone else suffered? If to be happy meant ignoring others' suffering then happiness was tainted, like stale pond water.

The Brush turned to Monique, swivelled his glance over her glistening black curls, the green wool dress she'd borrowed from one of her pals in the nurses' home. At six sharp she was due to return it, so that her pal could wear it for her night out. The hem rested on Monique's knees and showed off her nicely shaped calves. The Brush bowed over her hand.

I straightened up. The only way to accept being happy was to try to help people who weren't. All I could do to help Camille was to keep her secrets. I marched into the centre of the studio. Just tell us what to do and we'll do it.

A frilled cream muslin curtain stretched across the top half of the café door. Pattern of yellow polkadot-bees. More customers were banging in, filling up the tables. Blue smoke hovered in wreaths below the dark yellow nicotine-stained ceiling. Félix tipped back his chair, took a draught of pastis. Helping how? I can't see you two knowing one end of a paintbrush from the other. I'd like to see the mess you'd make!

Monique tilted the yellow ceramic water jug back and forth. You know nothing about it. There's nothing wrong with just having a go. Anyway, it wasn't about painting. It was more like carpentry. A sort of carpentry, anyway.

Mme Lydia had directed us to re-position the two ladders, prop them against a bare patch of studio wall. We climbed, steadied ourselves. She handed up our tools. She said to the Brush: I suggest you shoot this in close-up as much as possible. The viewer won't see the Master, but he'll assume he's there, just out of camera range, giving instructions. To Monique and me she said: we'll pretend that this is a real studio session. That the Master is here, telling you what to do. I'll point with my stick, to show you where to place the cut-outs, just get going, you'll find out how to do it by doing it. We fluted: yes, madame.

Mme Martin lifted the ciné camera, peered into it, adjusting her focus. The Brush turned to Mme Lydia. If it doesn't work out today, we can just stop. We can always come back on Monday, when the other assistants return, and shoot the film then, with them. No hardship for us to spend a couple more days in Nice, I assure you.

Mme Martin said: don't discourage our kind helpers, my dear. I'm sure they'll be fine.

The ciné camera clicked and whirred. Monique and I were placed close enough together that we could hand the light hammers and the pins across, to and fro between us. One would dangle a flapping cut-out, pinching it by its edge, while the other adjusted her stance, steadied herself on the slender step. Tentatively we tapped, knocked. Shapes in blue, pink, violet, orange and crimson flopped between our fingers. The wall kept collapsing onto me in a flurry of paper, I had to push at it, flatten it, prop it up, it wanted to wrap me up in itself, I had to fight back. Quite soon my arms ached from stretching. My calves ached from tensing when I leaned forward against the very top of the ladder. I worked barefoot, so that I could flex my toes, grip the rung with my arched soles as strongly as possible.

In between takes we sat on the floor. The Brush and his wife conferred, often disagreed, Mme Lydia joining in. Three times they shot the brief scene. The Brush insisted he wanted to continue filming with the other two assistants: back in the summer, when I filmed them that first time, they were doing so well, I'd like the continuity. I wanted to yell at him to shut up.

The café filled up. Onto the yellow tabletop the patronne dumped a small dish of cracked green olives. She lifted a hand. They're on the house, dears. She patted Monique's arm. So nice to see you out with your friends. The sisters will be pleased to know you're here, enjoying yourself.

Clem and I are film stars now, Monique said to Félix: we were being filmed! He smiled gallantly, spread his hands. Well, you're certainly both beautiful enough.

Camille rested her head on her fist. She stroked a finger up and down her glass of cordial. Félix added: and you too, of course, madame. Camille shook out another cigarette from her packet. Félix said: so when can we see this film?

A little later in the morning, Mme Lydia and Mme Martin went into the salon to fetch the Master, for the second scene.

Mme Lydia had checked with him: having rested and dozed, he felt stronger, ready to take charge. To begin with, the Martins were going to shoot the Master actually making one of the cut-out pieces. Monique would hold the big painted sheet of paper while the Master carved into it with his shears.

While we waited, the Brush lit a cigarette. He dismissed me. Thanks, my dear. You've got a job to do elsewhere in the hotel, haven't you? Scoot!

I sat down on the floor, amid a litter of coloured paper bits, near where I'd dumped my things earlier. My shoes stood neatly side by side. I said: look, they're just like a nice married couple. Not yet bored with one another. Still with plenty to say. Still faithful.

He turned, frowned. I said: this is my day off. I wish you'd let me stay. Just for a little while. I wish I could watch the Master working.

I sent the Brush a cool blackmail glance. He said: he asked for Monique specifically. All right. You can stay for ten minutes, but don't get in the way.

I pulled my shoes back on, scrambled to my feet. I'll tidy up.

I busied myself at the trestle table loaded with painted sheets. Some cut into, others not. Thick paper coated with colour. Washes of gouache. The studio assistants had painted them three days previously. Monique had come in early that evening and given them a hand, she'd loved it, she confided to me, you could be so bold swooshing the tinted wetness to and fro, you had to work fast to complete each sheet before the paint dried, so that you kept a uniform colour. The Master had been pleased with her work, had praised her. The following morning Mme Lydia had called to me where I was hoovering the rugs in the salon. Are you there, Clem? She came out of the studio, carrying a bucket full of big brushes in soak. She kicked the door shut behind her. Voice scratchy as sandpaper. The assistants went off last night without cleaning up properly. I couldn't ask Monique to do their job. Not fair on her. Find somewhere to rinse these, would you? The assistants use the kitchenette here, but I would prefer you didn't, I'm about to make coffee. I took the bucket downstairs to the service cloakroom, held the paint-clogged brushes under flowing water from the cold tap, stubbing them onto the porcelain, flexing the thick hairs back and forth. The gouache ran in streams of blurring colour across the sink, swirled into the plughole.

Camille woke from her cigarette trance. Filmed? With a proper ciné camera? Why?

Félix said: so who took the film, anyway? A proper cameraman, was he? Not the great Madame Lydia? No, she'd want to be in front of the camera, that one. Such a high opinion of herself she's got. Handmaid to the Master! I suppose for an old spinster she hasn't done too badly.

Don't mock, Monique said. It's not true, anyway. She's very modest, very self-effacing. Her sole aim in life is to make it possible for the Master to do his work. She is an amazing, selfless person. A sort of saint. She gives of herself constantly, completely, and asks for nothing back.

Félix laughed. Hope he pays her well, then. She'll never find a husband now. She's much too old.

Monique drew her chair away from his, turned her back. I said to Camille: no one you know. Her name doesn't matter. Just some woman who likes taking pictures.

She's married to a painter, Monique said, who's a friend of the Master's. They're not from round here, they're Parisians.

They've been travelling along the coast, photographing other artists, artists' houses. They came over here specially.

So pleased with herself for knowing so much. She wouldn't stop showing off but rabbited on. You should see their clothes. So well-dressed, both of them. They must have a fair bit of money. They're staying here in town at the Mimosa all weekend. Madame Lydia set the whole thing up, it was her idea.

She turned to me. Actually, Clem, don't forget, she and her husband both shot the film. They took turns.

Mme Martin had sauntered back in to the studio: Madame Lydia's just coming in with the Master, she was finding him a clean handkerchief.

Monique had stayed sitting on the top of her ladder. Hands in her green lap, looking about, whistling softly to herself. Her dress had ridden up above her knees but she hadn't noticed. She was absorbing the impact of the paper shapes; thinking. Yes, you do look very fetching posing there, the Brush had said. We all admire you, but let's take a break. Come down, little one.

Monique jumped, blinked. She scowled at him. Wearing her borrowed outfit, not having to be a carer, she could be cheeky. She was Mme Lydia's pet, the Master's too, she could get away with answering back. She twiddled her thumbs, lifted her chin. In a moment. I like it up here. A different perspective. If I had a sketchbook with me I'd draw the tops of your shoes, the top of your head. So glossy in this light!

Mme Martin joined me at the trestle table. I was lifting the coloured sheets of paper by their thick edges, patting them into place. Only pretending to work. Waiting for the Master to appear.

Mme Lydia's strong, clear voice reached us through the door

open into the salon. Wait here just a second, maître. Let me first just get rid of little Clem, and then I'll take you through. If I don't, she's bound to ask you what you think of her drawings, and you're so kind that faced with her you'll soften the truth. You'll tell her you've every intention of talking to her about her work, at some point, when you know you won't, you've time to do no such thing, and nor are you well enough to waste your energy in such a way.

The Master murmured. Mme Lydia said: all right, I won't send her away now. I'll speak to her tomorrow, on your behalf. These girls will eat you up, given half a chance. It's better to be honest with them at the outset and not give them unrealistic ideas. You know, Monsieur Martin has seen her drawings, he glanced at them earlier this morning when he came in, he says she has a minor talent at most, she hasn't got what it takes. You mustn't lead her on to think otherwise. It isn't fair on her.

Word-blows striking me in the stomach. I put my hands flat on the table, bent over them, tried to breathe. A hand touched my forearm. Mme Martin being sympathetic. I shook my head. If I'd been a dog I'd have bitten her. She gripped my elbow. She wasn't being nice at all. She was saying: don't touch those painted sheets! Get your hands off that paper!

Camille clenched her fist around her empty cigarette packet, squeezed it. She dropped it on the yellow tabletop. Félix said: there's a *tabac* next door. D'you want me to get you some more? Got any change? Camille spoke to Monique in a calm voice. So do tell me. What was his name? The man who helped do the filming. What did you say he was called?

Monique was such a daft innocent. If someone asked her a

question she replied with the truth. There were no secrets for her in her virtuous daily world, none in her cheery weekend world either. She said: Monsieur Hubert Martin. He was working with his wife. She was very knowledgeable. They were working as a team, taking turns with the camera.

Camille's mouth opened then shut. She lowered her head, wrapped her arms around her waist. Squeezing herself as tightly as she'd squeezed the cigarette packet. Trying to disappear.

The lights in the studio blurred. Wetness on my cheeks. I straightened up. I tried to go numb, made of iron, a machine who could tell her feet to walk her away. My feet stuck to the floor. Mme Martin let go of my arm. Her soft red mouth opened and said something. She looked sorry. What good was that. Monique had heard too. She twisted round, gripped the sides of the ladder, began climbing down. Well, I said: I must be off. Monique called: wait, Clem. The Brush fiddled with the camera.

Cast-off pieces of coloured paper littered the floor where I stood. Cut into. Shapes taken away from them. My insides had been cut out of me thrown down thrown away I was a hole in a piece of paper I was nothing.

Mme Lydia's voice called through the doorway. Here we come!

The others turned to welcome the Master. I stooped, snatched up the discarded fragments of paper nearest me. I gathered a fat swatch, slithered them into my arms. I had to save them or they'd be chucked into the bin. I slid out of the far door, opposite the door into the salon, rushed through the anteroom. I skipped out by the servants' entrance, ran upstairs to the maids' dormitory. Nobody about: they were all at work. I lay down on my bed, clutching the pieces of paper.

The café was yellow like the stains on the armpits of blouses, sticky-aired, steamed up with cigarettes. I tilted my glass of pastis. Félix said: hey Clem, slow down, you drink too fast. People's voices skittered back and forth across the tiled floor, between the plastered walls. Dance music pounded from the radio. The noise pummelled my eardrums. Camille leaned forward: I need to get out of here. I need some fresh air. Monique said: wait, I'll come with you, you mustn't walk back alone. Camille said: no, don't. Leave me alone, you fucking do-gooder. She slammed out.

I said: I can guess where she's gone.

More trouble loomed for Camille. Perhaps I should follow her, keeping well out of sight. If I caught up with her, would she turn on me, call me another fucking do-gooder? Perhaps she needed to be left alone for a while. When you were hurt you couldn't bear anyone to see, it only increased the pain, you had to hide like an animal. Being wounded made you deeply ashamed, you needed to crawl away into the dark. Not that that helped much. Sooner or later you had to get out of bed, face the world again. Pretend you were fine. Don't let them see they've hurt you. Why not? Because then they might try to hurt you again, hurt you worse. So fake it ha ha ha all's well.

I said: never mind, Monique, I'll go and look for her in a bit. I'll make sure she gets back to the hostel.

We'd finished our drinks, drained the puddles of melting ice at the bottom of our glasses. The evening dwindled, halted. Monique folded herself up like a cloak: I'm so tired. I need to find my bed and sleep. Before I fall over.

Back to the nuns, Félix said.

Yes, Monique said, back to the nuns.

She shook hands with him. She kissed me on both cheeks, whispered in my ear. Sorry. I realise I put my foot in it just now. Take care, Clem.

She didn't want Félix, she'd made that clear. So I felt all right about staying on with him. I wasn't betraying her, snitching her boy. He and I pooled our money, found we could afford a second round of pastis, a ham sandwich to share. I laughed and nodded and joked. The raw, harsh drink scoured me, I kicked in a bubble of yellow liquid, yellow light, dissolving.

Right. Time to brave the outdoors.

We hovered on the pavement. Well, Félix said, so what next? Warmth from the alcohol filled me, wind round my neck a chilly collar. A noose. As well be hung for a sheep as for a lamb. Those were Camille's thoughts, surely, not mine. She was upset, desperate. She might do anything. Cut her wrists. Throw herself into the sea.

Come for a walk? I said. Let's continue the evening's yellow theme. I want to take a look at the Hotel Mimosa. D'you know where it is? Show us the way?

We knocked along arm in arm through dark streets. Lit-up windows of cafés and restaurants went past like comic strips, people inside acting out their stories. Talking to one another. Kissing. The flare of street lights, silvery flow on the drawn-down steel shutters of shops, the crisp tapping of people's feet.

Félix steered, matching his pace to mine. That soothed me, our rhythmic pavement dance. After a while he said: I need to piss. Mind if we call in where I live, Clem?

He rented above a greengrocer's just a bit further into the old town. His landlady was out, visiting family. Félix had his own key. We fell into the dark entrance, out of the sharp cold. He went outside to piss in the privy in the back yard, then I did. Come upstairs for a minute, let's get warm. We slid up the narrow stairs behind the shop, into his cramped box. While I washed my hands at the little sink in the corner, he drew the curtains, lit the stove. He turned, gave me a questioning look. I stood still in the middle of the room. He put his arms round me. Beautiful Clem, I really like you, you're so nice. His hands burrowed inside my coat. His lips rubbed up and down over mine. I didn't fancy him as much as before, but enough that I decided to go ahead. I kissed him back, let him unbutton my dress. Part of me felt ashamed. You should only do this with someone you really wanted, otherwise you were cheating. But I was curious. What would it be like? His hand rummaged under my clothes.

We thrashed on the narrow mattress. Like drinking too much, trying to lose myself. Soon he shouted out, collapsed on top of me. He put his hand to my cheek. He muttered: now you're my girlfriend. Lovely Clem. He fell asleep. I got dressed and left.

29. Bedsitting room in the Bon Secour care home, La Ciotat

DENIS

Clem seated in her armchair loomed in semi-darkness. Her room smelled of oranges and bergamot: the scent Angela and Phyllis had brought her as a present. They had filled a large empty catering tin set on the white iron side table with flowers: white daisies, mauve freesias, white roses, small pink lilies, lilac sweet peas.

We need more light, Angela said. She put down her camera, peeled off her indigo linen coat, threw it aside.

Sister Marie-Claude stepped to the window, grasped the loop of the plastic beaded cord in both hands, adjusted it. The shiny white slats of the venetian blinds opened to their full extent. Sunshine dazzled in onto the nun's face. She stepped back, flapping a hand, returned to her position by the door, next to Sister Marie-Cécile. Dressed alike in their grey and white habits, yet so different: one thin and angular as a heron, the other round as a robin.

In the Hotel Regina, Clem remarked, the *persanes* were blue metal. They folded right back, so that you could see out. These blinds here put bars across your vision. Not satisfactory.

There, in the hotel, you saw Matisse's pictures, Angela said, but here, we can see yours.

The few I've got left, Clem said. Cardboard doesn't last. I stored them in the shed, which was a mistake. Most of them rotted away or were eaten by mice. Myself, I wouldn't mention my work in the same breath as the Master's.

Phyllis was settling a green cushion at Clem's back, putting a glass of water at her elbow. Clem was wearing a long, collarless orange linen coat unbuttoned over a loose white shirt with a narrow pale pink stripe, sky-blue baggy trousers. Also she sported Phyllis's normcore sandals: over breakfast she had declared her need for footwear with open toes, and Phyllis had obliged. The sandals displayed Clem's pink-painted toenails. Her single anklet dangled silvery discs. From her earlobes hung a pair of chandelier earrings strung with beads. She spotted me surveying her jewellery and smiled. In my youth, she said, girls in my village might wear a gold cross on a chain, or a Miraculous Medal. Married women would have one pair of earrings, their wedding earrings. That was it. Nowadays women can wear any kind of decorations they like.

She stuck out her foot and wiggled it. Sister Marie-Claude started forward with the pink blanket. Let me tuck this round you. You're sitting in a draught.

No, Clem said: I've put on my glad rags, they may as well be seen. Haven't worn this outfit for years. I'm going to make the most of it.

Very natty, too, Phyllis said.

You'll be wanting tattoos next, I suppose, said Sister Marie-Cécile.

They had those in my youth, Clem said, but only sailors wore them. Handsome young men in the bars in Marseilles, their arms tattooed with their sweethearts' names. Tricky if you changed sweethearts, like I did.

I sat to one side, to keep out of the way, staying in Phyllis's eyeline in case she needed to signal to me to do anything.

Business-like in a khaki shirt, indigo jeans, her blue sandals, her iPad on her knee, she perched on a wicker stool opposite Clem. Angela lifted her camera. Try to forget it's here. Just look at Phyllis. She'll ask you questions to get you going. Just talk to her.

Sister Marie-Claude said: Clem's had a bad night. I hope this won't take too long. She needs to rest.

Clem said: I can speak for myself, thank you. It's true I'm tired, but I want to do this.

Just as long as you won't get upset, Sister Marie-Cécile said.

That's up to me, Clem said.

Her face looked looser, somehow. As though she'd let go of something overnight. She turned to Phyllis. Go on, then.

Phyllis said: we want to talk to you about your paintings. But to start with, to put things in context, we want to ask you about your working life, how you've earned your living. You've taken various different jobs to support yourself as a painter. Will you tell us about your very first job?

Paid or unpaid? Clem asked. I started working at home when I was six. I suppose you mean my job in the Regina. It was housework but on a grand scale. A huge place, endless corridors, endless flights of stairs.

Phyllis prompted her. What kind of people were staying there?

There were a few English guests, Clem said. No Germans of course. That soon after the war, Germans didn't show their faces. Lots of Parisians. They used to smile at our Provençal accents. Mine's less strong than it used to be but in those days it was pronounced. Sing-song. Guests used to ask me questions just to hear my reply, so that they could laugh. But everybody's got an accent of some sort. When you speak

French, Phyllis, your English accent is a little marked, but it's charming.

Clem was swerving back to the conversation we'd started earlier, over breakfast. Angela and Phyllis had arrived after Clem had gone to bed; too late to be introduced. In the morning, handing jam and lengths of baguette across the pale blue tablecloth, they had begun to get to know her. She had insisted on joining us in the retreatants' dining-room, sharing our coffee and fruit. Phyllis ate hungrily, not attempting to restrain her appetite. She must be happy, I thought. Clem said: you two can speak French? That's good. So we shan't need Denis to translate. We can do the whole thing in French, and if I speak too fast for you to understand just stop me.

Phyllis nodded at me as though to say: this is fine, all's well. Clem said: I'll tell you more about my job in the hotel in a moment. I didn't stay in it long, in any case. I left Nice in rather a hurry. I left my boyfriend too.

She cocked an eye at Angela. No, boyfriend is not the right term. He was a nice boy, that Félix. Handsome. But he wouldn't have done for me for long. Nor I for him.

Her hands began jumping about. She forced them together, controlled them. Now, at last, she seemed willing to open up, because Phyllis and Angela had joined us. Obviously they made her feel safe, in a way that I didn't.

Clem said: that evening, after leaving Félix's digs, everything speeded up. Several things seemed to happen all at once. There was no time to think about what to do, only to act.

She paused. That grey and black sentinel, Sister Marie-Claude, stationed with her back to the door, shifted from foot to foot, emitted a tiny yawn. Sister Marie-Cécile, next to her, turned her head. They whispered to one another, exchanged half-smiles. Friends, colleagues, conferring. How long will this go on? Give them a chance. Look, it's doing Clémence good. She's perking up.

Phyllis and Angela sat and waited, and I copied them. I tried to be patient rather than felt it. My mind kept racing ahead, refusing to settle in the present. I wanted to open the window wider and let in more air, I wanted to hear only bearable things and then to be gone, I wanted a decent cup of coffee rather than the watery stuff we'd been served earlier. Clem had swigged it back, chasing her caffeine fix. Pouf. Much too weak.

Phyllis caught my eye. She shook her head, very slightly. I realised I was tapping my hand on my knee. I stopped. I sat back in my chair. I blew out my breath, smiled at Phyllis.

Clem said: the magazines my mother read had stories in them. Serials, in weekly episodes. All the stories had the same sort of shape, and always ended well. My life doesn't seem to have been like that. It's had lots of starts, lots of stops, quite a few pauses.

She turned her head towards me. Sorry, Denis. I know we went through some of this on the beach. But I needed to say it to Phyllis and Angela too.

That's all right, I said. Take your time.

And now, looking back, Clem went on, I can't be sure at all of the exact sequence in which things happened. I can't remember the dates, either. Certain events have stuck, and others have just vanished. I'm worried I'll get things completely wrong.

Phyllis said: we can sort out the dates later on. And we'll find the right sequence then as well, the one that suits, when we do the editing.

So, for example, Clem said, concerning that evening at the café. I had forgotten to empty my pockets before going out.

The maid collecting up our work dresses and aprons for the wash found mine flung across my bed, she found the pair of earrings I'd kept, and the anklet.

Clem turned her head, setting the gilt chandeliers at her earlobes swinging. Yes, these. I thought you should see the evidence.

What was she talking about? Angela and Phyllis both glanced at me. I shrugged.

Clem said: that girl was so stupid. She took them to the housekeeper, because I wasn't around to ask, and of course the housekeeper saw straight away that they couldn't belong to me. She immediately checked with the guests in the suites I'd been cleaning. Madame Lydia told her the truth, that they belonged to the Master. Madame Lydia insisted that the Master would not want to press charges, but I got the sack anyway. The housekeeper gave me my two weeks' money and turned me onto the street. I just had my coat, my satchel with my few things, also the bits of painted paper from the Master's studio. The housekeeper hadn't thought they had any value, they couldn't be stolen property, she assumed they were just rubbish. Luckily she hadn't thrown them away.

She looked at me again. Do you remember them, Denis? I kept them in the drawer of the dining table and we made collages with some of them, one wet day.

Yes, I said, I remember that. And I've got the blue piece that you sent me, I brought it with me, I've got it here.

Clem went on. Sorry. I know I've begun in the middle of the story. But it feels the closest at the moment.

That's all right, Angela said, just keep going. Any gaps we need to fill in, we can do that later.

One gap we can fill in right now, Clem said. Will you show us the piece of paper, Denis? You and I both know what it looks like. But I want Angela and Phyllis to see it. I want it to be recorded on camera.

She felt down the side of her chair. Let's see if it matches the colour of the piece I've got.

30. Colour photograph (precise date unknown) by Yvette Martin of Matisse at the Hotel Regina, Nice

Wearing wide-legged grey trousers, a V-necked, dark turquoise cardigan with big white buttons, the top two undone, over a loose white vest revealing his throat, the top of his chest, Matisse sits in his wheelchair. Barefoot. Right foot planted on the ground, left foot tilted to show his instep, a piece of paper lying against it; apparently just fallen from the dark green cutout he holds in his left hand while with his right he carves into it with a large pair of scissors. His relaxed, informal clothing – workman's gear, invalid gear – clearly frees him, lets him concentrate. No more suit and tie. Never again. He doesn't need them now. He's stripping himself of everything he doesn't need.

31. Night scene, Nice

CLÉMENCE

The wind had died down, and the night felt less cold. A person could hover and not shiver. The Hotel Mimosa was a small establishment, three streets back from the grand ones under the palm trees fronting the bay. A yellow electric sign hanging like a flag above the entrance illuminated it. A yellow square in the darkness. Blurry yellow light cast on the hotel's glass front door. Darkness beyond the glass. If a night porter was inside, surely he was asleep. Just in case he wasn't, I kept my distance.

A slender woman in a tightly belted coat, its collar turned up, was pacing casually along the opposite pavement. She had tied on a headscarf and pulled it forward, half-hiding her face. A lady tourist. Just idling about, just taking the evening air, hands in her pockets, click of her high heels. Any moment now her little dog would reappear from doing his business behind a lamp post and she'd pick him up, fondle him.

She turned, began sauntering back again. I approached her. She threw me a tight look. I put a hand on her brown knitted sleeve: Camille, come back with me, there's no point hanging about here. Her white face framed by the headscarf, the tatty brown fur collar. She shook me off. I'm all right. Leave me alone.

A car engine rattled in the darkness at the end of the street. A taxi emerged from the shadows, pulled up outside the front door of the hotel. Two people, just shapes in overcoats, got out. A woman. A man.

Camille breathed: there he is.

She wandered across. Unremarkable, just another hotel guest, returning from a walk. The Martins turned. The taxi revved. Camille came up with the Martins. She reached forward, as though to embrace the Brush. His cry. High, sharp, a seagull's call. A scuffle, Mme Martin screamed, the Brush crumpled, collapsed on the pavement. Light inside the hotel doorway snapped on, an oblong of gold. The night porter and the taxi driver were bending over the Brush, Mme Martin kneeling by him, Camille backed away across the road towards where I stood, dropped something in the gutter. She stood still for a moment, glanced at me, then strolled off, disappeared into a side street.

I picked up the knife. Wet, slippery. I retreated further into the shadows. The huddle of people broke: Mme Martin turned her head, looked up. I took another step away, almost tripped, turned round, ran. Beyond the corner I caught up with Camille, meandering along in the darkness between street lights, whistling gently. I grabbed her, hauled her down a black tunnel of cobbled alley, kept going until my breath caught my legs were giving out my heart's blood thundering in my throat my ears.

Cafés and bars were still open, lit boxes in the dark street. I picked one small enough, ordinary enough, pushed in. Sage green and white chequered tiled floor. Blue fug of cigarettes. Camille dropped onto a wooden chair. Its low brown back curved round her, propped her. I fell into a matching chair opposite. Pale moon on the wall jerked arrow hands. Only nine o'clock. The barman looked up. Two brandies? Sure. The punters, all men, were smoking, reading their papers. A sturdy chap in blues, with thick dark hair, glanced at us. Shrewd eyes, a fatherly type. You girls all right? I nodded. The other drinkers left us alone. They'd seen everything, they weren't bothered. Just one of them peered across, a small man with a creased, reddish face, a black moustache like a stripe of paint. He winked at me and I turned away.

I dipped my hand into my coat pocket. My cautious finger-tips found the blade. I shut the penknife, shoved it deeper down, folded my handkerchief around it. My fingers felt sticky. I moved them back and forth on the soft cotton. When I brought my hand out it was clean.

One sip of the harsh brandy: a kick to the throat. It made me sit up, want to spit. Camille took a gulp, wiped her hand across her mouth. She said: that's better.

I whispered: are you crazy? What did you think you were doing back there? Are you insane, doing something like that?

Camille said: not at all. But goodness, I must look a mess.

Her hair had come down at the back. Cheeks reddened with cold. I said: it doesn't matter. We've got to think what to do.

Do be quiet, Camille said.

She removed her hairpins, shook out her hair, then scooped it up with both hands, twisted it, drove her hairpins back in, smoothed it neat. She got out her powder compact, dabbed on whiteness. Tiny silk-backed powder puff. Humming to herself. She clicked the lid shut, caught my eye. Proper powder. I'd forgotten I had it with me. So much better than those tear-off leaves. They don't really work. But they're useful when you're travelling, of course.

My shaky stomach, my unjointed limbs. So cold in this place, underneath the mugginess. Too cold to take my coat off.

The men had piled in around the stove, blocking its heat. Pity I didn't smoke, that might warm me.

I said: with luck you'll get away with it. Monsieur Martin will want the police to think it was just a casual mugging, you were after his wallet, he won't want to let on he knows you, he'll want to hide that from his wife.

That story might not work. Mme Martin hadn't seen Camille, but she'd spotted me. Had she recognised me? Would she think I'd done it? Nasty little girl out for revenge on a critic who merely told the truth.

What, you think he's still alive? Camille whispered.

She took out her lipstick, streaked it over her lips. She pressed them together, sealing the colour, checked herself again in the compact's mirror. A scarlet bow that lifted as she smiled. That's more like it. Now I look like myself again.

Her red mouth printed itself on the rim of her glass. I kept my voice down. Listen, will you? For tonight you should stay at the hostel as usual, then first thing tomorrow you should take the train to Paris. I've got a friend there, my friend Berthe, I'm sure she'll help you, she works for a family at the British Embassy, I'll send her a telegram, she'll come and meet you off the train.

I heard myself babbling. Camille frowned. Creases between her eyebrows. But I meant to kill him, you know.

I whispered: shut up. People will hear you.

Camille said: I don't care if they do.

You were very upset, I said: you only wanted to scare him. That's what you'll have to say if you get caught, if you get arrested.

Camille said: he's done nothing, according to their view. He lied to me, he betrayed me, he abandoned me, he lied to his wife. For them, those aren't crimes. For me they are.

Losing the baby, I said, that upset you, you're not yourself, that's why you lost control.

Camille sighed. No, it wasn't that. The baby was an accident. Poor little creature. She put away her compact and lipstick, closed her bag. You think I'm crazy, a poor crazy girl to be pitied, but I'm not.

The red-faced man slid his eyes towards us then away again. Camille gave a delicate yawn. She picked up her glass. She said: I made up my mind. I acted. I did what I meant to do. Now it's over I feel exhausted, but I don't feel sorry, you know. Not at all.

She sipped her brandy. I said: we'd better go. I'll see you back to the hostel, then I'll go back to the Regina, and first thing in the morning I'll take you to the station.

Camille said: in a minute. What's the rush? I'm famished. I haven't eaten since I don't know when. God, I'd love a plate of fried potatoes right now this minute.

The wire basket on the *zinc* contained two hardboiled eggs. Those will have to do, come on, Camille, we can't stay here.

You're paying, aren't you? she said. I've no money left.

I hesitated. I'd forgotten. I haven't, either.

The red-faced man pushed back his chair, raised a forefinger. Half mocking half serious. Nice girls don't put on make-up in public. You should be ashamed of yourselves, you little tarts.

In a calm voice Camille told him to fuck off. He started getting up. A fellow in the corner reading the newspaper put it down, raised his head. His chipped front tooth. The milk delivery man. Ah, he said, my little friend from the hotel. You don't want to bother with her, chum. She bites. Poisonous, her bite is. The dark-haired man said: leave it. Just leave it.

The barman said to us: you want me to call the police?

217

The sturdy dark-haired man looked us up and down, sighed. I'll pay for you. He waved towards the door. Now scram. Get lost. Go home to your mothers.

I tugged Camille out. Clip clop over the tiled floor. Her very shoes sounded insolent. She strolled along peeling the eggs one after the other, stuffing them into her mouth, throwing the shells down on the pavement as we went. Now that I've eaten I'll be able to sleep. Pity I've no salt. And a piece of bread and butter, now, I could do with that.

She wouldn't hurry. She was savouring her eggs. The moon sailed in and out of clouds. Camille raised her head, put a hand to her cheek. The wind's got up again, it's freshening, dampening, can you feel it? There'll be rain before morning, I dare say.

Once I'd seen her slide into the hostel, past the doorkeeper nun too sleepy to take much notice of anything, I returned to the Regina. I was just ahead of the servants' curfew so I wasn't expecting trouble. The housekeeper was waiting for me, however, and yes, I was indeed in trouble: I was a thief. So I ended up taking the train to Paris with Camille next morning. For the second time, we fled together.

32. Man, escaping

DENIS

Sunlight whitened the street. Sun had been shining all morning
and would go on shining whatever I felt. That was comforting,
somehow. I'd get over this. I'd make sense of it. Confusion
of thoughts confusion of bodies. We piled into the hired car,
parked just outside the care home.

Angela and Phyllis insisted on giving me a lift as far as
Marseilles. That's the least we can do.

First of all they'd suggested I stick around. We'll complete
the interview with Clem, there's a lot still to cover, her progress
as a painter, her experiences in the war, her entire adult life,
pretty much. We could all three move to a hotel, you could just
lie low, do whatever you want, swim, sunbathe, and then we
could get together in the evening.

They wanted to keep an eye on me. They meant well. I said
no.

Next they'd offered to drive me anywhere I wanted to go.
To the airport, for example. If I was so desperate to leave, why
not take the plane? I refused. I had my train ticket, I might stay
in Marseilles for a while, or I might move my departure date
forward, get a train home immediately, either way I'd be fine.
Phyllis said: but will you, though? You've had a shock.

You want to look after me, my darling, I said, and I'm truly
grateful, but right now I need to be on my own.

All right then, Phyllis said: we'll take you to the station in

Marseilles, and then it's up to you what you do, of course.

Once in their car, zipping along, I wanted to jump out of it, escape the motorway's high speeds. Only a short drive, but it felt endless. Time had vanished. Just the terrifying present. Like Clem's mandala turned vicious. My innards churned, tightened, churned. Angela drove calmly, alertly, she was only doing seventy, but I lost all speech, robbed of speech by speed, all of me clenched, resisting, praying for this to be over, other people's reckless driving, swerving in and out of lanes with no signals, we were all much too close to each other going much too fast. Pink-flowered oleanders shot backwards at us, the black tarmac streamed ahead shimmering in the heat, four lanes of metal bullets. The air con emitted cool air but I was sweating.

Like bumper cars but faster. Clem was one car and I was the other. Over and over she hit me head on, sent me skidding. When we turned off onto the slip road to Marseilles I could let go. Knees shaking. All of me shaking. We left the bypass, cruised towards the city centre.

Phyllis peered over her shoulder. You all right, D.? You're very quiet.

I'm fine, I said.

La Ciotat, the care home, the nuns, were far behind us. Clem had gestured at the camera. She had said: I need to put a frame around what happened. I'm sorry, Denis, but that's the way it is. It's too hard otherwise. This is the only way I can tell you.

Angela kept filming. Sister Marie-Claude leaned against the door, hands folded over her grey overall. Sister Marie-Cécile, standing next to her, glanced at her watch. Phyllis leaned forward a little, encouraging Clem with her eyes.

Clem lifted the blue teardrop shape of paper in one hand.

With the other she lifted the piece she'd sent me, the blue sheet with the teardrop cut out of it. She put the shapes together. The one fitted perfectly into the other, it took its place inside it. They belonged together. You could hardly see they'd ever been parted, cut away from each other. She said: you see now, don't you.

So you stole some of Matisse's cast-off bits of paper from making the cut-outs, I said: so what? You've admitted that already. Why make such a song and dance about it? OK, so you stole an actual cut-out as well. What do you want me to do about it? Hand it in to the Matisse Museum in Nice? Inform the police? Will you please explain? I've come all this way, I've tried to be patient, but I've had enough.

The two nuns tut-tutted. Phyllis lifted a hand. So, Clem. Go on. Just say it.

33. Black-and-white photograph (precise date unknown) by Yvette Martin of Matisse in bed in the Hotel Regina

Matisse's head has sunk between the pillows. White hair and beard, white nightshirt. He has turned his face to look at Mme Lydia, who gazes back at him. She wears her white overall and white plimsolls. She has drawn her chair as close as possible to his bed. She is holding his hand. She looks tense, controlled. She is like a wire, transmitting energy to him fingertip to fingertip.

34. Apartment interior, Paris

CLÉMENCE

Paris was mucky and wet. We trudged over the greasy pavements lining the quays. The river slopped along swollen and grey. Clinging to our shared umbrella Camille and I swerved around puddles. People barged past. Cars cruising along too close to the pavement sent up sprays of dirty water we had to dodge. Camille chucked back curses in return. She said: one day I'll have a car, I'll be the one doing that.

The woman who opened the door had large dark eyes under arching dark brows, silvery-white hair drawn back. She wore a black-and-white striped blouse, a calf-length grey skirt, a grey cardigan like a jacket, with black velvet edging the cuffs. Two of you! I was only expecting one. My husband obviously got it wrong.

The rain pulsed down. She said: you poor wet creatures. You'd better come in.

She seized my streaming umbrella. Where did you get this? That's my spare. Did my husband lend it to you?

She shook it so that drops flew out onto the step. Such a well-travelled brolly. Up and down it goes. Paris, the Midi, Paris. Always on its own these days. It used to be one of a fine pair.

She rammed it into the hat-stand, where it dripped onto the metal trough. The apartment's upstairs. Go ahead, and I'll follow.

We unlaced our sodden shoes, left them on the mat. She showed us into a small salon, with red and pink patterned wallpaper, a sky-blue rug, a sunflower-yellow one. The lid of the piano against one wall sprouted a gold and green tuft: a fern in a brass pot. Two little red armchairs stood close together, ready for a chat. Sit down. Are you thirsty? I'll fetch you something to drink. And have you eaten? You're not hungry? Very well then.

Camille whispered: did you see her ring? A real beauty. She's got class, this lady.

Mme Matisse returned, carrying a loaded tray. She poured red syrup into narrow glass tumblers decorated with gilt swirls, topped them up with water from a grey ceramic pitcher. She saw me looking. Tea glasses, she said, from Morocco. They drink mint tea there, did you know that? But this is grenadine.

She seemed to understand how shy we felt. While we drank, she carried on chatting into our silence. Putting us at our ease. Some American friends gave me the grenadine, and a bottle of champagne too. They smuggled in plenty of dollars with them, now they've got a suitcase hidden under their bed in the hotel full of francs, they can buy whatever they want. And they're very generous. Whenever they come to visit they bring me something nice to eat or drink.

She topped up our glasses. Her hand holding the heavy jug shook slightly. I wanted to jump up and help her, but she might have felt insulted, so I kept quiet.

You can stay until you find your feet, she said. We're in a state of chaos, we're packing up some things in the studio, but you won't mind that. At the moment I'm the only one here, so there's plenty of room for you.

We needed shelter. Very well, she would take us in. Perhaps she liked helping her husband, feeling of use to him. Given that he had Mme Lydia cushioning his every move, he didn't seem to need his wife too much. Had he sacked her, as the housekeeper had sacked me? Or had she sacked him, for employing a live-in assistant who was so much younger, and perhaps even more devoted than she'd been? Did she prefer Paris to the Mediterranean? How could she? You and I are compatriots, she told me. I too was born in the south.

I expected Mme Matisse to prod us for our stories, but she didn't. She simply accepted us. Later, getting to know her, I realised that this was how she and her friends had behaved all through the war, when people were fleeing, homeless: you gave them food, somewhere to stay, you tided them over, you let them be.

She took clean sheets and pillowcases from a carved wooden cupboard. Make up your own beds, will you? I'm not so good on the stairs as I once was. The spare room's in the attic. A rather primitive arrangement, but I'm sure you'll manage.

Once we were upstairs, Camille said: did you notice her outfit? Beautiful material. Beautifully cut. Out of date, though. Terribly pre-war.

We're not exactly fashion-plates, are we? I said.

The cramped space under the roof, walled in plywood, held two camp beds, a washstand with a china basin and jug. Cotton rug with red and black zigzags. Camille put one hand on her hip, swayed forward two mincing steps, turned, minced back. She said: of course I was lucky, working in the dress shop. I could buy the samples at a big discount. So I was always well turned out. Shame I can't go back there. I could do with some new clothes, and so could you.

She meant that she'd been sacked for getting pregnant. Out! She was wearing the clothes she had on when I first met her, but now with a belt around her newly slender waist, the white silk blouse billowing out above it.

We took turns to stand on the single chair and put our heads out of the skylight. Rain spattered the hinged pane of glass I held up with one hand, gripping the window frame with the other. A ripple of grey-blue: a mansard roof sloping down. The pitch of it cut off the street below. No moon visible in the dark grey sky above the grey roofs. No stars.

Camille said: I wonder what he told her when he rang her up?

I don't know, I said. He just said it would be all right.

Shooing me inside the Regina's back entrance, the house-keeper had told me to go straight up to the dormitory, pack my belongings, leave first thing in the morning. Her lips pinched and pursed. You had your second chance, you wasted it, I wash my hands of you. Her white collar, unbuttoned, lolled open. She fingered it, began re-fastening it. What are you staring at, you little drunken wretch? I edged past her. Climbing the stone stairs, I felt sodden with tiredness. I bullied my heavy legs: lift, lift.

The dormitory door nudged open. A red nightlight burned on a wall bracket. Beyond it: darkness. I crept through by feel, clutching the ends of cold iron bedsteads one by one. The other maids were blanketed humps. Someone snored, muttered.

I reached my bed at the far end of the row. Above the clear glass of the ox-eye window, the clouds pushed past the moon, sheared off. The pale light let me see just enough. I shed Annette's dress, folded it on top of my pillow. I fumbled my own clothes on. I gathered my possessions, packed my satchel. I slid the Brush's drawing of Camille under my spare jumper, stuffed in the penknife. Dark blots on the white square of my handkerchief.

I placed my jumper and coat ready for the morning. Be precise. Everything in the right order. *Be prepared.* The Guides' motto. This time Girl Guide Captain Monique couldn't help me. Be prepared to flee.

I trod out again, very quietly. No one woke, no one saw me go. Down to the third floor. Along the dim, hushed corridor, over the carpet someone else would be hoovering tomorrow. A silvery girl loped beside me, from long mirror to long mirror: arched doorways showing that other world. A dark garden with moonlit paths, a silver pond flicking with fish. That glass bowl of goldfish in the Master's picture. Trapped. The police arriving, smashing the bowl, the goldfish flapping and dying on the carpet.

A glimmer under the door of his suite. I tapped on the heavy wooden panel. Silence. I tapped again. A faint voice said: who is it?

I said: it's Monique.

The voice said: well then, my dear, come in. The door's not locked.

A ball of yellow light haloed by gold-hazy shadows. A bulky dark shape: that armchair of his, low and wide, that I'd seen in one of his paintings. Next to it, the little metal table bearing the yellow-shaded lamp. Even in the darkness the room felt clear. Open spaces through which you could move easily. I knew its shapes of air. Over there, on that wall, his daughter was dreaming, under a quilt of grey clouds. People were drifting past whom I'd never see again. The room was peeling me off, shedding me.

The Master lolled against cushions, his knees swathed in a blanket, a cardigan around his shoulders. Rolled up in softness. He rubbed his eyelids. He'd been dozing, and I'd woken him.

Do come closer, my dear, he said.

He reached for his glasses from the side table, put them on.

Round owlish eyes. A white owl shape, his feathers all plumped up. Talons disguised as white felt slippers. I was that country mouse, pinned in shivery grass.

He studied me. Sleepiness cleared from his face.

Not Monique, I see, he said, which is a shame. But on the other hand, how delightful to be visited in the middle of the night by a pretty girl. Should I know you? Have we met?

I said: no, not really, monsieur. I'm Clémence. I'm the maid who cleans in here. Used to, I mean.

Ah, Mademoiselle Clémence. I remember now.

What did he remember? I stood stiff and still in front of him. A mouse-criminal, about to be pounced on, my head bitten off, my guts torn out.

He flapped a wing, sketched a wave. Do forgive me for not getting up.

I said: please excuse me for disturbing you.

He changed from owl back into gentleman. Not at all. Such a charming visitor as yourself is always welcome.

He smiled. There. We've got the polite speeches out of the way. Now tell me. What can I do for you?

I fished in my skirt pocket, held out the two pencils I had picked up the day before. These are yours. I wanted to bring them back before I left. I'm sorry I took your other things, as well. I shouldn't have done that.

He looked me over. If you're not in a great hurry, why don't you sit down? Why don't you find a chair and bring it over?

I lifted a padded stool, carried it across, settled myself in front of him. His hands curled over the ends of his chair arms. Pale-skinned, a bit swollen, with blue veins, liver spots.

He said: if you would be good enough to keep me company for a little while, I should be very grateful.

He released his grip, flexed his fingers. As though he were checking they still worked. That in the morning they'd seize the scissors, the shears, obey him. Blades opening like an eagle's beak, snapping on thick paper. He said: I am feeling rather anxious. I am waiting for Madame Lydia to return. She has been called out, a friend of ours in trouble, taken to hospital, and she has gone to offer her support to his wife.

That struggling creature on the pavement, the gold flash as the doorway of the hotel lit up, the high cry. Had Mme Martin mentioned seeing a girl there? She would tell the police, though, when they questioned her.

A knife injury, apparently, he said, but it appears not life-threatening. The Martins, yes, of course, you know them. You met them earlier today.

He spoke mildly, slowly, as though he didn't have energy to spare. Lying back, he seemed collapsed, as though he too had been stabbed and his strength was leaking away. His strength was Mme Lydia and she had taken herself off. She was his blood, his breath.

My poor Lydia, he said, spending the night sitting up in a hospital. She needs her rest. Now she's got this extra worry and bother on top of all the trouble I cause her.

I said: I've caused you bother, too. I'm sorry.

Keep the pencils, he said. I've got plenty. You can write your love letters with them. Go on, put them away.

He concentrated, lifting the carafe from the side table, pouring and sipping water. He looked grim, as though something hurt. He saw me watching him and attempted a smile. You can keep the jewellery too, if you want it. You're welcome to it. It's over there, on top of the bureau. You can take it with you when you go.

229

I said: thank you.

He set down the glass. His hand fell back on the blanket. A cheap anklet, a pair of cheap earrings. Nothing to make a fuss about. Young women are so beautiful in their natural state, they don't need adornment, decoration, but they don't know that, they think they have to paint their faces, put on fancy clothes. Not true at all. They're beautiful exactly as they are.

Except when you want them to put on exotic costumes, I said.

His eyebrows twisted up. Yes, but that's just a fantasy. That's a game. A game I don't play any more, in any case.

I said: I wasn't planning to wear those things in the street. I'd look silly going out in them. I wore them for dressing-up, but once was enough.

Of course, he said. You're another one who wants to learn to draw, aren't you? You and a thousand other girls, all dreaming of becoming artists. Why do you want that? Don't you know how hard a road it is to follow? First of all you've got to train, and that takes several years. Who'll pay for it? Then you'll most likely fail to make a living at it, and then what will you do?

His questions weren't real questions, waiting for a reply, but criticisms: I was wrong to want what I wanted. Had his family said similar things to him? How had he survived? Perhaps by staying silent. I stared at his feet in their pale felt slippers.

You'll need to find a patron, he said, a man like me, someone experienced, with a bit of clout, to help you. Just don't get married and have children. That's what I told your friend Monique. For a woman who hopes to become an artist that's fatal. Unless your husband can afford to pay for a children's nurse, of course.

He moved his head slightly, and the light from the lamp glinted, reflecting off his spectacles. You think about it. You'll find that I'm talking sense.

He was old enough to be my grandfather. White-haired, white-bearded. Well-meaning. He had tried to help Monique. He was trying to help me. You had to be polite to grandfathers, thank them for their advice.

He smiled at me, a grandfather patting a small girl on the head. I paint because it brings me such great pleasure. Simple as that. But it's a big jump from being a maid to being a painter. You need to be an athlete! I wish you *bon courage*, my dear.

I said: I ought to go. You must be tired. It's late.

Sunday tomorrow, he said. Monique may come in and help me again, after she's been at her devotions. Madame Martin, too. Lydia will ring them both in the morning, to find out. Poor Hubert will doubtless be kept in hospital for a day or so, but he will want to carry on with what we've begun.

The dark air felt stuffy, stale. He was breathing gently, regularly. The mound of his stomach rose and fell.

He said: probably you think I'm a monster of selfishness, ruthlessness.

I was selfish and ruthless, too. Girls weren't supposed to be, so we hid it under being nice, we acted it in sly ways, to avoid being found out, punished. You could survive that happening. You just had to start again.

Life as a painter is harder for women, the Master said. You're going against your nature, to some extent. A lot of women turn aside, to graphic design, interior design. Domestic forms of art. That suits them better.

And then he painted the results. The wallpapers, woven rugs, patterned cloths. Once they were part of an oil painting they were high art. Some of the nuns at school had done water colours: holy pictures for us to slip into our prayer books. They had sewed banners for processions, they'd embroidered hangings for altars, they had stitched priests' vestments. For God, not for themselves.

The Master said: being disciplined is the only way to get work done. I haven't got much time left. I've got to keep going. Not allow myself to be distracted. You don't understand that, I expect. Probably you want to be loved. Most women do.

Such shrewd, ironic eyes. He was teasing me, testing me. I'd never see him again, so I could say what I thought. Why do you assume you know about me? Who are you to say? It's up to me how I live. I'll manage, I assure you. And don't men want to be loved too?

He plucked at the cardigan, drawing it more snugly under his chin. He folded his hands in his lap and stared at me.

I said: I'm leaving tomorrow morning, first thing. I stood up, pushed the stool aside.

You're in trouble, aren't you? he said. Have you lost your job? Do you want to tell me about it?

In Mme Matisse's attic, Camille and I shook out sheets. Camille flung one on, then flapped out another. She said: so long since I've done this. My landlady always did it for me. Give us a hand, Clem?

Proper mitred corners. Tightly tucked in. Fat pillows eased into cases, beaten to fit snugly. The art of bedmaking, perfected at the Regina. My magic to keep control. I'd be OK. Held. Oh, Mum. Why hadn't she written back to me?

Camille surprised me, patting my shoulder. Thanks, dearie. And thanks for getting us here.

I sat down on my camp bed. A narrow shelf of rigid canvas stretched onto poles. How did soldiers sleep on these? Surely we'd been more comfortable at Guide camp, curled in folded, pinned blankets on groundsheets. In the morning, at the open mouth of the tent, the sweet smell of dewy grass.

Camille said: now I'm on home ground I'll manage fine. No one knows where I am, I'll be safe. And you too.

I hadn't mentioned Camille to the Master. I just admitted I'd been given the sack, and had nowhere to go. He said: you don't want to return home to your parents? Very well, then. I'm going to telephone my wife in Paris, see whether she can put you up.

He wrote down the address. He gave me the money for the train fare, added extra on top. Call it a loan, if you prefer. Sort it out with my wife. I'll telephone her first thing tomorrow. By then you'll be on your way.

He'd given me such a wad of francs that surely I'd be able to pay for Camille's ticket as well as my own. We'd travel third class, the money might just stretch. Thank you, I said.

Don't forget your sketchbook, he said. It's over there, with the other things. Madame Lydia was wondering what to do with it. Whether she could trust the housekeeper to give it back to you or whether to wait until she saw you. Take my spare umbrella, too. Madame Matisse will be glad to have it back.

We shook hands. We said goodbye.

His eyelids lowered, he settled into a doze. I made for the back way out of the suite, through the anteroom. I knew there was a rubbish bin there, by the door to the kitchenette. I threw the sketchbook into it.

Rain sprinkled the attic window. I emptied my satchel onto my camp bed, began to sort the contents. Camille pounced on the nude sketch of her done by the Brush. You've got this? I thought I'd got rid of all his masterpieces.

D'you want it? I asked.

No, Camille said, you keep it. Since it's a drawing of me, it's mine really, so I'm giving it to you. One day you may need some money, you could sell it. He might be famous by then, it might be worth something.

He's going to recover, you know, I said. Monsieur Matisse was sure of it. He'll be able to go on working.

Good for him, Camille said. Good old Hubert Martin.

She took a pen out of her handbag. She wrote in the lower right-hand corner: *for Clem, with love.*

It ought to be signed with his name, to give it proper value. I'll sign it for him. No, I'll initial it, that's what he used to do.

She dashed off the initials H.M., handed the drawing back. Now I'm a forger, in addition to all my other crimes.

Next morning Camille and I helped Mme Matisse lay the table in the kitchen for breakfast. She'd been out and bought a baguette. She came in all frosted and crisp with cold. She took up a serrated knife, tapped it on the long loaf: I am in a state of rejoicing. Shops full of bread again. Coffee off the ration. I can't believe it. After all these years. I have to pinch myself, to make sure it's real.

She filled our cups, she opened a jar of redcurrant jam. A friend in Normandy sends me this, it's home-made.

The friend had also sent her a slab of butter. In the Regina, we'd had margarine occasionally, never butter. Camille and I were desperately trying to do everything right, not to be nuisances, so we scraped on the butter thinly, knowing how expensive it was. Mme Matisse watched us, nodded. Now, you're going to need to find jobs. How about dressmaking?

Millinery? I worked in a hat shop when I was first married, my husband earned practically nothing, so I kept us afloat. Can you two sew? The clothes shops are opening up again, there'll be work. On the other hand, I don't know that I've still got contacts in the rag trade.

She pushed the jar of jam towards us. But a theatre workshop. That might be the thing. My husband worked on a couple of theatre projects at one time. Let me see what I can do.

I hate sewing, Camille said. I'd rather design hats than put them together. But Clem here, she can sew all right.

Beggars can't be choosers, Mme Matisse said. Start low, work your way from there.

She fixed us up double quick. Two days later, in the workroom of the Folies Bergères, Camille and I sat side by side at the long table, stitching lines of threaded sequins onto velvet-covered buckram head-dresses and bodices. Patterns of spirals and stars. Behind us, the shallow drawers of a row of cabinets held pearl buttons, bits of diamanté, dyed feathers, ribbons, reels of thread, glittering beads. Other workers, older than we were, more experienced and skilled, gathered lengths of stiffened and spangled net and tulle into tiny full skirts with high bustles. They were dedicated and expert, very proud of their exquisite confections. They transformed the dancers into circus ponies prancing on their hind legs and tossing their manes and tails, into peacocks with jewelled spread fans, parrots swinging on perches. Parrots in fishnets and high heels.

When the dancers lost their youth, at thirty or so, they had to retire. Some ended up in our workroom, and sewed, and told tales of their past triumphs: after-theatre suppers with rich men, lovers who sent bouquets. Children? You tied them to dressing-room chairs while you were on stage. These ex-dancers boasted of the presents winkled out of admirers. How else did you save for a pension?

Same problem being a model, Camille said. It's too insecure. I shan't go back to it. I suppose this place is all right, as jobs go. But I'm not staying longer than I have to, that's for sure. It's too dull.

Dull meant safe. But sooner or later you wanted adventures again. You took risks, you took the consequences. One girl came back to work soon after *a misadventure*, told us all about it though I tried not to listen. A self-induced, botched miscarriage, then into hospital, where the operation was completed with no anaesthetic, just to punish her. Camille yelled at her to shut up. Look at this poor kid here, she's going green.

I wrote to Monique, telling her Camille and I were safe and well. I wrote to my parents too, telling them where I was and that I had a job. This time, my mother replied. We will always forgive, we resign ourselves, I pray for you, you can always come home.

What would she forgive me? I wouldn't tell her. She wouldn't have to know. Yes, I'd go home at some point. But certainly not yet.

I used Mme Matisse's telephone to contact Berthe at her employers' home over on the Right Bank. Berthe suggested we all meet up for an aperitif in a few days' time. Roger's so busy, he's always dashing about, and this weekend is already all booked up, but after that would be very nice.

What about an entire night out? I said. Surely we could do it on the cheap.

Girls in the workshop had described the jazz clubs opening up in basements around St Germain. Hot, smoky atmosphere, brilliant bands. Can't we go to one of those? Berthe vetoed my idea. Not our sort of thing, they'll be full of riff-raff.

Anyway, she hinted, Roger preferred the older, more stylish

Paris, the city as he imagined it having been before the war. Chic cafés and restaurants, yes, floor shows with gorgeous girls kicking up their legs, yes, he was up for that; grimy dives run by weirdos, no. Berthe added: Roger will pay for the drinks, don't worry, he's very generous, and he can afford it, he's on a good salary, he'll want to treat us.

Camille and I beat through the rain to the smart place he fancied near the Arc de Triomphe, arrived early, bagged a booth by the door. Camille leaned back and studied her fingernails, a weary woman of the world, but I turned country mouse again, peeping at the glittering bar, the painted pillars, the gilt-framed mirrors reflecting the lights. Lots of young people with white teeth Camille said must be Americans were lording it, talking merrily, drinking tall glasses of beer. They wore what looked like workmen's blues, very clean, very well-pressed.

Various passing chaps tried it on. You're all alone, girls, may we join you? Camille flicked her eyes over them, pursed her lips, waved them away. We can't look too bad, then, she said, despite our outfits!

Mme Matisse, clearing out her cupboards, had come across some of her daughter's discarded clothes, donated us a couple of frocks. Rather old-fashioned, skimpily cut and short. I expected Camille to object to cast-offs, after the nuns' charity, but she didn't. She'd chucked the brown knitted coat into the river, insisting I go with her to witness the death. The sad brown woman sank, surfaced, sank again, drowned. That's it! Camille said. That's what good little Catholic girls do when they're pregnant and unmarried, you know, they drown them-selves. No way I'd ever do that, I said.

Mme Matisse offered us darned blouses, re-knitted jumpers,

turned dresses. They'll tide you over, dears, until you get your first pay packets. Camille fingered the crepe. Good enough quality, yes, thank you, this will do quite nicely. And if we cut this frock up, we can use it to lengthen these other two. Mme Matisse mocked her. Even during the war I took pride in my appearance, as did my daughter, I'm glad to see you do the same.

You wouldn't know, from the way she spoke, that she'd done anything but worry about clothing coupons. Yet she'd been in the Resistance, Monique had told me, she'd been caught, put on a train for Germany, taken off it, dumped in prison for several months. A different punishment to that meted out to her daughter. Images of the beatings the daughter had endured punched my dreams at night. Her back lacerated, streaked with blood. Her mouth open, screaming. Here was her mother stroking her old frocks, running her fingers gently along their seams.

Camille had left a trunkful of clothes, a box of belongings, at her former landlady's across the river. Wasn't she going to go and collect them? She shook her head: I'm not ready to do that yet. For the moment I'm lying low. Anyway, she may have sold them, who knows? It's you, Clem, who should be thinking of your future.

There they are! I waved. Camille laid a hand on my elbow. Calm down. Let's take a look at this hero.

Roger was boyish and eager-faced, with curly dark brown hair cut short, gleaming with brilliantine. He sprang with energy, holding the door open for Berthe, ushering her in, lightly cupping her elbow. He steered her towards our banquette. So gallant, bowing and shaking hands, pulling out Berthe's chair for her, lighting Camille's cigarette. Berthe translated. He's saying keep the packet, lots more where that came from.

Berthe unbuttoned her tight little jacket, shook out her crisp striped skirts, crossed her legs, twirled a foot in its high-heeled shoe. Roger gazed at her, let out words like barks. Berthe put up a hand to her glistening hairdo. He's saying he can't get enough of me, he says roll on December, not long to go, marrying me he says he'll be the happiest man alive.

Roger put his arm round her waist, kissed her cheek. Camille said: you're getting married in England?

Yes, Berthe said, and then we'll come back here. Roger's contract with the Embassy doesn't end until next autumn. So Roger suggested we move to England after that.

Roger didn't seem to mind her talking for him. He winked at her. She translated again. He's happy just sitting here with three pretty girls, admiring us. He says what would we like to drink?

I showed Berthe Monique's letter, received that morning, replying to mine. *After Christmas I'm going to go and stay with the Dominican nuns in their convent for several weeks, to see what the life's like, to test my vocation. If all goes well, which I think it will, I shall spend some time sorting out my affairs, taking care of my family, and then I'll enter as a postulant. After that, not quite sure when, it'll be my Clothing, and then the novitiate.*

Berthe and I sat in silence. Roger lifted his glass. Cheer up, ladies. Chin-chin. Here's to our futures and to frolics and fun. Tell them about your plans, sweetheart.

Egged on by Roger, Berthe was planning to study for a teaching qualification. You're so bright, my darling girl, much brighter than I am. Top of the class in every way. Berthe had returned to the English classes she had neglected, and now suggested I should learn to speak the language too. Then when you come to visit us in London, Clem, you'll be able to talk to Roger properly.

To start me off she wrote me out a couple of English verbs

and their conjugations. The verb *to be*. The verb *to love*. I recited them to myself as I stuck my needle through piled sequins, strung them out along velvet. I am all right. I have been all right. I shall be all right again.

Mme Matisse gave us latchkeys, let us come and go as we pleased. Real freedom, such as I'd never had. At night I could go for long walks, exploring the city, and nobody knew where I was, and I could just vanish among the crowds. Once or twice Berthe, Camille and I went out for cheap suppers together. People here didn't cook with olive oil. They didn't have our southern vegetables. Usually we were offered platters of nameless meat with boiled potatoes. I tried to be polite, I learned the names of the dishes, I kept my opinions to myself.

Mostly Berthe spent her free time with Roger. That was how it was: they were engaged, she saw less of her girlfriends. One of Roger's acquaintances, one of the chauffeurs at the American Embassy, who could speak a fair bit of French, took me out a couple of times. Tall, fair-haired, with a friendly grin. Petrol no problem, so he drove me to the Bois de Boulogne, parked in deep under the trees. He taught me some vocabulary: *heavy petting, going too far*. But I wasn't a *cocktease*, he complimented me: I was *hot stuff*. When he told me he had a week's leave and was off to Deauville with his wife and baby, that was that. He didn't approve of French morals, it turned out. French women were *easy lays*.

In early December I rang Berthe and asked to see her on our own, without Roger, so that we could talk freely in French without her having continually to translate. No Camille, either. I thought our conversation might upset her. I told her Berthe was going to give me an English lesson. Camille said: well, in any case, I'm going to the cinema.

She had made a new male friend. An older man, whose wife had been shot by a German sniper as the last battles raged in the Paris streets, as people surged out to anticipate the early days of Liberation. Part of a crowd flooding towards the Champs-Élysées she had been picked off by a soldier firing randomly in retreat. The widower owned a clothes shop, with a sideline in corsetry formerly dealt with by his wife, and had suggested Camille come and handle that part of the business. If it turns out OK, Clem, then, well, we'll see. No, she wasn't ready to introduce him. Let's see how it goes. She had a new alertness, merriment. No more fucking artists for me, young Clem. Tra la la.

Sunday afternoon. Sun glimmering in the pearly sky, a chilly wind. Bent into it, people scudded along, determinedly taking the air after lunch. Berthe and I met in the Tuileries gardens, sat on a bench close to the round pond, wrapped in our coats. Stone goddesses stalked past. Dark green hedges curved behind them. Berthe said: right, I'll test you on your verbs.

I began reciting the verb *to be* in the present tense. I am. I am sure I am pregnant. I am terrified. You are. You are my friend.

I dropped into the future tense. They (he/she) will disapprove. That is an understatement, I added.

The claw feet of our iron chairs shifted in the gravel. The carousel turned, half-empty. Just a few children, bundled in thick coats and scarves, gripped the horses' manes, rose up, fell down. Their parents stood watching. One small boy flew a red kite. It swayed and dipped, staggered up again. Toddlers on leading reins lurched forwards. Mothers pushed prams.

Berthe recited part of the verb *to love*. I love you. We, you and I, love each other.

She patted my knee with her gloved hand. It will be all

right. We'll think of something. For a start, have you talked to Madame Matisse?

In the studio Mme Matisse, wearing a blue-checked apron over her black Sunday dress, a blue scarf tied around her hair, was hammering shut the lid of a packing-case. Her mouth clamping a row of nails, she nodded at me. I fetched a broom, began to sweep up the litter of straw on the floor. Tap, tap, tap. She took out the last nail from her mouth, knocked it in, straightened up, stretched. At her direction, I began wrapping in newspaper certain pots, jugs and dishes stacked on a nearby card table.

He used to use those in his paintings, she said. Now that he won't be coming back to Paris, he wants them with him, old friends sitting around his bed. I'd have thought he had enough bits and pieces down in Nice as it is. But what he wants he must have. So off they'll go tomorrow.

She must still love him, even though they no longer lived together. Why else would she be so willing to help him? She had ceded her place to Mme Lydia, but hadn't stopped being alert to his needs. Her standards of devotion were clearly very high. They must have given her life a focus. She wasn't abandoning them just yet. They'd had three children together. That connected them, in ways I knew I did not understand.

I dragged the second packing-case from its corner, began filling it with a preliminary layer of crumpled newspaper. Mme Matisse opened a fresh box of nails. She listened to my blurted tale.

I said: I know there are places girls can go, there are women who'll help them. It happened recently to one of the girls I work with, she told us about it.

Whack! Mme Matisse banged her hammer onto the side of

the packing-case's open wooden mouth. Her steel nail sank into the wooden lip. You're not to do that, Clémence. It's very dangerous. You might die.

She scooped up a big handful of straw, thrust it in. What about the child's father? Is he willing to acknowledge the child and marry you?

I said: I'm not sure who the father is. And I don't want to get married. And I don't think I'm cut out to be a mother.

You're still very young, certainly, Mme Matisse said, and yet some young women manage it at your age.

She took up a wrapped pot from the array I'd set ready, and balanced it between her palms. Already I'd forgotten which pot precisely it was. Just a nameless shape: bulky and fat.

Listen, she said. In return for your story I'll give you one of my own. I'm taking you into my confidence, Clémence. It's a delicate matter.

Short, shiny lengths of straw clung to her apron bib. She brushed them off, re-tied her turban-scarf. Just as neatly she wrapped up her words, she laid them tenderly in the depths of the packing-case, tucked extra wadding around them. I adopted my daughter, you see. I took her in, brought her up as my own. Why did I do that? Well, you must understand, her mother was witty and charming, very stylish and chic, she was gifted as a seamstress, she loved fabrics, she could do anything with them, but she earned very little, she could not afford to keep a child. She and Monsieur Matisse could not marry, in any case, there were family difficulties, on his side at least, and so they parted. That was an unhappy time for them both. But anyway, it finished.

She nailed down the packing-case lid. Tap, tap, tap. Marguerite's mother scrabbled under it, gagged by newspaper, she was being packed off, sent away, not allowed to return. Mme Matisse began wiping her dusty hands against each other. My own hands were black with newsprint. She said: we're too dirty to use the bathroom, we'll go into the kitchen, wash at the sink there.

I said: do you think she changed her mind afterwards?

Mme Matisse ran the tap, scrubbed and rinsed her own hands, handed me the bar of soap. She drew forward the coarse linen towel hanging from its hook. Perhaps. She may have done. I don't know. Her initial arrangement with Monsieur Matisse was that she would not keep in touch. They thought it was better that way.

She wrapped the towel around my fingers, began to dry them. She trapped my fingers between her own. A sort of caress. It was all a long time ago. But I do know that at the time she was relieved, she was glad her child would have a home. She was sorry to part with her, but she felt it was for the best.

She put a pan of milk to heat on the stove. She was a practical person, Clémence. So was I. Someone's got to be practical. One genius in the family is enough. Looking after a genius is a full-time business.

She frowned. Thinking of Mme Lydia perhaps. She spooned chocolate powder into a jug, jiggled the pan of milk. You must learn to be practical too. For example, you must keep on with your job as long as you can, they won't get rid of you until the baby shows.

She poured the milk into the jug, whisked the mixture, rotating the little wooden paddle between her hands until the froth rose.

I asked: what was the name of your daughter's mother?

Camille, Mme Matisse said. She was called Camille. You can

imagine it was a bit of a shock when you first introduced your friend, when you first arrived. It's a common enough name, I suppose. A nice name I think.

We drank the hot chocolate. A bit too rich. She said: I'll take you to see my doctor. He'll look after you until the baby's due. In the meantime, you must decide what you are going to do afterwards.

I reported back to Berthe that evening. I sat on her chintz-covered bed in her room in the English family's flat in the 8ième and watched her doing her hair, brushing it up, letting it fall down, brushing it up again. Berthe turned from the mirror. She came and sat down next to me. She touched my cheek. Yes. That's the best solution. It's obvious.

That evening, in between rumbas and sambas, she consulted Roger. He spoke in the conditional tense. He would be happy to do anything she wanted. He added in the subjunctive mood. If she were really sure.

So that was the arrangement we made. Berthe spelled it out like a grammar lesson. She was as practical as Mme Matisse. As I was learning to be. Berthe and Roger wanted children. Accordingly, they would be having their first child in six months' time, as soon as I gave birth to him. They would take him back to England later in the year and present him as theirs, and he would grow up with them and be well cared for and they'd bring him to visit me so that he and I might know each other as godmother and godson.

The future tense. I shall hand him over I shall give him up I shall abandon all claim to him.

35. Railway station, Marseilles

DENIS

I sat on a bollard on the vast forecourt of the station in Marseilles. Classical statues posed around its edges looked on. For the first time in years I longed for a cigarette. To plug my mouth with, so that I would not start crying.

The sun was beating me up. A sufficient hurt. One that I could name, deal with. In the hierarchy of pains it came lower down the list than the anguish caused by Clem's announcement. Cross it off. Get up and leave it, move on, forget it. Goodbye pain.

I believed Clem. I didn't believe her. A fantasy. A family romance. Yet if it were true. If she'd really done what she said she'd done.

How could she and Berthe have deceived me so completely?

I had a stomach ache. I wrapped my arms around myself, bent over.

Traffic roared in the distance. The noise sealed me into itself. Cars and motorbikes howled as I longed to do. Perhaps if I stayed here long enough I'd stiffen into rigor mortis. Turn into one of those statues. For pigeons to crap on.

You all right?

Deep voice. His shadow falling across me. I refused to look up. Signal meaning go away, leave me alone. No drugs, no tracts, no beggars, I've no spare cash, just fuck off.

A touch on my shoulder. I flinched. The deep voice came

again, patiently. You all right? His Provençal accent. A sort of friendly music. I looked up. Blue and white trainers, creased knees of heavy blue cotton trousers, a white T-shirt. Close-cropped black hair flecked with grey. His sunburned face, puckered; his eyes directed at me like a beam of brown light. You remember me?

Gérard the taxi driver from La Ciotat. He gestured towards the station entrance. I was bringing some tourists to catch their train, dropping them here, I left the cab round the back and came over to buy a sandwich, then I saw you, and you don't look so good.

He sat on the neighbouring bollard. You need some water? You want to move into the shade? I think perhaps you should.

He made his questions sound ordinary. Just checking out a traveller in trouble, doing what ordinary goodness prompted him to do. Roger and Berthe's so-called goodness had hurt me. Gérard's released warm tears to mix with the sweat running down my face.

Gérard said: you want to tell me about whatever it is?

I wiped my face with my handkerchief. I said: how long have you got? You want the ten-hour version or the ten-minute version?

He said: how about the thirty-minute one? I have to pick up some people a little later, right now I need a cup of coffee, I'm making for the coffee bar on the concourse, why not come with me? I think you should come inside, out of the heat of the sun. It looks as though it's not doing you any good.

Espresso hissed and dribbled from a metal tap. We collected wooden stirrers, sachets of sugar, found a free table, sat down. Gérard pushed aside a couple of grease-stained paper plates. Brown hairs glinted on his brown forearms. He sipped his coffee. For a while we remained silent, and I was grateful for his delicacy, giving me time to collect myself, not pushing.

I heard myself sigh. He looked at me. So what's up?

I told him as briefly as I could. Clumsy, banal words. I was recounting a kitsch fairy tale.

Gérard listened. He didn't hurry giving his opinion. He sat for a while, thinking, then blew out his breath. Hey, you know, in fact that's a pretty ordinary story. It probably happened to lots of women of that generation. So you've lost one mother, so you've gained another. In fact you had two all along. A double dose. Won't that do? What are you complaining about?

I tried to smile. At nearby tables people were studying their phones, they were pushing back chairs making screeching noises on the tiled floor, that's what you did with children you pushed them back and forth you scolded them for whining if they complained. My dream of the dancers in red, chucking me between them like a ball. Ha. Train announcements by computerised voices instructed me with metallic charm go away never come back.

Gérard said: my own mother got divorced, I had a stepmother after that, so I had two mothers too. My mother was a bit of a cow. My stepmother wasn't that great, either. I brought myself up, more or less. But look at me. I survived. Even though I had a pretty tough time.

Pull yourself together, Denis. That was my mother talking. Which mother?

My coffee had slopped over onto the Formica tabletop. I blocked the creeping puddle with a paper napkin. Brown wetness sank into the crisp whiteness, turning it soggy. I pushed it aside. Apparently, my mother, my birth mother that is, wanted to tell me the truth once I was eighteen. But my adoptive mother insisted they'd promised never to tell me, it would hurt me too much, they should stick to their promise. They had a row about it, apparently, and then stopped seeing each other. So I never did get told the truth. Or what my mother says is the truth. I don't know that I believe her fancy tale. Perhaps I just don't want to.

Gérard drank his coffee. Be all right. Just be all right.

I don't know how, I said.

His brown face creased. He folded his sturdy arms on the tabletop, sat there looking serious and puzzled. Give it time. Get through today, and tomorrow things will start to feel better. And the next day a bit better still. And so on.

A nice straightforward narrative of improvement. I ought to try it. I couldn't think of anything better, could I? Ah. I could make a list. A list of Gérard's qualities that I had experienced so far. *Kindness. Goodness. Tolerance. Wisdom. Humour. Generosity.* A taxi-driving saint. One passenger after another leaning forwards, telling him their troubles, confessing their weaknesses, and Gérard counselling them. Take it easy, man. One step at a time.

I said: thanks. I'll be fine.

He said: you're sad. Nothing wrong with feeling sorry for yourself. We all have to do that from time to time. You have a good wallow, then you get out of it and continue living. You'll manage it.

He glanced at his watch. Sorry. I've got to go in a minute.

Thank you for the coffee, I said.

He got up. He didn't screech his chair. He pushed it back gently. It slid a little way away, stood obediently still. No jumping up and down no shouting don't go don't leave me. Good well-behaved chair.

He said: you'll be back, you know. You'll want to see your mother again. You've got my card still? I'll pick you up from the station, I'll drive you there.

I got up too.

Still plenty of life in her, I said. A new lease of life in fact.

Given to her by her two admirers. Phyllis and Angela relishing her every word, shaping her experience to fit into a collective story about outsider artists, amateur artists, the ones western culture labelled Other. Down with the myth of the solitary white male genius: old hat. Down with notions of perfection: they'd gone out with old-fashioned Christianity. All artists were flawed, all artists were struggling, they lived not in solitary ivory towers but on massed council estates, and they needed and cherished each other. Perhaps Angela would get the film commissioned for TV. One of her celebrated arts documentaries. Frieda, popping downstairs to collect the rent, might mention watching it. Oh yes, I'd reply, that character in the outlandish get-up, in fact she's my mother, did I never mention I was adopted, strange that, sit down and have a cup of tea and I'll tell you all about it if you like.

Gérard and I shook hands. I said: you didn't get your sandwich. I'm sorry. You're going back to work hungry.

He hesitated, then put his brown arms round me, embraced me. Scratch of his stubble. His body, warm against mine. *Allez-y. Bon courage.*

In the booking office I changed my tickets. Yes, there was a train leaving in an hour's time for Paris, then an easy connection for the Eurostar. *Sans problème, monsieur.* Phyllis and Angela had said: why not go on to Collioure, as you originally mentioned you might? Spend a few days there? Or stay in Bagnols? That's a quieter place, you could find a nice cheap

250

hotel, then see how you feel, whether you want to come back here, talk to Clem some more. No, I'd said, no. I can't stay in the same country as that woman. I've got to leave.

My rage with Clem propelled me all the way back across France, through Paris, to the coast. As my train approached the Tunnel, rage left me. Perhaps because it had worn me out. My eyelids wanted to slam down. Too much emotion, all these new facts banging at me, the sight of Clem the smell of her the sound of her voice. Give me instead the quiet of a library. Nice neat rows of computers. Classification systems that let you navigate calmly, efficiently. Indexers and archivists who knew their jobs. Dig out biographies, newspapers, memoirs. Check what I could of Clem's story. Did any of its details exist online? I could start now, if I wanted, using my phone. No. I was too tired.

No special cheap offers on Eurostar this time: I was in Standard Class. No Ted grumbling and muttering. Ha. I could teach Ted a thing or two, an insult or two. I was as rude as he was. I hadn't said a proper goodbye to Clémence, nor to the two nuns. I'd just bolted.

Perhaps I'd write to Clem. Perhaps I would propose coming to see her again. Perhaps at Christmas. Perhaps sooner. She'd said: I want to know about your life, I want you to tell me all about it. She looked at me anxiously, her hands twisted around those wretched bits of blue paper. Shock had made me want to lash out. I wanted to hurt her. Show her what you could do with words. I'd fled, so that I couldn't cut into her with words.

In the middle of the Tunnel I decided I needed a drink. To celebrate my confusion. Formerly I'd believed I was half-English and half-French. Now it seemed I might be wholly French, or I might be half-French and half-American. In fact not half or wholly French so much as Provençal. How much did all that matter?

I had survived this far. Clem had survived too. I should toast both of us. And the memory of my adoptive mother. Who'd done her best, kept the promise of her Girl Guide troop. Kept me clothed and fed, got me educated, sparred with me, loved me in her own way, which was all anyone could do. And my adoptive father. Who'd helped me with my maths homework, hoped I'd pursue a career as a salesman, sent me for boxing lessons, feared and despised me as a poofter. Loved me in his own way, yes, I supposed so.

The memories continued flooding out even as I got up and walked down the carriage towards the bar. Those people, my parents, all my parents, had slashed at the wall separating us. They were pouring through, surrounding me, exclaiming. Calm down, I said to them, I'm listening, but please don't talk all at once. Take it easy. One at a time. No good. They clamoured in their Babel tongues. English, French, Provençal, American.

I bought myself a ring-pull can of gin and tonic, returned to my seat. Less legroom than in First Class. I tilted my plastic goblet. No ice clinking. No offers of refills. No smartly uniformed cabin staff pushing their cart along, dispensing coffee and wry remarks.

Fuck. Maurice. Any moment now he might be arriving in my flat. He wouldn't be expecting me to turn up: I'd assured him I'd be away for several days longer. Hell. What to do?

Sweetness of bubbling tonic, sharpness of the alcohol. Go and stay with a friend. Don't let on, don't make him feel bad, don't make him feel unwelcome. How crass of me. Should I phone him? No, we were deep under the sea and there was no signal.

I swigged my gin, stared at the grey plasticised-cloth seat-back of the passenger in front. Don't get stressed, Ted's wife had begged: you know it's so bad for your heart. Have a heart, Clem might want to say to me: please try to understand why I did what I did.

We left the Tunnel, shot into the evening sunlight, coasted in towards Ebbsfleet. My phone rang. Frieda. She sounded snippy. You're on your way back now? Good. So I'll see you soon? There are things we must talk about.

I said: what's up? What's the matter?

You told me you'd be having one visitor, not two, Frieda said: I just think you should have let me know, that's all.

Maurice was going to visit his sister in northern France, I said. He must have brought her with him to London. I agree, he ought to have let us know.

Not his sister, Frieda said: he's brought a child. No, I don't want to talk about it now. I'll wait until I see you.

36. Black-and-white photograph (precise date unknown) by Yvette Martin of a bedroom at the Hotel Regina

The shadowy room, almost completely cleared of furniture, seems enormous. Shutters pulled across the tall window. Rolled-up mattress on the wide single bed. Two pillows balanced one on top of the other. Folded blankets, folded counterpane. The door to the corridor angles half open. Beside it on the floor stands a suitcase bound with a leather strap, a raincoat lying on top of it, a furled umbrella leaning against it.

37. The paper chapel

CLÉMENCE

His huge studio-room in the Regina was full of sunshine, as it was the first time I saw it, but now sunshine filtered and made subtle. He had walled his studio in paper, transparent enough to let the light from the windows behind shimmer through.

He'd constructed an almost lifesize model of the chapel he was designing for Monique and her sister nuns in Vence, he'd built it around himself, surrounded himself with it, he was its animating force, though he'd have denied that he was imitating the power and glory of the God hidden inside the tabernacle on ordinary chapel altars, he'd have insisted he was just an ordinary working artist relishing a new project, he collaborated with his indispensable team, the makers of ceramic tiles, of wooden benches, of glass windows. He was a modest man, as Monique had always said. Also, as he'd told me, he was ruthless. He wanted to get it right.

He half-sat, half-lay, propped by pillows in the centre of his paper chapel, he'd had his bed moved in so that as soon as he woke he could get to work swiftly and easily. Flexible like a membrane, the chapel curved round him, held him, sheltered him. When it was ready it would open, pulse around him, push him out. How energetic that paper body, and how easily torn. He understood that: he'd lived through two world wars, he had witnessed what we could do to one another. We made, we damaged, sometimes we tried to mend, to repair. Like his mother working at textiles, like Amélie constructing hats. Stitching and re-building ruined cities. Marking, every month, what destruction meant, then getting on with renewal.

Waking inside his paper model of the chapel, he contemplated the paper altar set slantwise facing both the nuns' paper stalls and the nave, the line of close-set paper windows, arched openings reaching from ceiling to floor, the pierced paper door set flat in the side wall opening into the confessional painted pale pink inside, whorled like a listening ear. Nothing but pure paper, sturdy and vulnerable and changeable. You could tear it down cut it up cut bits out of it gather the scraps in your hands, pleat and fold them, launch them as birds, start again building.

He invited me in. Clem, you belong here too, you can come and go you can invent your Glorious Mysteries of the rosary what are they I don't know yet you can fill in the face of the Madonna to suit yourself and do you see the chapel when built as a ribbed white block roofed with blue tiles patterned like waves of the sea undulating under the blue sky the chapel will endure a certain time perhaps another hundred years who knows perhaps it will get blown up perhaps it will be used as a cowshed a dance hall a greenhouse I don't know but you and I shall not endure dear Clem we shall die back like the wild flowers on the hills of Provence, we shall rot down like the plums fallen in the orchard grass, people's prayers will continue rising up fresh as the grass and the wild flowers in spring, the wild thyme.

And here inside the chapel inside my room, its fragile walls of paper so easily torn down and burned or shredded, here inside you will find everyone you have ever loved, we shall all be there, and Camille and Berthe and Monique and Roger will be there too, and Madame Lydia and your parents and your little brother and the Martins, Amélie and Marguerite and Marguerite's mother, Félix and the American chauffeur and the doctor and all your other lovers, and your child Denis he will be there too. The chapel will be a song in light and it will be sheet music and it will be a story that you will help to write, a word that you have laid like a tile, in the right place. And there will be no priests interceding, there will just be us, the people, holy and ordinary, being born in all our blood and mess: connected.

38. Figures in a kitchen

DENIS

The small, thin, black-haired boy looked to be about ten years old. He sat well back on the pink-flowered cushions of the wicker armchair near the kitchen window, all folded in on himself, knees drawn up and pressed together. As though he were still hiding curled behind the suitcase inside the boot of Maurice's sister's car, arms round his head. He wore a blue tracksuit, scuffed grey and white trainers. The summer night was warm, but even so we had tucked a blanket around his shoulders, like a shawl. I thought it might make him feel safer. Outside, the dark garden pressed against the glass, perhaps for him like something threatening. I wanted him not to feel afraid. His narrowed brown eyes, with charcoal smudges under them, flicked over our faces, back and forth. He hadn't spoken yet. He looked apprehensive. He couldn't tell what would happen next. Nor could we. We had to make a plan.

Maurice sat at the table opposite him, glancing at him from time to time, clearly trying to reassure him. He rested his forearms on the blue tablecloth. He was wearing the jeans and soft red cotton shirt from the day of our outing together, so recent. He had got up in slow motion when I arrived, raising one finger in a clear gesture: don't alarm the child. The angel of the Annunciation in medieval paintings looked like that, forefinger pointing upwards. First Joyful Mystery of the rosary: behold, I bring you glad tidings, if unexpected ones, you shall have a son. You always wanted a child, didn't you? Here he is.

Maurice had shaken hands with me. I have taken advantage of you, as you see, but I felt you had a good heart, I trusted that even if you were taken aback at first you would give us shelter.

Frieda had remained standing by the door into the hall. She was wearing an embroidered black waistcoat over a low-necked pink T-shirt, a black skirt patterned with roses. Grey, cosy-looking slippers. Perhaps she'd just settled down for an evening of TV when the visitors arrived. I was used to her in more flamboyant footgear: high-heeled mules, cowboy boots. The slippers domesticated her. I wasn't used to that, either.

She said: let's be clear about what's entailed.

I said: I don't know whether I have a good heart or not. I'd like to think I have but I'm not sure.

Frieda exclaimed: good heart or not, that doesn't matter, Mr Maurice here is telling me this is a straightforward affair of justice, human rights, but it's going to involve us in a lot of trouble, he hasn't given me the chance to say whether or not I agree. And this is my house, don't forget.

Her neat little terraced house, so carefully maintained, cleaned, regularly re-painted, the brickwork re-pointed, the steps always swept, the windows washed. I was part of that work. Surely I ought to have a say about our visitors: whether they went or stayed.

Maurice remained poised, composed. Unlike Frieda who had hurried to greet me, exclaiming, as soon as I opened the front door. Hardly giving me time to dump my rucksack she had rushed me into my kitchen. What are we going to do? Just tell me, what d'you expect me to do?

My dear landlady had then found her manners. She started

off by fidgeting, jumping up and down to reach for my tea caddy, my teapot, set out mugs, then gradually she'd calmed down, gone upstairs for a tin of biscuits, arranged a selection on a plate, offered them to our guests.

Maurice surveyed a tumble of brown oblongs dotted with black. They looked stamped, pressed. You could imagine the machine pushing them out onto long trays, cutting them, in some hot factory. They staled easily, I remembered, became soft rather than crisp. You bent them, broke them in two.

Garibaldis, I said, though as children we called them squashed fly.

Maurice picked up a different oblong biscuit, a pale one, held it between his long fingers, turned it round, inspecting its speckles of sugar, its deckled edges.

These are called Nice biscuits, he said, but I've never known why. Made in Nice, I suppose, and that's it. Biscuits with a definite nationality. Citizen biscuits.

I wanted to say: yes, all right, Maurice. You don't have to go on. I understand. Do I? No, of course I don't. I can try to imagine what this child has been through, but I need facts.

He turned his brown eyes on me. The polite guest, waiting for me to speak.

Don't explain more than you feel you need to, I said. Just tell us anything you think we need to know right now. The rest can wait.

Keep on speaking in English, please, Frieda said: or else Denis here will have to translate and that will complicate matters even further.

Maurice said: I'm telling you what my sister told me.

He talked slowly, unemphatically, not raising his voice. Clutching his chocolate digestive, the boy kept his eyes on him. The sound of Maurice's voice, even speaking a foreign language, seemed to soothe the child; he sat back. The deep tones were weaving him a safety net. He needed that. He had relatives already settled in this country, it appeared, and therefore the right to be reunited with them, but he had been left behind, separated, arriving in a different convoy, then stuck in the Calais camp, with no papers confirming his name, his status.

An unaccompanied minor, Frieda said. Yes, I recognise that term.

Maurice's sister had got to know him, heard his story, one of many similar ones, yes, but what could you do, she would do what little she could. Better to rescue one child than none.

That's taking up a sentimental attitude, you know, Frieda said. A political solution is really what's needed.

That's all very well, but it's likely to take some time, Maurice said, while the politicians go on squabbling over whose responsibility these children are. The UK is supposed to take them in, under the Dubs agreement, but it's dragging its feet.

Yes, I said, that is shameful.

So in the short term, Maurice said, my sister decided to act.

The matter was urgent: not only was the child traumatised by what he had endured so far but at risk of being displaced again. The French authorities wanted to close the camp, disperse its inhabitants into the provinces, many of the children would most likely flee, might never be found. Accordingly Maurice, after a discussion, had decided to bring the boy across. Maurice had driven in to the camp as a visitor, a well-known volunteer bringing donated supplies to his sister's team, and he had driven out again as a people smuggler.

Frieda turned her head towards the boy. I glanced at him too.

He was grubby, lank-haired, with scars of mosquito bites on his wrists and neck. He had relaxed, lain his dark head against the fat pink cushion propping him. Biscuit crumbs down his front.

Maurice said: I was lucky. As it turned out I had no trouble. It was a busy time, they didn't search every car. I just sailed through.

I said: you were already planning all this on the Eurostar? When we first met? That's why you gave me your phone number?

Yes, Maurice said, I picked you because you seemed the right sort to help me if I needed help. I needed somewhere to take Shal once we arrived in the UK, I didn't want to abandon him in yet another refugee holding centre, and you offered me your place.

You manipulated me, I said.

Yes, Maurice said. I'm sorry, but I couldn't be sure what you'd say if I told you the truth. I could see you were a kind person. You were very open to talking to me, spending time with me. I just took it from there.

He selected another biscuit. Ah. Petit Beurre. I didn't know you could get these in England.

His elegant hands. On the Eurostar those hands had tilted the silvery pot, he had poured me coffee. Now he sat in my flat, drinking tea. Not a suppliant. A dignified, well-behaved guest. He was expecting me to play my part in turn: the welcoming host. He was expecting me to behave as a decent human being. He was depending on me not to let him down.

Clem's eyes meeting mine. Clem's voice. I did what seemed best at the time. I'm sorry, Denis.

I said: you're on holiday at the moment, aren't you, but

you've got a job to get back to. You've got your family too. So after that it will be up to Frieda and me. Right?

Maurice nodded. I'd like to see him settled, and I'd like to keep in touch with him from France. My sister would too. Anything we can do from that end, we will do. And then eventually, once we've found his relatives, I'd like to come and visit him, as often as I can.

Frieda suddenly spoke. Obviously, I'm not going to throw him out on the street. He's got this far, we must take him in. He has landed among strangers, we must do our best for him.

Perhaps the child would show us what he needed. Perhaps you learned from the child about what to do. That crying child in the supermarket days back. My instinct to pick her up, comfort her. There were two of us. We would cope.

Frieda leaned across, collected our empty mugs, put them next to the teapot. She lined up the milk jug, the half-empty plate of biscuits, the bowl of sugar lumps. She placed her hands on either side of this assembly, as though bracing it.

She addressed me. I've got the spare room on the top floor, and my sewing room next to it. Our visitors can use those.

I spoke to Maurice. In the morning, we'll contact a refugee organisation, we'll contact a solicitor, we'll work out the next steps to take.

I looked back at the boy. He needed a good wash, some clean clothes, a haircut. None of that mattered for the moment. He had fallen asleep.

Acknowledgments

Thanks to all at Sandstone Press, in particular to Bob Davidson and to Moira Forsyth for her scrupulous care in editing. Thanks to Charles Walker for his unfailing wisdom, expertise and humour, and to all at United Agents.

Thanks to all my friends, and to my family.

Thanks to Hilary Spurling, whose biography of Matisse, among the many books I read for research, was invaluable.

www.sandstonepress.com